Praise for *Murder at the Courthouse*

"The people of Hidden Springs are warm and caring, if a little gossipy, but secrets lurk beneath that friendly surface—dangerous secrets that turn deadly when a body shows up on the courthouse steps. This intriguing new mystery had me reading late into the night."

—**Lorena McCourtney**, author of the Ivy Malone Mysteries and the Cate Kinkaid Files

"Gabhart's tiny town of wacky characters is a delightfully fun read. Needless to say, the mystery is only part of this memorable story written by one of today's bestselling authors."

—*CBA Retailers + Resources*

"A. H. Gabhart has created a bevy of quirky characters who are not as simple as they appear on the surface. *Murder at the Courthouse* will keep you engrossed and entertained."

—*Killer Nashville*

"A comfortable, enjoyable read."

—*New York Journal of Books*

"The plot will keep readers anxious for another story set in Hidden Springs."

—*RT Book Reviews*

Books by A. H. Gabhart

Murder at the Courthouse
Murder Comes by Mail

Books by Ann Gabhart

The Outsider
The Believer
The Seeker
The Blessed
The Gifted
The Innocent

———

Words Spoken True

———

Angel Sister
Small Town Girl
Love Comes Home

———

Christmas at Harmony Hill

THE HEART OF HOLLYHILL

Scent of Lilacs
Orchard of Hope
Summer of Joy

HIDDEN SPRINGS MYSTERIES

2

MURDER COMES *by* MAIL

A. H. GABHART

Revell

a division of Baker Publishing Group
Grand Rapids, Michigan

© 2016 by Ann H. Gabhart

Published by Revell
a division of Baker Publishing Group
P.O. Box 6287, Grand Rapids, MI 49516-6287
www.revellbooks.com

Printed in the United States of America

Library of Congress Cataloging-in-Publication Data
Names: Gabhart, Ann H., 1947– author.
Title: Murder comes by mail : a Hidden Springs mystery / A. H. Gabhart.
Description: Grand Rapids, MI : Revell, a division of Baker Publishing Group,
    [2016] | Series: The Hidden Springs mysteries ; 2
Identifiers: LCCN 2016000102 | ISBN 9780800727055 (softcover)
Subjects: | GSAFD: Christian fiction. | Mystery fiction.
Classification: LCC PS3607.A23 M875 2016 | DDC 813/.6—dc23
LC record available at http://lccn.loc.gov/2016000102

Scripture used in this book, whether quoted or paraphrased by the characters, is taken from the King James Version of the Bible.

Published in association with the Books & Such Literary Agency.

16   17   18   19   20   21   22   7   6   5   4   3   2   1

To my sisters,
Jane and Rosalie.
Sisters share lifetime memories
and make the very best friends.

1

When he was a little boy, his mother told him a drunk jumped off this bridge and survived. Jack watched the swirling brown eddies in the river far below him while his toes curled inside his shoes trying to grip the narrow strip of roadway on the air side of the railing. He didn't see how anyone could walk away from this jump, but his mother, who didn't believe in idle gossip or idle anything for that matter, never told stories unless they were true. She said Jack's father knew one of the men who went out in a boat to fish the drunk out of the river below. The man hadn't even broken a bone, or maybe he'd broken all his bones. Jack couldn't remember now which she'd said.

Jack stared down at the muddy water until there didn't seem to be anything but the water and him and wondered if that could happen to him. He supposed not. For one thing, he wasn't drunk, although he'd have bought a bottle of something as he came through Eagleton if he'd had the money. Money. He was tired of thinking about money. Maybe he should say tired of thinking about not having money. Tired of doing things he shouldn't because of money. Better to simply end it all. Fling himself out into the air and let the river swallow him.

A tremble started in his legs, and he ordered his hands to let go of the railing to get it over with. But his mind no longer seemed to have any real connection with his body.

His eyes locked onto the water again. It was mud-puddle brown. Not the nice bluish green he'd visualized on the way here. Even when he was a little kid and lived here in Kentucky close to the river, he'd never gone swimming in water this nasty. A person could get sick swimming in the river during the dog days of summer. At least that was what his mother used to tell him.

He shut his eyes for a second. He had to quit thinking about his mother.

Besides, he wasn't going swimming. Everybody said the fall killed you when you hit the water. He'd be dead before he swallowed any of the filthy water, and what would it matter if he did? Dead people didn't have to worry about germs. About anything.

His knees practically rattled inside his skin as the trembling spread through him until even his scalp shivered under his hair. Only his hands weren't trembling as they kept a paralyzing grip on the railing behind him.

All he had to do was turn loose and it would all be over.

2

How did he get into these things? Michael Keane wrestled with the steering wheel of the old bus to keep it rolling on a fairly straight course down the road. The bus could have gotten an antique vehicle tag when the First Baptist Church of Hidden Springs had acquired it for church outings ten years ago. Since then the only thing that held it together was Pastor Bob Simpson's constant entreaties to the Lord.

Michael told Pastor Bob he needed to pray for donations for a new one, but the preacher smiled and said God had supplied this old bus. It would surely make one more trip. So far it always had. Of course that was with the pastor behind the wheel tuned in to his direct line to the Man upstairs. As Michael fought the old bus around the curves down toward the river, he was pretty sure the words stringing silently through his head might not be the exact same ones the reverend used to keep the wheels rolling.

Behind him, nineteen members of the Senior Adult Ladies Sunday School Class chattered and fanned themselves furiously with folded church bulletins they must have stuffed into their purses for just this occasion. Nobody suggested putting the bus windows down. They were going to a play in Eagleton, and a few beads of sweat were a small price to pay to keep their beauty-shop curls intact. Aunt Lindy was the one exception. She had sensibly lowered her window as soon as she boarded the bus and thus turned her seat into an island of wind all the other women avoided.

Michael met her steady blue eyes in the mirror. She was the reason he had given up his day off to ferry the women to Eagleton for the matinee performance in place of Pastor Bob, who had been called to do a funeral this afternoon.

"You'll enjoy it." Aunt Lindy all but commanded him that morning when she called.

"Can't you find another driver?" Michael had looked out the window of his log house at the perfect blue of the lake where he planned to spend the day out in his rowboat drowning worms. "How about Hal Blevins?"

"You know Hal hasn't been the same since his bypass surgery last year. What if our bus breaks down?" Aunt Lindy paused to give Michael time to imagine Hal having heart failure by the side of the road while a busload of little blue-haired ladies watched. "Besides, Clara's first husband's niece is in the play. You remember Julie Lynne. The two of you dated when you were in high school, didn't you?"

"One date." In those days Julie Lynne Hoskins had been too tall, with a frizzy brown mop of hair that she continually hacked at with a brush to fight it back from her face.

Aunt Lindy had pushed him to ask Julie Lynne to the homecoming dance. She said Julie Lynne needed a date and they'd have fun together. They didn't. At the dance, the two of them sat in a pool of awkward silence amid the thumping music. He tried to get her to dance a couple of times,

10

but she just shook her head without raising her eyes from her clenched hands in her lap. That was the last time he'd listened to his Aunt Lindy's advice about girls.

Shortly after that, Julie Lynne's family had moved away from Hidden Springs, and he'd lost track of her until their tenth high school reunion. She hadn't come, but one of the girls reported spotting her in a store catalog, modeling underwear.

That was amazing enough, but now here she was onstage in a play that some of the ladies on the bus behind him weren't too sure was proper. He was kind of looking forward to seeing how Julie Lynne had changed.

He wasn't so sure he was as interested in her seeing how he had changed, or maybe how he hadn't changed. After all, here he was still in Hidden Springs, not having done much of anything yet, just passing the days being a deputy sheriff in a place that hardly ever needed a deputy for anything but directing traffic and collecting property taxes.

But that was fine with Michael. Arresting people wasn't on his list of favorite things to do anyway. He liked having plenty of time to fish and read about the War Between the States and keep Aunt Lindy happy. She wasn't looking very happy at the moment as she glared at Edith Crossfield across the aisle from her.

Edith had been talking nonstop since they'd met at the church thirty minutes ago. Michael tuned her out after the first mile, but now he tuned in again to see what had Aunt Lindy riled.

"There are simply some things you shouldn't do as a church," Edith was saying. "I mean, we have to have standards."

A couple of seats back, Clara James flushed red and muttered something to her seatmate, but Clara wasn't about to take on Edith head-to-head.

Aunt Lindy had no such reservations. "If you're that worried about your sensibilities being insulted, Edith, you could always get off the bus and go back home."

Michael slowed the bus a little to add emphasis to Aunt Lindy's words.

"Get off the bus?!" Edith swung around to face her attacker. "And what would I do out here two miles from town, Malinda?"

"Michael can call Lester to come pick you up and take you home."

"In his patrol car?!" Edith sputtered. "And lose my ticket money? I think not."

"Then hush and enjoy the trip." Aunt Lindy turned her face back to the front as if the exchange were over.

"Well, I never, Malinda." Edith flapped her makeshift fan double-quick. "I'm not one of your high school students. I've got a right to say what I think, and I think we should have been more selective about which play we're seeing. Even if Julie Lynne is Clara's niece and all, that doesn't mean we have to support something indecent with our attendance. But seeing as how the Sunday school class was going, I thought it my bounden duty to come along. I always support the doings of the church. You know I do, Malinda. Better than you most of the time, I might add. Not that I'm keeping count or anything, but . . ."

She was still droning on as Michael wrestled the bus around the final curve to the bridge spanning Eagle River. On the other side of the river the road straightened out a bit, and if the bus could make it up the hill, they might actually get the rest of the way to Eagleton without incident. That is, unless Aunt Lindy tired of Edith's harping. Who knew what might happen then?

He glanced at her in the mirror, but she wouldn't meet his eyes now. She was staring studiously out the window, her short steel-gray hair lifting off her forehead in the breeze from her open window. Her lips were set in a thin line that made Michael cringe, but Edith Crossfield prattled on, multiplying her words, letting the sheer volume of them steamroller her opponent.

Michael was so busy waiting for the explosion from Aunt Lindy that he didn't notice the man perched precariously on the wrong side of the bridge railing, leaning toward the river below, until one of the ladies behind him gasped and pointed. After a shriek, even Edith fell silent.

The man had picked the middle of the bridge for his jump. People always picked the middle of the bridge. While he was working in Columbus, Michael and his partner, Pete Ballard, had talked down a few jumpers, but they'd lost a couple too. One a doped up sixteen-year-old boy, and another, a middle-aged woman. Michael's stomach lurched at the memory.

Michael braked to a stop about fifty feet away from the man, who kept his eyes on the water and didn't seem to note their presence.

On the bus, the ladies found their voices, with Edith speaking up first. "What's he trying to do?"

"I think he means to jump," another lady chimed in.

"Who is he?" Two women spoke that question in concert.

"What does that matter right now?" Aunt Lindy frowned

13

at the other women and then looked toward Michael. "Do something, Michael."

"I'll try." Michael watched the man through the windshield. The man looked stiff, as though his muscles were holding out against this idea of jumping. Maybe there was yet hope.

Michael winced at the noise the doors made when he slowly creaked them open. Who knew what might spook the man into answering the pull of the water?

"Aunt Lindy, call Betty Jean. Tell her to get the sheriff or somebody out here, and better have her send an ambulance." He spared a glance back at the wide-eyed ladies. "Everybody, stay on the bus."

He could only hope they would listen as he climbed down to the ground. Behind him, Aunt Lindy's phone beeped as she punched in the number.

"I hope this doesn't take too long," Edith Crossfield said.

"Why, Edith! What a thing to say!" her seatmate responded.

"I don't care. If a fellow wants to do himself in, he should choose somewhere that it doesn't bother other people instead of coming out here and messing up everybody else's plans. If we don't hurry and get to Eagleton, we won't have time for lunch before the play, and I didn't eat all that much breakfast."

Michael was glad when the woman's voice faded away behind him. If he had to listen to much more from her, he might be crawling over the railing to join the poor sucker who suddenly jerked his head around to stare at Michael.

"Stop!" he shouted. "Don't come any closer or I'll . . . I'll jump."

"Okay, buddy. Take it easy." Michael held up his hands and slid two steps closer before he stopped about ten feet away from the man. Still too far to lunge and grab him if he turned loose of the railing. Besides, even if he could grab him, he might not be able to hold him.

The guy wasn't too tall, but probably weighed in at over two hundred pounds. His thinning hair that had been made to obey the comb with some kind of goop now stood up in points where he must have run his hands through it prior to climbing over the railing. His loose shirttail added to his disheveled look. Not that it mattered whether a guy had his hair combed and his shirt tucked in when he was ready to jump off a bridge, but the more serious ones generally did.

Michael inched a bit closer and tried to remember his suicide intervention training. "What's your name, buddy?"

"What difference does that make?"

"None, I guess, unless you don't want to end up a John Doe."

The man jerked back from the words as though he'd been struck.

"Easy, fellow." Michael kept his voice calm. "I was just asking your name."

"Jack." The man hesitated a moment, then added, "Smith. Jack Smith."

A fake name for sure. That held out more hope of talking the man back over the railing. If he was intent on killing himself, he wouldn't mind Michael knowing his real name.

"I'm Mike." Michael leaned against the bridge railing as if they had all day to shoot the breeze. "You from around here, Jack?"

"You don't know me, do you?" The man looked worried.

"No, should I?" Michael shifted on the rail and took a step closer to the man.

"No. Nobody knows me." The man looked back down at the water. "I expected it to be bluer."

"Been a lot of rain upriver the last couple of weeks. Keeps the river sort of muddy. But Eagle Lake's nice and blue. Maybe you'd like to go fishing out there."

"I'm not planning on doing any fishing."

"You don't like to fish?" Michael didn't wait for an answer. "I'm a big fisherman myself. It's a good way to relax and get back to nature."

The man glanced over at Michael with a dumb-joke kind of grin. "I was thinking of getting back to nature on a more basic level. You know, dust to dust." He looked back at the water. "Or maybe mud to mud."

Michael eased another step closer. He could almost reach out and touch the man now. Sirens wailed in the distance. The man's head jerked around, the dumb-joke grin gone. Michael should have told Aunt Lindy to ask them to come in quiet.

"Cops. They're always trying to spoil a party," the man said.

3

"I just want to help you, Jack." Michael kept his eyes on the man even though a car was coming up behind him. Not the ambulance or the sheriff. The sirens were still a mile or more away.

The man looked down at the river. "I thought it would be easier, you know." He glanced over at Michael again. "If you really wanted to help me, you'd give me a push."

"You know I can't do that. So come on. Why don't you just swing your leg back over the railing there. I'll help you." Michael moved closer.

"Get back!" The man teetered on the edge from the force of his words, but his hands were still clamped to the railing. So tight his knuckles were white.

Michael scooted his feet to make the man think he was shuffling back a couple of inches. "Okay. I'll stay back, but don't you want to tell me your story first?"

"If I told you, you'd tell me to go ahead and jump."

"It can't be that bad." Michael kept his voice even, with no idea whether it was bad or not. The man looked like a regular Joe, but then so did the worst miscreants sometimes. "But whatever it is, we can talk about it."

A car door slammed behind him, and Michael dared a glance over his shoulder. Not good. Hank Leland was headed toward them, camera in hand. The newspaper editor must have been on this side of town and tuned in to his police scanner. No other way could his old van beat the ambulance and sheriff, who were speeding down the hill with sirens screaming and lights flashing.

Poor Jack Smith, alive or dead, would be this week's big story in the *Hidden Springs Gazette*. That and the snail-paced response time of the emergency vehicles. Hank never passed up an opportunity to get in a shot or two at the county officials. He claimed it boosted circulation.

The sirens cut off, and in the sudden silence the click of the camera was easy to hear. The man pulled his gaze away from the water to look past Michael.

He made a sound that might pass for a laugh. "I thought here in Hidden Springs a man could find a little peace and quiet to do himself in."

Michael took another look over his shoulder. Things were going downhill fast. Hank was right behind him, focusing furiously. Even worse, some of the Sunday school ladies had climbed down from the bus and a couple of them, Sue Lou Farris and Judith Phillips, were tottering toward the bridge, their white hair flashing in the bright sunshine. They had their phones up and ready to capture all the action. The two pudgy Aunt Bea–sweet women competed for who could take the worst photos.

The sheriff climbed out of his car and moved purposely toward the two women to shoo them back as fast as his heavy frame allowed. He swiped at the sweat on his face while he talked to them. It took something big to pull Sheriff Potter out of his air-conditioned office on a hot, muggy July day like this.

At the ambulance, Gina and Bill bustled around opening doors, pulling out their equipment. Not that any of that would help if the guy jumped. Any minute they'd be rushing toward Michael and the man as though they expected the guy to climb back over the rail into all the commotion and lie down on their stretcher.

A few men in pickup trucks had chased after the sirens to be in on the action or maybe just to be sure the ambulance hadn't been headed after their mother, father, sister, or brother. The ambulance didn't go out all that often with sirens going full blast.

"I don't believe this." The man fixed his eyes on the two women protesting the sheriff's pointing them back to the bus. "This is just too crazy. One of them could be my mother."

"Your mother?" Michael jerked his attention back to the man.

"Tell her I'm sorry. That she wasn't the reason I ended up bad." With those words, something changed in the man. He was no longer a mass of fear unsure which way to lean.

Michael was already diving for him when Hank shouted, "He's going, Mike."

At the very instant the man turned loose of the rail, Michael grabbed him in a kind of sideways tackle. A half second later the man would have been gone, but in that vulnerable moment of unbalance, Michael managed to topple him back over the railing onto the road. The man groaned when his head banged hard against the pavement.

Michael stayed astride the man, afraid to turn him loose, while at the same time wondering if he might have killed the poor guy in the process of trying to save him. Behind him, Hank Leland's camera still clicked. Michael looked around straight into Hank's viewfinder. "Put that fool camera down and grab his shoulders, Leland, so I can see if he's breathing."

Hank dropped the camera to let it dangle by its strap around his neck. He had the grace to look a little shamefaced as he moved over to grab the man's shoulders. "Sorry, Mike, but you know real news doesn't show up often in Hidden Springs, and half the time when it does, I'm on the other side of the county covering a pig calling contest or whatever."

Michael slowly lifted up off the man. He didn't want to chance the jumper scrambling to his feet and taking a leap yet. One thing he had learned while working in the city was to never underestimate a person's strength or quickness. Adrenaline was a powerful stimulant.

"Is he dead?" Hank whispered beside him. "He cracked his head pretty hard."

"I hope not. That would make some headline. 'Deputy Kills Man, Trying to Save Him.'" Michael looked down at the man's closed eyes and then his chest. It was rising and falling. "He's alive," he said to nobody in particular.

"Good." Hank sounded relieved. "'Deputy—Hero of the Day' will sell more papers. Especially here in Hidden Springs where the citizens all already think you're a hero just 'cause you're so good-looking."

The stretcher wheels clattered on the roadway as Gina and Bill ran toward them. Sheriff Potter lumbered along behind them. Michael kept his hold on the man's legs, pinning him to the road. Even though the man hadn't moved a muscle since he'd fallen, Michael sensed a resistance in the muscles under his hands.

Bill knelt beside the man and opened his kit. "Move back," he ordered. Gina squatted down on the other side of the man, and Hank cheerfully relinquished his hold on the man's shoulders to pull his camera up again.

Michael turned loose of the man at last. He was about to stand up when the man's eyelids popped open to reveal blank, empty eyes, almost as if the man's spirit had made the jump and all Michael had saved was the empty baggage of his body.

But then his eyes focused on Michael. "You should have let me go. It would have been over then."

"Whatever's wrong, fellow, we can get you help," Gina told him as she shined a light in his eyes. "Jumping wasn't the answer."

The man didn't act as if he heard her. Instead he kept his eyes directly on Michael. "You'll wish you'd pushed me."

4

Michael drove the ladies on to Eagleton to see the play. There was no reason not to go. That was what the ladies kept telling one another the rest of the ride. After all, the tickets had been pricey and they'd lose their money if they didn't see the play. It was too late to give the tickets to anyone else, and it wasn't as if the man had actually jumped. Everything had turned out fine. Michael had seen to that, and then they would beam his way.

Michael felt their beams even with his eyes firmly fixed on the road as he guided the old bus through the traffic in Eagleton. Once, when he glanced up at the mirror, he'd even caught Edith Crossfield looking at him kindly. He squirmed a little in the driver's seat under all the benevolence and discovered a broken spring.

They were trying to make him out as some kind of hero, and what had he done, really? He hadn't crawled out on a ledge or over the railing to rescue the man. He simply sneaked up close enough to jerk him back from the edge, giving the poor chump a concussion to boot. That didn't make him a hero. Keeping people from slipping off the edges was part of his job as an officer of the law.

Not that all that many people in Hidden Springs danced on the lip of danger, or even trouble. A few did, of course. While Hidden Springs might be a little town time seemed to have forgotten, regular folks, not saints, still lived there. So, as a matter of course, trouble showed up now and again. The good thing was that in Hidden Springs, folks generally managed to deal with one round of trouble before another round started.

Michael liked it that way. He liked being able to keep things under control, maybe even make a difference in the town. His friends from back in the city told him he was deluded. They said he was wasting the best years of his life in a lazy little town that wasn't likely to make headline news unless one of its citizens happened to buy the winning jackpot lottery ticket. That did have a one-in-several-million chance of happening, since people in Hidden Springs slapped down their money for the opportunity to strike it rich here the same as any other town.

Not Michael. He didn't need to throw his dollars away trying to win instant wealth. He was content with what he had. Content with his ordinary life in Hidden Springs where he grew up. His ancestors, generations back, lived in Hidden Springs—from Jasper Keane, the founding father, right on down to Aunt Lindy. Michael fit in Hidden Springs.

After the play, that's what Julie Lynne said she'd never done. Fit in Hidden Springs. And never could. The whole bunch of them trooped backstage with Clara to see her after the final curtain came down.

"Please just Lynne." Her eyes danced through the lot of them as if she could barely keep from bursting out laughing.

She came out of the hole-in-the-wall dressing room to speak to them, barefoot and still wearing the flesh-toned body suit she'd worn for the last scene. Michael suspected she would have been just as relaxed in the buff. Her formerly kudzu hair was now honey-blonde tresses flowing silkily down her back. Her eyes were an unusual blue-green. Nothing like they were in high school.

"Contacts and a great hairdresser," she told her aunt when Clara said she hardly recognized her.

Michael couldn't spot even a trace of the girl who shared that disaster date with him. He stayed behind the other ladies in hopes nobody would bring up how they went to school together, since he figured she wouldn't have a bit of trouble seeing the boy he used to be.

Julie Lynne hugged Clara without touching much but their cheeks. "I would have known you anywhere, Aunt Clara. You look just the same as the day I left Hidden Springs. You people must have a fountain of youth there." She turned on the other women. "And there's Miss Janet, my old Sunday school teacher, and Mrs. Jenkins. You lived down the street from us. How is that Paula Jo? Paula Jo and I used to giggle till we were sick, and you'd tell us we must have turned our giggle boxes upside down."

She didn't give Mrs. Jenkins time to tell her about Paula Jo, which was just as well. It wasn't a story Mrs. Jenkins relished telling all that much anyway, since Paula Jo was living in a leaky old trailer and working on her second divorce. Julie Lynne's eyes jumped over to Aunt Lindy. "And Miss Keane, the meanest teacher in Hidden Springs, maybe even the whole world."

"Thank you." Aunt Lindy smiled, not a bit upset by her description.

24

"X plus Y equals something, I'm sure." Julie Lynne laughed. "I never was that great at math. And you had a nephew. What was his name? I went out with him once. Disaster of the decade."

Some of the ladies tittered and peeked back at Michael.

Julie Lynne finally looked directly at him. She'd been sliding her eyes across him occasionally almost the way a cat might rub against someone's legs to get attention. "You?"

"Mr. Disaster in person." Michael stayed where he was, but the ladies in front of him stepped aside, ready to watch another show.

Julie Lynne gave him the once-over and then touched the tip of her tongue to her top lip. "You ask me to dance again, Mike, and the dance floor won't know what hit it."

Michael smiled. "I'm still not much of a dancer."

"Oh, but I've learned lots of new steps since I left Hidden Springs." Julie Lynne kept her eyes locked on him as if all the ladies around them had vanished into thin air. "And I'm a great teacher."

Aunt Lindy cleared her throat and stepped between Michael and Julie Lynne. "Well, it has certainly been nice seeing you again after all these years, and we did enjoy your performance. It must be exciting to be an actress."

"It has its moments." One corner of Julie Lynne's mouth twisted up in a sideways smile as she slid her eyes from Michael to his aunt. "Just like life. And the same as life, we play some of the scenes right and some of them wrong. Except in life, you don't get the chance to play the scene over."

"Have you a lot of scenes you wish you had played differently, Julie Lynne?" Aunt Lindy didn't bother remembering to call her only Lynne.

"Of course. Don't we all?" Julie Lynne raised her eyebrows at Aunt Lindy and then let her smile come back full force as she looked back at Michael. "Actually the worse things about acting are the layoffs between parts. As a matter of fact, once this run is over in a few days, I'll have a week or two of downtime. Maybe I'll come for a little R & R in Hidden Springs. You'd put me up, wouldn't you, Aunt Clara?"

Shock colored with a dash of dismay flashed across Clara's face before her inbred hospitality came to her rescue. "Well, of course, Lynne. My door's always open to family, but I'm afraid you might find us a bit dull, dear."

"Extremely dull," Aunt Lindy stuck in as if trying to do what Clara clearly couldn't. Snatch away the welcome mat before Julie Lynne could step on it.

"Dull sounds delightful right now." Julie Lynne aimed her smile squarely at Michael.

"Besides, it's not all that dull." Edith Crossfield launched into the story of Michael pulling the guy back over the railing at the bridge. Several of the other ladies chimed in with their versions.

During the third recap, Michael grabbed his opportunity to exit. He grinned and waved at Julie Lynne, then made his escape to bring the bus around.

The streetlights were blinking on in Hidden Springs by the time Michael pulled the bus into the First Baptist Church parking lot. The trip home was uneventful. Nothing vital fell off the bus, the ladies settled on the first fast-food restaurant they saw, and the Eagleton Bridge was empty of jumpers.

Aunt Lindy hadn't done much talking on the way home, but then Aunt Lindy wasn't the type to waste her breath making small talk about whether or not it looked like rain or about the sun going down when any idiot knew the sun went down every day.

She did have something to say as Michael drove her home. She waited until they were turning into the street leading down to what some in Hidden Springs called the Keane mansion. It was far from mansion size, no bigger than most of the other houses on Keane Drive, but the stone structure sat impressively on the end lot with ancient oaks around it to prove it had been there a very long time.

A Keane had founded the town and Keanes had played a major part in the town's history ever since. But now the town was down to its last two Keanes.

Aunt Lindy accepted being the reigning Keane in Hidden Springs as the natural order of things. Should anything ever threaten the town's existence, Michael had no doubt she would marshal whatever defense necessary to save the town. He also knew she was determined to keep the next generation of Keanes in Hidden Springs. If indeed there ever was a next generation of Keanes.

So Michael wasn't surprised when, without preamble, she said, "I would advise you not to encourage Julie Lynne if she should decide to carry through with her threat to visit Clara."

"But, Aunt Lindy, just last week you were telling me I needed to settle down, get married and produce some little Keanes."

"Not with Julie Lynne Hoskins."

"What's wrong with Julie Lynne? You practically forced me to ask her out when we were in school. You must have thought we'd get along then, and I'm beginning to think you might be right." Michael kept the smile off his face. "You have to admit she's grown up nicely."

"Yes indeed." Aunt Lindy kept her eyes forward and her voice unperturbed. "And no telling what it cost her to do the growing. Still, I suppose if one is going to take one's clothes off in public, it's best to be sure everything is properly filled out and inflated."

"It looked all natural to me."

"I'm not going around in circles with you on whether or not Julie Lynne's curves were all her or part fiberfill, Michael. I'm merely pointing out that encouraging her would be foolhardy."

Michael finally let himself laugh. "If we ever discover the woman who meets both our qualifications, she'll probably tell me to get lost."

Aunt Lindy didn't laugh. "If she did that, then she definitely wouldn't meet the qualifications I would have for her. If indeed I did have such qualifications in mind. Which I do not."

Michael pulled into the circular drive in front of the house. He stopped in front of the entrance. "I'll walk you around to the back door." He turned the key off and reached for the door handle.

"No need in that." Aunt Lindy gathered up her purse.

Aunt Lindy lived in three rooms in the back, while she let the ghosts of Keanes past haunt the rest of the house undisturbed. Once a year she flung open the heavy doors into the front rooms to decorate for the ghosts and all of Hidden Springs to come to a Christmas tea. It was a Keane tradition.

That was where Michael used to imagine he would get married. In that huge front parlor at Christmastime. He could see himself in a black tux and a woman in a lacy gown beside him with the eight-foot tree sparkling beside them.

Then, when he was a mere lovesick teenager, it had been Alex wearing the white wedding gown. Even now, he could see no one else there beside him, but he had a hard time believing Alex would ever be ready to share that wedding dream.

Alex Sheridan was on the fast track, an attorney in DC with clients whose names made headlines. She thought Michael should be on a fast track somewhere too, instead of poking along here in Hidden Springs. The idea of Alex settling down in Hidden Springs was too ludicrous to even consider, and the idea of him in DC was worse than ludicrous. It was terrifying.

For a while last year Alex actually made sounds of coming to Hidden Springs and letting her uncle add a Sheridan to the Sheridan on the shingle in front of his lawyer's office on Main Street. Then Reese Sheridan's health had improved and one of Alex's big-name clients got embroiled in some sort of meaty scandal in DC. Michael hadn't seen her since, except for a brief appearance at Aunt Lindy's open house last Christmas. Alex had zoomed in and out that day. They hadn't even had time for a good argument.

Now Michael hurried around to help Aunt Lindy out of his old truck. He walked her up the porch steps to the door with its etched glass panels. No light shone from inside. "You should leave a light on in the front hall."

"Why would I do that? I have never been afraid of the dark."

"It's not the dark. It's what's in the dark."

"There's nothing in the dark but my house. Our house." She fished her key out of her purse. "I've been locking my door if that makes you feel any better, although I can't imagine anybody bothering me here."

"Probably not, but some kid might think it was funny to try to scare you."

"If you mean one of my students, I sincerely doubt that ever happening. They would know better." She turned the key, pushed the door open enough to reach inside, and flipped on the porch light.

"Even one you give a bad grade?" Michael teased her.

"They get the grades they earn. I don't give them anything." She peered up at him with narrowed eyes. "If you're trying to get a rise out of me, you should know better too."

"Right. Sorry, Aunt Lindy." Michael touched her shoulder to stop her before she went inside. "And don't worry about Julie Lynne. She'll never come to Hidden Springs."

"You could be wrong there. She might very well show up here, but who said I was worried? I know you'll do the right thing. You always do." She reached up to lay her hand on his cheek. "I'm proud of the way you saved that man out on the bridge. It could have so easily gone the other way."

"It was just routine. I did what any other police officer would have done."

"You kept him from jumping."

"I didn't keep him from wanting to."

She frowned a little. "Wonder what would bring a man to such a state?"

"Who knows?" Michael shrugged. "Money trouble, drugs, women. Depression. It could be anything."

"Your grandfather always said every man has his demons. The successful man is he who learns to control his."

"I think this guy needed crowd control." He remembered the look on the man's face as he lay on the road staring up at Michael.

"Thanks to you, he will have a chance to work through his problems now. We should pray for him."

After she went inside, Michael waited until the light came on in the window of his aunt's sitting room and then headed home. As he drove through the woods to his log house on the lake, he hardly gave a thought to Julie Lynne chasing him down in Hidden Springs. He kept seeing the jumper and hearing his words. *"You'll wish you'd pushed me."*

It hadn't exactly sounded like a threat. More like a promise.

5

The next day the weekly issue of the *Hidden Springs Gazette* hit the stands at the local Save Way grocery and the Hidden Springs Grill. Folks could also grab a copy off the front counter in the *Gazette* office, which operated on the honor system. Three quarters in the bowl on the counter bought a paper off the top of the stack.

On the day the paper came out, Hank Leland always stayed out of sight behind the partition that divided the offices from the pressroom until the first flush of buyers passed through. He claimed that was so people would read the news for themselves and not simply stand there wanting him to give a narrative report of what he'd written. Others around town claimed it was more likely Hank wanted a clear path out the back way in case somebody took issue with one of his stories and showed up ready to punch him in the nose.

Either way, Annie Watson kept guard at the front desk. Annie had worked on the paper through three different editors and knew exactly how many words would fit in a column inch and the difference between a nickel's clink and that of a quarter in the payment bowl on the counter.

Michael didn't bother picking up a copy on the way to work. Noon would be plenty early enough to see what kind of story Hank had come up with on the jumper, but when he went in the sheriff's office, Betty Jean Atkins was already well into the middle pages of the paper. Behind her, the coffee-maker made its final gurgles to extract every drop of water out of its innards, and the computers hummed with their cursors flashing at the ready.

Betty Jean peered over the paper at him. "The hero in the flesh."

Michael groaned and poured a cup of coffee. "How bad is it?"

"Not bad at all. Great pictures." Betty Jean turned back to the front page. "Hank will have to print another run for all the girls to have copies to get you to autograph."

"Yeah, right." Michael sat down at his desk and thumbed through his phone messages. As usual, not much happening. A bicycle missing at the trailer park. Maybe stolen. Maybe borrowed. A rock through a window out at the high school. Some kid who must not have been straightened out by Aunt Lindy yet.

"Where's Lester?" Michael looked up.

Lester Stucker was the other deputy in the office. Michael didn't need to ask where Sheriff Potter was. He'd be at the grill loading up on caffeine and cholesterol for the day.

"School starts in a few weeks. He's probably out checking his whistle and making sure the crosswalks are painted. Or maybe he's patrolling the bridge, hoping for another nut to come along so he can be a hero too." Betty Jean stood up to fill her coffee mug. "Heaven help the nut if one is out there. Lester would push him the wrong way for sure."

"No way for you to talk about a fellow deputy." Michael kept flipping through his messages. Buck Garrett, the state detective for the area, had called, but it didn't sound urgent. A Dr. Philip Colson wanted him to call. Michael noted the Eagleton number and wondered why a doctor was calling him.

Betty Jean took a sip of coffee and then shook the paper at him. "Well, don't you want to know what it says about you? Or have you already read it?"

"Nope."

"Nope, you haven't already read it, or nope, you don't want to know what it says?"

"Both." Michael kept his eyes on the notes in front of him.

Neville Gravitt, the county clerk, stuck his long, narrow head in the door on his way to his own offices. "You did a fine thing, Michael, and we're all thankful you're here working for us in Hidden Springs."

Michael looked up, so surprised by Neville's speech, he couldn't think of a response. Neville's face disappeared and his footsteps went clicking on up the tiled hallway. The phone rang and Betty Jean picked it up. "I'm sorry he's not available for comment at this time. Would you like to leave a message?" She jotted down something and hung up.

When it started ringing again almost immediately, she punched the hold button. She did the same with the second line on the phone on the sheriff's desk. Then she slapped the newspaper down in front of Michael. "If you're going to be a hero, you'd better read up on what you did to get there."

"I was just doing my job, Betty Jean." Michael pushed the paper away.

Betty Jean pushed it back. "Maybe so, but newspapers

make heroes, and Hank has hit the jackpot with this bunch of pictures. That's the second call from a reporter, and it's not even eight thirty yet."

"Reporter?"

"The *Eagleton Herald* and Channel 22 news. Channel 22 is sending out a camera truck to film the bridge and the hero." She waited a second for that to sink in. "I think you'd better get ready, Mr. Hero of the Day. Things must be slow in the big town this week."

Michael reluctantly looked at the paper. Four photos covered half the front page. The first showed the man on the edge with Michael reaching toward him. In the next, the man had turned loose of the railing and was leaning toward the water. The third showed Michael hauling him over the railing, and the last was of the man being loaded onto the stretcher. The headline screamed in bold block letters, DEPUTY SAVES JUMPER.

"Not a very imaginative headline," Michael said.

"I thought about 'Deputy risks life to save stranger.'" Hank was in the doorway. "But headlines are better short and concise."

"I'd think they needed to be true too." Michael looked over at Hank. "I was never in any danger."

Hank shrugged a little. "Readers favor the dramatic over factual any day." He sneaked a look at Betty Jean, who had yet to acknowledge his presence. "Hi, Betty Jean," he offered warily, not crossing the threshold into the office. "What do you think?"

"You don't want to know." Betty Jean sat back down at her desk and hit a few keys on her keyboard.

Hank had used up his welcome at the courthouse long

ago. "That's where you're wrong. I always want to know what my readers think."

"Who says I'm a reader?"

"Betty Jean, you injure me." He started to step into the office.

Betty Jean's glare stopped him in his tracks. "How can we help you this morning? Do you have taxes to pay? Want to report a burglary? A missing person, perhaps an editor?"

"How about a hero interview?" Hank offered.

"Sheriff Potter doesn't allow media in the office area." She narrowed her eyes on the editor. "You have been apprised of that rule previously. It has not changed."

"Come on, Betty Jean. I hardly said anything bad about the sheriff this week. Why, I mean he beat the ambulance to the scene yesterday. I gave him credit."

Betty Jean got up from her desk to yank the paper out of Michael's hand. She opened it to an inside page and read, "'Sheriff Potter, who showed up on the scene after the crisis was over, was very effective in keeping back the curious. After allowing Deputy Dawg to leave the scene, the sheriff graciously gave a statement to this reporter. No, he didn't know the man's name or why he wanted to jump. No, he had no idea why the man would pick this bridge or where the ambulance was taking him, but he was sure it would be somewhere where the man would get the care he needed. If the reporter wanted to check back with his office tomorrow around noon, more information could be available at that time.'"

"I didn't write Deputy Dawg." Hank looked a little worried. "Did I?"

"Deputy Dawg. Deputy Keane. Close enough." Michael laughed and stood up. "I better take a turn around the block and make sure all the stores are still there. Tag along, Leland, if you want some exercise."

"He could certainly use that," Betty Jean muttered as she took the phone lines off hold.

Hank didn't let her get the last word. "Hey, Betty Jean, I'm thinking about starting up a love connection section in the want ads. If you want to send in an ad, I'll give you a special rate."

Michael grabbed the editor's arm and pulled him through the doorway before Betty Jean threw something at the man. Betty Jean's consuming desire in life was to be a bride, but so far she hadn't met anyone with a consuming desire to be her groom. She was into her thirties. Michael wasn't sure how far, since her age seemed to go up or down to match whichever man she had her eye on at the time. She had all kinds of excuses when the men she picked didn't call. She needed to lose weight. She talked too much. She didn't talk enough. She was too smart. Working for the sheriff, who also happened to be her uncle, scared men away.

Michael used to tell her she was too picky, but all that did was make her mad. Nowadays, he pulled out his sympathetic look and merely nodded when she related the trials and tribulations of husband catching. Except of course when she said she was too fat. Then he was quick to assure her that wasn't the case. He didn't want to come in one morning and find his desk out in the hall.

Hank fell into step beside Michael. He fingered the little notebook in his shirt pocket but left it there. "You get the feeling Betty Jean doesn't like me?"

"She'd like you better if you weren't married."

"Sometimes I think I'd like me better if I wasn't married."

Hank glanced over his shoulder to see if anybody was close enough to hear him. "I didn't say that."

Michael laughed.

"Yeah, you can laugh." Hank sighed. "Single. Handsome. A hero. The girls will be lining up for a smile from you."

"I hope you weren't planning to interview me about my love life." Michael pulled open the courthouse door and stepped outside.

"That wasn't my intention, but I'm sure it would increase circulation. So come on. Give me all the juicy details." Hank grinned and pulled his notebook out of his pocket.

"It would put your readers to sleep. I just work and fish and read."

"And play hero."

"Let's drop the hero tag." Michael gave Hank a look. "Who knows? That man might not have jumped even if I hadn't come along. He had a pretty tight grip on that railing."

A pencil stub appeared in the editor's hand. Michael admired the man's ability to write on the run. While nobody else could make heads or tails of his notes, Hank rarely misquoted anyone. That was why the city and county officials preferred not to talk to him. It wasn't that he got what they said wrong, but he did have a talent for getting them to say the dumbest things.

"You get the guy's name?"

"He said Jack Smith, but that's pretty generic. Probably not his name."

"The hospital admitted him under Jack Jackson. He had some kind of ID, and then there's the car, of course. The sheriff had T.R. tow it in. You could probably find out plenty from checking it out."

"I'm sure the sheriff has taken care of that. Why don't you ask him?"

Hank touched the lead of his pencil to his tongue. "I figured I'd ask a friendly source first and take my lumps with the sheriff later."

"You could try not being so antagonistic. At least in print."

"Sweet and cuddly news doesn't sell papers and I got to sell papers. Rebecca Ann just went to the orthodontist. They want to do braces. Kids cost a bundle. You remember that if you ever take leave of your senses and consider getting married."

"I'll keep that in mind."

Out on Main Street, Jim Deatin was propping up some tires in front of his auto supply store. When Michael spoke to him, Jim straightened up and wiped the sweat off his forehead with a near salute. "Way to go, Michael. We're proud of you."

After they walked on up the street, Michael said, "I don't think I'm going to enjoy this, Hank. How about printing a retraction? Say Deputy Dawg was in Eagleton yesterday and actually Hank Leland was the hero of the day."

"Nah, nobody would go for that. Besides, it's your big blue eyes in the pictures. Good shots if I do say so myself."

"Too good. I sort of wish you'd been on the other side of the county at that hog calling contest or whatever."

"Don't worry, Mike. It'll just be a couple of minutes of fame and then the big-town boys will find a new hero." Hank frowned down at his notebook. "But you owe me the first interview and you aren't telling me a thing."

"I don't know a thing. The man was on the outside of the railing when we got to the bridge. He said his name was Jack Smith. He didn't give any reasons he wanted to jump. I was talking him back from the edge when some crazy photogra-pher came along and tripped the poor sucker's trigger and he turned loose of the railing."

"You don't mean me?" Hank looked up from his frantic scribbling.

"The description fits, but actually it was two photogra-phers. Sue Lou Farris and Judith Phillips snapping shots of him with their little camera phones. They're what set him off for some reason."

"That could do it for sure. Those old girls are scary. They're always bringing in pictures and wanting me to print them in the paper." He shook his head as he reviewed the scribbles in his notebook. "Okay, we've got up to him turning loose. Then what?"

"You don't need me to tell you that. You were there. I grabbed him, yanked him back over the railing, gave him a concussion."

"Did he say thank you?" Hank peered over at Michael.

"Suicides don't thank you for saving them. At least not right that day. Sometimes later they might be grateful, but mostly they tend to go out and try again."

"He said something. I heard him."

"Then why ask me if you heard him." Michael wanted to forget what he said. He wanted to forget the whole thing. Move on.

But once Hank grabbed hold of a question, he wouldn't turn it loose until it was answered. "I wasn't close enough to make out all the words. Something about pushing him. You didn't push him, did you?"

"You think I would push him?" Michael frowned over at Hank.

40

"No way. A hero saves people."

"Stop with the hero stuff," Michael said.

"Then tell me what he said." He had his pencil poised over the notebook.

Michael gave in. He didn't know why it mattered anyway. They were simply the words of a desperate man not thinking clearly. "He said I would wish I'd pushed him."

"Huh?" Hank scowled at Michael. "What do you think he meant by that?"

"How should I know? I'm no psychiatrist. The man obviously had problems or he wouldn't have been ready to make a dive into Eagle River."

"There hasn't been a suicide there for years. Not since I've been here in Hidden Springs and that's been . . ." Hank paused a minute to think. "My golly, that's been thirteen years next month. How many do you think have jumped there?"

"I remember two, but I've heard stories about others years ago."

"Maybe I'll do a history piece on all the jumpers." He scribbled in his notebook. "How many do you think there might be?"

"Beats me. You're the reporter."

"Yeah, and you aren't giving me much to go on with this Jack guy. You think you'll be investigating into who he is or why he wanted to jump?" Hank peered over at him.

"I don't look for the sheriff to make it a high priority. The man's being taken care of. Nobody else was hurt. Case closed." Michael was tired of talking about the jumper.

"There's his car."

"He can claim it when he gets out of the hospital."

"You think they'll keep him in very long?"

"I think three days is routine. After that, the psychologist or whoever can keep them longer if the person still seems to be at risk." Michael remembered the phone message from a Dr. Colson. He could be the doctor treating the jumper. "Most of the time the person has sobered up by then or is back on his medication and they send him or her out to start the cycle all over again."

"You think our Jack was drunk or on something then?" Hank was scribbling again.

"I didn't say that. From all outward appearances he was sober as a judge."

Hank looked up from his notebook and grinned. "That doesn't mean much in this county. Judge Routt probably has pockets for his bottles inside his robes."

Michael acted as if he didn't hear him as they passed the Laundromat. Inside, Janet Ericson with her toddler twins in tow was loading washers. She looked up and waved. The boys looked up and waved too.

"Maybe I should stop and take some pictures." Hank stuffed his notebook back in his pocket and lifted the camera around his neck. "Babies sell papers almost as good as heroes in Hidden Springs."

"No doubt better. Go ahead and grab a photo op while you can." Michael waved at the boys through the window. "They're getting their grins ready for you."

Hank hesitated, but then dropped the camera back against his chest. "I've got about a hundred pictures of those kids. People will think I'm their uncle or something if I publish any more. Besides, cute as they are, they're not the hot story today. The jumper is."

"But I don't know anything else to tell you. In fact, from

the sounds of it, you know more about our jumper than I do." Michael waved at the twins again and kept walking.

"I am the reporter." Hank hurried along after him.

"So what do you know that I should know?" Michael glanced at him.

Hank grinned. "Guess you'll have to wait for the paper like everybody else."

"It's a long time till next Wednesday."

"One week. Seven days. One hundred sixty-eight hours, give or take a few."

"It'll be old news by then." Michael shrugged. Hank might know something. More likely he was trying to fish for more information from Michael. That wasn't going to work. Michael didn't know anything to tell him.

"Yeah, enjoy your spot in the sun, Mike." Hank fell into step beside him. "You'll probably look handsome on television. Just remember not to smile too much. You end up looking like a used car salesman or a politician when you smile too much while the cameras are rolling."

"Or a newspaper editor," Michael said. "Did you get paid for the pictures?"

"I'm not in the business for my health."

"Glad to hear it. At least Rebecca Ann will get her braces."

Hank laughed and swatted Michael on the shoulder. "Life is good, Mike. Life is good."

"I guess our jumper didn't think so."

"The story's bigger than him now. He'll have to go along for the ride and 'fess up to whatever his problem might be. Maybe it'll turn out that he's got some kind of terminal illness." Suddenly Hank looked uneasy. "You don't think he had anything catching, do you?"

"If I find out, I'll be sure to let you know." Michael left him in front of the newspaper offices and went on down the street past Roxie Rockwell's insurance office and Reece Sheridan's office, where Reece was probably inside snoozing at his desk. He crossed the street in front of Paul's Billiard Hall to go back to the courthouse.

It really didn't matter what the jumper's problem was, but Hank's questions had awakened Michael's curiosity. If Hank did know more about the jumper than he was telling, Michael didn't want to wait and read it in the paper next week. Maybe instead of just calling, he'd drive over to Eagleton and talk to that Dr. Colson if it turned out he was treating the jumper. As usual, not much was happening in Hidden Springs, and odds were, no reporters would be looking for him in Eagleton.

6

Dr. Colson couldn't make time to see Michael until one thirty. So it turned out the Channel 22 news reporter found Hidden Springs before Michael made it out of town. Kim Barbour bounced across the courthouse yard like a puppy let off its leash. When Michael refused to do the interview on the bridge, tears popped up in her wide brown eyes, but after a couple of quick blinks, she settled for the courthouse steps.

The cameraman, who looked as if he'd been shooting on location more years than the pretty young reporter could claim living, listened impassively as she explained in depth the type of shot she wanted. When she rushed into the courthouse to find a mirror to check her hair and makeup, he shuffled over to Michael.

"The kid's been in the business three months and she's telling me about shadows." The man blew out a weary breath and shifted his gaze from the courthouse door to Michael. "You and me both know the truth is, this little doll was hired for her big brown eyes and cleavage, but she fantasizes it was her brains. Anyway, be a pal, and just go along with her so we can get this done with as few tears as possible."

Michael was all for that, and the tears that tumbled out during the interview had little to do with him. The girl reporter kept stumbling over her own questions even though she had them carefully written on cards. By the third retake, the questions were getting old. What had he thought when he saw the man on the bridge? Had he been concerned about his own safety? Did he know what had brought the man to such a desperate step? How did it feel knowing another human being was still alive because of his quick actions?

Michael tried to remember Hank's advice and not smile too much as he repeated his answers. He'd just wanted to help. He'd never been in any danger. No, he didn't know the man, had never seen him before, but people had all kinds of problems, etc., etc.

Attracted by the Channel 22 van, a few townsfolk clustered around them, ready to smile and wave if the camera happened to turn their way. Hank bounced here and there snapping shots with his own camera, mostly of the pretty young reporter. A couple of times he caught Michael's eye and flashed him an idiot smile.

When Kim Barbour was finally satisfied with the shoot, she turned toward the onlookers with a dazzling smile and told them the segment would air at six. Then she followed the cameraman to the van and headed for the bridge. They were still there when Michael passed over it on his way to Eagleton a half hour later. The cameraman looked like he might be laughing as he gave Michael a little salute when he drove by. Kim Barbour, on the other hand, planted her hands on her hips and glared at Michael as if she'd like to give an eyewitness account of him jumping off the bridge.

Of course, he could have gone to the bridge to let her get her location shot. He just hadn't wanted to.

Everybody was making way too much of the whole episode. Besides this Kim, he'd already talked to two other reporters on the phone. Same questions. Same half-baked answers. Same mountain out of a molehill. The poor guy probably would have climbed back over the rail, crawled into his car, and disappeared if Michael hadn't happened along with his busload of silver-haired ladies.

At the Eagleton Hospital, Michael waited by the elevators for the doctor to come down from the restricted fourth floor, but the elevator doors were still closed when the doctor appeared behind him.

Dr. Colson was a few inches shorter than Michael and what Aunt Lindy would call wiry. He led the way back down the hall to the stairs. Great exercise, he told Michael as he took the stairs two at a time to the second floor. He didn't wear a doctor's coat, but wore crisply pressed black pants and a white shirt with a Daffy Duck tie. His hospital identification tag was clipped to a belt loop.

He ushered Michael into an empty patient room. "We won't be disturbed here." The doctor waved Michael to the only chair and perched on the edge of the stripped bed. "Housekeeping likes to give the ghost time to move on before they redo a room when a patient dies, and this poor soul took leave of his life early this morning."

Michael resisted the impulse to take a quick look around and kept his eyes on the doctor. That peculiar hospital odor of medicines, antiseptics, and sickness soaked into his head and brought back the weeks he'd spent in the hospital after the car accident that killed his parents and almost killed him when he was a teenager. The scent was imprinted in his memory. Still, there seemed to be something a little different about the smell here. Maybe ghosts had an odor. Or if not ghosts, then death.

The doctor stared at the far corner of the room, as though pinning his imagined ghost there with his eyes. "This one surprised the nurses. Male, thirty-five, no history of heart problems, a routine appendectomy. They kept him for ob- servation last night. It appears they didn't observe well enough."

"Hard for his family," Michael murmured.

"Yes. So young to die." Dr. Colson shook his head. "But death can come at any age. Young or old. Actually, you look to be about his age, Deputy Keane. What? Thirty, thirty-one?"

"Somewhere around that." Michael didn't see any reason to tell the man his age.

"Then if you need your appendix out, you might be wise to go to Baptist General on the other side of town."

"I'll remember that."

Dr. Colson got off the bed, opened the drawer in the bed- side table, and pulled out a book. "Well, look at this." He held the book around for Michael to see the title. *Teasing Secrets from the Dead.* "A book by a forensics doctor. I've sometimes considered getting into the forensics field. Ferret out why the criminally insane do the things they do. Has to be fascinating work, don't you think?"

"For some perhaps."

"You don't sound very enthusiastic, Deputy." The doctor gave a short laugh before he stared back down at the book in his hands. "But it does seem an odd book to find in a recently deceased patient's room. Makes you wonder what secrets his own death might reveal."

"I suppose an autopsy can answer that." Michael reminded himself that the doctor was a psychologist. It was his job to figure out what made people tick, but Michael hadn't come for a lesson in psychology. He'd come to find out more about the jumper.

Still holding the book, the doctor sat back down on the edge of the bed in almost precisely the same spot as before. "Death is funny, isn't it? Most of us run from it and it chases after us with a vengeance in spite of all we do to elude it. And then some people run toward it and can't seem to catch it no matter how hard they try."

"You mean like our Jack Smith."

"Smith?" The doctor looked up from the book with a puzzled frown.

"The jumper. He told me Smith, but I think he used Jackson here at the hospital."

"Jack Jackson, yes. Not a very likely name, although I suppose there are Jack Jacksons as well as Jack Smiths born into this world."

"Is Mr. Jackson still a patient here?"

"Yes, we'll keep him a few more days. Then reevaluate his case."

"Have you found out anything about him? Family? Friends? Job?"

"I can't give out that information. Patient confidentiality and all that, but I can tell you his condition is stable. He shows every indication of a complete recovery physically. Mentally remains to be seen."

"Good to know the knock on the head when he fell on the road didn't do any permanent damage," Michael said.

"Yes, that is fortunate. Concussions can be deadly." The plastic-covered mattress crackled as the doctor shifted his position to stare straight at Michael. "Of course, deadly was what the man wanted, wasn't it?"

"So it seemed yesterday. People often change their minds, however, after a near brush with death."

"Indeed." The doctor smiled.

Michael didn't smile back. The clatter of a rolling tray out in the hallway was muted by the closed door. A door Michael was ready to go back through to find fresh air and sunshine outside the hospital. But first he'd ask his questions. "Why did you contact me regarding your patient, Doctor? If you can't talk about his case."

"I attempt to find every means possible to help my patients. I thought perhaps our Mr. Jackson or Smith, whichever it may be, said something to you on the bridge that might be useful in his treatment, but I certainly didn't expect you to make the trip here." Dr. Colson's tone of voice made the last a question.

"I'd like to talk to Mr. Jackson. Tie up some loose ends."

"Oh no, I'm afraid that won't be possible. He's under suicide watch, and not in any mental state to deal with details, although I'm not sure what loose ends Mr. Jackson could have in your town." Again the questioning tone without the direct question.

Michael refused to be intimidated. "There are some unanswered questions."

"There are always questions without answers, Deputy." Dr. Colson's smile was back.

"It's my job to find answers."

"And it's my job to discover the right questions for those answers." Finally the doctor asked a direct question. "Did our Mr. Jackson reveal anything to you in his moments of distress on the bridge that might give some clue to his mental state?" The doctor looked down at the book in his hand and slowly stroked the slick cover before he opened it carefully to where a page was dog-eared.

The light above the hospital bed glinted off the small patch of scalp showing through the doctor's carefully arranged hair as he gave every appearance of reading the open book while he waited for Michael to answer.

Michael wasn't sure what kind of game the doctor was playing with him, but whatever it was, Michael had no interest in taking part. He'd come for information about the jumper. Nothing more, and if what he knew could help with the man's treatment, he had no reason to withhold it from the doctor. "Actually, I had the feeling the man didn't really want to jump. That if we hadn't happened along, he would have eventually climbed back over the railing, gotten into his car, and driven away."

"But the paramedics said he did try to jump, and that you jerked him back from the brink at the last second." The doctor looked up from the book.

"That was later. Once we came on the scene, it was as if we had called his bluff and he had to go through with it. Perhaps to save face."

"Kill himself to save face?" The doctor looked like he barely kept from laughing. "I think you should leave the psychoanalyzing to professionals."

"You asked what I thought and I told you."

"Fair enough. But are you saying he jumped because he had an audience?" The doctor raised his eyebrows a little.

"Actually he was about ready to give it up and climb back over the railing when something pushed him back the other way."

"Something pushed him," the doctor repeated as if he were taking mental notes. "What might that have been?"

"You may think it's strange."

Again the humoring smile. "My business is connecting the strange with reality."

"It was just circumstance that put us on the scene. I was driving a busload of church ladies to a play in Eagleton. I told them to stay on the bus, but two of these women love to take pictures. They must have thought a man about to jump off a bridge was their photo op of a lifetime. They weren't about to pass it up."

"They took pictures?"

"As fast as they could click the camera buttons on their phones."

"I'd like to see those photos." Dr. Colson showed his first real interest. "Seeing Mr. Jackson's face while he was considering suicide might reveal something about his emotions at his moment of greatest despair."

"I can check with them, but they weren't really close enough to get much detail. However, the editor of our local paper showed up at the bridge too. He took some pictures."

"Yes, I called the *Gazette* an hour or so ago after Mr. Jackson revealed a reporter was on the scene. Mr. Leland was kind enough to send me copies." The doctor smiled briefly. "The photos put you in a very favorable light, I must say."

"I was lucky our man was sort of teetering or I'd have never gotten him back over the railing."

"So you think he was wavering even then?"

"I think he lacked the courage to jump and wanted someone to push him. At least he told me I would wish I pushed him. That I'd be sorry I saved him." As soon as he spoke the words, Michael wished them back. He needed to let it go, forget what the man had said instead of dwelling on it.

Dr. Colson gave Michael his full attention. "Why do you think he said that?"

"I don't know, Doctor. Maybe that's something your examination can reveal. It sounded like he felt guilty about something he'd been doing."

"What do you think that might be?"

"I have no idea." Michael shrugged a little. "But he obviously had problems. Maybe an addiction of some sort."

"Addiction? Interesting." Dr. Colson tapped his chin as though that helped him think. "What addiction would you guess?"

The doctor didn't blink as he stared intently at Michael, who suddenly felt like an uncooperative witness or maybe one so bent on helping in an investigation that he was making things up. He forced himself to sit still and meet the doctor's eyes. "Who knows? Some kind of demon pushed him toward the edge of that bridge."

The doctor wouldn't let him back away from his words. "We all have our demons. I daresay even you have your share."

All at once, the hospital smell crept out of the corners, dark memories firmly embedded in the odor. Michael tried to keep his face blank, but it was obvious Dr. Colson sensed Michael's unease.

Michael spoke up before the doctor had time to offer him a counseling session. "None that have me climbing over bridge railings. The fact is, if Mr. Jackson is involved in something which might endanger others, you have an obligation to report that activity to the police."

"Absolutely," Dr. Colson conceded. "What activity do you suspect?"

"I don't suspect anything. Simply doing a routine follow-up here." Michael wasn't sure if speaking to a psychologist was routine after keeping somebody from committing suicide, but it sounded more professional than saying he was checking out a premonition.

Dr. Colson seemed to be a step ahead of him. "I don't suppose it would be very heroic to save a child molester."

Michael stood up, ready to end the conversation. "Whenever you feel Mr. Jackson's mental condition improves enough to allow it, I want to talk to him." He handed the doctor one of the sheriff's old campaign cards with the office number scribbled on the back.

"I will let you know when or if he's agreeable to such a conversation. The man hasn't committed a crime. At least none we are aware of." The doctor glanced at the card, then placed it in the open book he still held as if to mark his place. He closed the book and smiled up at Michael. "But you can rest assured if I find out the poor man's demons pose a threat to others, you'll be the first to know." Dr. Colson laid the book on the table by the bed.

Michael didn't look at the book even though he had the feeling the doctor would leave it there for the housekeeping staff. With his card still inside. "If any relatives show up before you release Mr. Jackson, they can claim his car with the proper paperwork."

"I'll pass along that information." Dr. Colson held his hand out toward Michael. "It's been a pleasure, Deputy Keane. I appreciate your willingness to help me understand our Mr. Jackson. And his demons. I've always been interested in the criminal mind. Not that Mr. Jackson necessarily fits that profile."

Michael wasn't going to go down that trail again. "Let us know when you release him."

"Why? I doubt he'd make another attempt from the same bridge." A puzzled frown wrinkled the doctor's forehead.

"Probably not, but we can send out an extra patrol just in case."

"You must not be very busy down in Hidden Springs."

"It's a small town."

"A nice, peaceful job for you, I suppose." The doctor followed Michael out of the room.

"I like it."

"A satisfied man, happy in his work. A rare thing these days."

Michael was glad the doctor didn't follow him down the hall to the stairs. He didn't know which he was happiest to escape when he went out the front doors—Dr. Colson or the hospital odor. Either way, he took a deep breath and left the ghosts of the hospital behind.

7

The Channel 22 news crew was long gone when Michael pulled off beside the metal sign at the end of the bridge. The state put up the marker years ago detailing the history of the Eagle River Bridge, date of construction, the politicians who took credit for the project, the engineering design. Nothing very interesting except that it was one of only two bridges in the United States with a curve. Most people stopped reading before they found that out.

Michael didn't even glance at the sign today before he walked out on the bridge. The road, once the only route to Eagleton, had been drained of most of its traffic by the interstate just west of town. The interstate added a few miles to the trip to Eagleton but guaranteed you wouldn't get caught behind Farmer Brown poking along, checking out the cows in his neighbors' fields.

Michael traveled the old road whenever he had the extra time. Sheriff Potter said it didn't hurt to let the citizens see a sheriff's car around their way on occasion. It helped get the vote out at election time, and the sheriff, working on his fifth term, was an expert at getting the vote out.

Heat from the afternoon sun rose in waves off the blacktop, and the railing was warm to the touch as Michael leaned against it and looked down at the river. The water was settling into a nice green color that made Michael imagine monster fish lurking in its depth. Funny how yesterday's muddy water had caused the jumper to hesitate, maybe saved his life.

A beat-up Chevy pickup rumbled down the hill and stopped beside Michael. The right front fender had been crunched in some accident so long ago that the creases in the dent were rusting through and some twigs rested in the empty headlight socket as if a bird had briefly considered a nest on wheels. Orbrey Perkins had given up night driving years ago, so the lack of a headlight was no problem.

Orbrey braked to a stop beside Michael and leaned across the seat toward the passenger side window. "Is this where the guy tried to jump?"

"He was considering it strongly." Michael stepped away from the rail and over to Orbrey's truck.

"You find out what his problem was?" Perkins, well into his seventies, had long ago given up worrying about the time. He was fond of saying if God hadn't wanted him to talk, he wouldn't have given him a mouth. A fair number of folks in Hidden Springs figured God gave them legs to turn and go the other way when they saw Orbrey coming toward them on the street, because even a simple hello had a way of stretching into ten minutes or more.

Michael didn't figure he had to worry about that today. Another car would come along to nudge Orbrey on up the road. Michael rested his arms on the open window. "Nope. Could be he was just depressed."

"For the life of me, there's some things I can't understand.

57

To take a flying leap off here no matter what the reason."
Orbrey shook his head. "It don't make no sense."

Michael didn't say anything, but Orbrey didn't need much
encouragement to keep a conversation going. "I've known
four folks to pitch themselves off here. Five if you count Jerry
Cox, who changed his mind halfway down. Could be all the
others might have changed their minds halfway down too,
but he was the only one to live to say so. That was a story
now. Must have been nigh on thirty-five years ago now. Me
and the wife were already living on our farm out here then.
I heard tell Jerry died down in Tennessee a couple of years
back. Heart attack."

Sweat was soaking through the back of Michael's shirt. He
didn't mind talking to Orbrey, but there were better places
than the middle of a highway bridge in the July sun. "You
know, Hank Leland was talking about writing up a story
about the jumpers. You ought to go see him. I'll bet you
could help him out a lot."

"That would be a story, wouldn't it?" Orbrey reached
down into the clutter on his seat and pulled out a plastic-
wrapped peppermint. He looked at it a minute as if he knew
it was his last one before offering it wordlessly to Michael.
When Michael shook his head, Orbrey looked relieved and
slowly unwrapped it. "You know I just might go hunt Leland
up tomorrow. I could tell him some things. If he will ever
slow down enough to listen. The man's always in a rush
about some kind of deadline or something."

"He'll want to hear these stories. You tell him I told you
to come by." Michael kept his smile to himself as he thought
about Hank stuck listening to Orbrey. Maybe that would
keep the editor out of everybody else's hair for a few hours.

"I'll do it. Reckon Leland might take my picture?"

"I wouldn't doubt it."

Orbrey popped the mint in his mouth and got a good suck going. He pushed it over into his cheek to keep talking. "Leland takes a fine picture. You got to give him that. Them in today's paper ought to win a prize somewheres."

"You ever see the guy around before?"

"You mean in the last week or two?"

"Ever." Michael swatted at a sweat bee on his neck. "I mean, none of those folks that jumped before, none of them were strangers, were they? He had to know about the bridge somehow."

"I see what you mean." Orbrey rolled the mint around in his mouth as he considered his answer. "You know, his picture in the paper did remind me of somebody that used to live around here. Sort of a no-good, best I recall."

"You remember his name?"

"I ain't too good at names, just faces, you know. I never forget a face, and I ain't saying this fellow was the one I'm thinking about, just that he looked some like him. Family maybe." Orbrey looked directly at Michael. "But don't you have his name already? I mean, you got his car and all, or was it stolen?"

"Not so far as we know, and Jackson is what he said."

"No, that ain't right."

"Well, if you were to remember a name, you call me up, okay, Orbrey?" Michael pushed himself away from the truck window, thankful for a car approaching down the hill.

"I'll do it, Michael. The missus, she's better at names. I'll ask her." With a glance up at his rearview mirror, the old man reluctantly put his truck in gear before he raised his index finger off the steering wheel in farewell and slowly drove on toward the other side of the bridge.

When Michael got back to the office, Betty Jean had the phone to her ear. She rolled her eyes at him and pointed to the pile of pink While You Were Out messages on his desk held down by his stapler.

Michael shuffled through them while he waited for her to hang up. Buck again. Guess he'd better try to track the state police detective down to see what he wanted. He couldn't think it had anything to do with the jumper. More likely that stolen car Buck found abandoned out on the interstate last week.

Kim, the reporter, called to thank him for the interview and to remind him to tune in at six. Aunt Lindy called to tell him to stop by her house before he went home. No reason, but then Aunt Lindy didn't need to give him a reason. She said come, he went.

The rest were "way to go" notes from various citizens of the county. Betty Jean had written the message out on a couple of the notes. After that she just wrote "ditto." On more than a few of the ditto notes, the *o* had been decorated with smiles or frowns and one from somebody named Brittany had been turned into a radish with a top and roots, the whole works.

After Betty Jean finally hung up, she groaned loudly. "I'm not answering another call."

"The phones that bad?" Michael looked over at her. "What's going on?"

"We have heroes among us."

Michael counted through his notes. "Ten calls."

"I quit taking messages. They all were saying the same thing anyway. 'Tell Michael how proud we are of him. Keane

County is lucky to have a man like that serving us, yuk, yuk, yuk.' You get the idea." Betty Jean held up a list of names. "Uncle Al said I should get their names. The election's next year and it's always a good idea to know who your friends are."

Michael looked across the room at the page. There had to be thirty names. "That many people couldn't have called."

"That's just what I answered. I had Lester helping for a while but talking to all those females gave him hives, so I sent him out to wash the sheriff's car."

"Females?"

"Running four to one, I'd say. Maybe better than that. Half of them I don't even know."

"You know everybody in Hidden Springs." Michael gave her a doubtful look.

"I thought I did."

"Just tell them they've got the wrong number and hang up," Michael suggested.

"People don't vote for people who hang up on them." Betty Jean rubbed her ear.

"If you don't know them, they can't be voters." Michael looked down at the telephone messages he still held. "Do you know what Buck wanted?"

"To make trouble, same as usual. And Hank Leland called."

Michael ruffled through the notes to see what Hank wanted. Betty Jean stopped him. "You know I don't take messages from Hank."

"Right. I forgot the feud for a minute."

"I'm not feuding with anyone," Betty Jean said stiffly. "I treat Hank with the same courtesy I would any other citizen of the county."

"He probably votes."

"I should hope so." Betty Jean huffed a breath.

"He might put your picture in the paper sometime and some great-looking guy somewhere might see it and propose marriage."

"It could happen." Betty Jean scanned her list of names. "Three of these wanted to know your marital status. I put a star by their names. Should I have gotten their numbers for you?" She smiled up at him sweetly.

Michael laughed and surrendered. He never came out on top in any verbal exchange with Betty Jean. "No, that's okay. Names are enough. If it's written in the stars, then it will happen, right?"

"I gave up on the stars a long time ago." Betty Jean held up another pink note. "I did try to take one number. Alex called. I guess she must have been talking to Reece about our local hero."

Michael tried not to act interested, but the mere mention of Alex's name had a way of making his blood pump a little faster. He used to try to deny it, especially to himself. After all, Alex had rarely made anything more than cameo appearances in his life since they were kids and had vowed to be friends forever. Alex was tall, leggy, incredibly beautiful, and even more intelligent.

Ever since she'd shown up in Hidden Springs last year during that bad time after they found a body on the courthouse steps, Michael had quit trying to tell himself that Alex was no more than an old friend. That didn't mean he didn't still try to convince the rest of the world of that. So now he kept his voice low key. "She say what she wanted?"

"If it's you, all I've got to say is poor Karen." Betty Jean waved her pink While You Were Out pad.

"Karen and I aren't dating. I help with the youth group at her church. That's all." Michael wondered when he'd get to quit explaining that to people. Karen told him to stop explaining anything, but then she hadn't lived in Hidden Springs all her life the way he had. People seemed to think they had the right to know everything there was to know about him or at least do their best to find out.

"Some folks around town think there's more than that between you and Karen." Betty Jean gave him a look. "Or that there should be."

"Then they're wrong." Michael swallowed a sigh and explained one more time. "We decided it was better to stick to being friends. She's got her church. I've got my job."

"And Alex."

Sometimes Betty Jean wouldn't give it up. Trouble was, she was right. Not about him having Alex. He didn't. That didn't mean he didn't wish he did. "Alex and I are just old friends."

"Yeah and the sun's nothing but a little yellow circle in the sky."

"Come on, Betty Jean, I haven't got time to be playing your romantic games. She's an old friend. So did she leave a message or not?" Irritation or maybe eagerness leaked out in his voice.

Betty Jean raised her eyebrows but backed off. "Let's see. It was something like this. There was a recess in her big trial where she's trying to get some bigwig out of a jam he shouldn't have gotten himself into to begin with, and she heard the news. Wanted to let you know she always knew you were hero material. Said she tried your cell number but you didn't answer. When I told her you'd probably forgotten to charge your phone, she laughed and said that sounded like you."

"Glad I gave the two of you a laugh." Michael pulled out his phone. He had switched it off while he was with the doctor and then forgot to turn it back on. Cell phones could be a pain, but when Alex's number flashed on the screen, he was definitely sorry he hadn't remembered to turn the ringer back on.

"She said to tell you not to try to call her. The trial and all. But she promised to call back," Betty Jean said.

"Maybe in three months when she needs me to check Reece's furnace filter or whatever."

"She does set great store by her uncle Reece." Betty Jean gave him a sideways glance. "Does she have any other men in her life?"

"Dozens, no doubt." Michael did his best to sound nonchalant, but the words jabbed at his heart.

"Yeah, life's rotten sometimes." Betty Jean made a face.

The phone rang, but after a quick check of the clock to assure herself it was three seconds past five, she let it ring.

"Might be an emergency," Michael said after four rings.

"Then answer it. I've handled all the emergencies I'm going to handle today." She clicked off her computer and shoved some papers into a drawer. "Then again, the trial might be having another recess."

"That's not why I'm answering. I'm picking up because you haven't turned on the answering machine yet." Michael lifted the receiver. It wasn't entirely true, but then it wasn't Alex either. Instead it was Mrs. Hastings, who lived out on Bear Ridge Road ten miles outside of town. She was sure somebody was peeking in her windows and rattling her doorknob. The old lady thought that was happening at least once a week, sometimes more.

"Are you sure it's not the wind, Mrs. Hastings?"

"Wind? Are you daft or just hard of hearing, young man? I said I saw eyes staring at me through the window."

"Maybe a neighbor kid?"

"I don't care who he is. I want him arrested." Mrs. Hastings's voice hit a shrill high note. "I pay my taxes. I'm entitled to protection. What's the world going to think if you let an old woman get murdered in her own home?"

Michael held the receiver away from his ear and let her have her say. Her spiel didn't vary much week to week.

Betty Jean picked up her purse and mouthed "I told you not to answer." She waved and walked out the door with a wide grin on her face. She was usually the one who got stuck listening to Mrs. Hastings.

Michael caught a pause and stuck in, "We'll send somebody out."

The old woman's tone changed at once. "Deputy Stucker came last time, and I just know he scared away whoever was bothering me."

It was tempting, but this was Wednesday, the night Lester always took his mother to church. As much as Michael hated listening to Mrs. Hastings, Mrs. Stucker was worse. Besides, Lester wasn't there, and while it was unlikely anybody was actually rattling Mrs. Hastings's doorknob, someone might be messing around out there. It wasn't on the way home, but what was another hour? Jasper would wait patiently on the front porch for his supper, and the fish in the lake weren't exactly going anywhere. He still had Aunt Lindy to see to, and Alex would no doubt have some kind of high-profile dinner date that would push the hero of Hidden Springs right out of her mind.

Betty Jean was right. He shouldn't have answered the phone. Betty Jean was always telling him his biggest problem was that he thought he could solve everybody's problems and make everybody happy. She said he needed to remember that most of the time when you solved one problem for somebody, the person thought up two to take its place.

As Michael drove around the twisty turns of Bear Creek Road to scare away the boogeyman for Mrs. Hastings, he wondered if the jumper would be that way. Michael had come along and solved his problem of not enough courage to turn loose of the railing and jump. What problems had ballooned up to take their place?

He wished the doctor had let him see the man. Maybe if he saw him he could get rid of this uneasy feeling that the man might be right. Maybe it would have been better if he'd chanced driving the old church bus on the interstate.

8

Michael missed the six o'clock news. At six thirty he was still going through the motions of checking out Mrs. Hastings's phantom prowler. The old lady, Olive Oyl–thin and wearing a sweater buttoned all the way to the top even in the July heat, followed him around, complaining about how long it took Michael to get there. She obviously missed out on the news that he was a hero, and somehow that kept the trip from being a total waste. He could handle being an ordinary mess-up guy better than a hero any day.

He even managed to smile and nod when she let him know how that nice Deputy Stucker would have been quicker, how he knew what an emergency was, how he wouldn't have just come poking up as if nobody's life was in danger. What was the use in taxpayers paying for the likes of sirens and those flashing lights if he wasn't going to use them?

After he inspected her windows and door, he looked around in the old woodshed that was falling down under its own weight and peeked in the outhouse that had sunken into the ground until the door wouldn't open more than a crack.

Not a prowler to be found, Michael assured Mrs. Hastings as he backed away from her toward his car, promising that he'd be sure to send Deputy Stucker out if anybody bothered her again. As he drove away, he figured that would be tomorrow, as soon as Mrs. Hastings spotted his footprints in the soft dirt below one of her windows.

The next morning Michael was finishing his coffee when Hank Leland showed up at the Grill and plopped a handful of printed-out newspaper stories on the table in front of him.

"Isn't the internet the wonder of the universe?" Hank slid into the booth on the other side of Michael and called over to Cindy behind the counter. "How about some coffee and a blueberry muffin?"

"You've already had a Danish today, Hank," she told him.

"That was so early it was practically last night, and we're just talking about one muffin. What harm can one little muffin do?"

"Look in the mirror." Cindy gave him the once-over when she brought the coffee and muffin. "And check your blood pressure."

"It's this job and trying to keep up with our heroes." Hank pulled the saucer with the muffin closer to him as if he was worried Cindy might grab it back. "Did you see our local boy make good on television last night, Cindy?"

Cindy pushed her short red hair back from her face and beamed at Michael. "I sure did. Albert brought the little TV from home and set it up on the counter. Nobody so much as chewed until they went to a commercial. You looked very handsome, Michael."

"He did." Hank shot a grin over at Michael. "I expect he could probably get a job at one of the Eagleton used car lots now without a bit of trouble."

"If things get too slow here in Hidden Springs, I'll send out résumés." Michael scanned the headlines on the clippings. He was relieved none of them included the word *hero*.

"Things are always slow here in Hidden Springs," Hank said.

"Come around Sunday after church lets out and try keeping enough chicken fried to feed the Baptists and Methodists," Cindy said.

"I'm talking about news, Cindy." Hank took a gulp of his coffee.

"You mean like folks trying to jump off bridges." Cindy picked up the sugar shaker and swiped up a drop or two of spilled coffee. "I'd rather read about Zelma Ann's granddaughter winning a scholarship to that art school in Virginia."

"I told your sister I'd put that in the paper next week."

"That's the trouble with newspapermen. They don't ever want to write nothing but bad news. A kid gets in trouble, it's plastered all over page one, right enough. A kid does something good, then maybe a mention on page four in section three."

"The *Gazette* hasn't had three sections since last year's Christmas parade."

"See what I mean?" Cindy stuck her wipe towel in her apron and headed toward the kitchen.

Hank looked at his almost-empty coffee cup and then Michael. "What do you think my chances are on getting a refill?"

"About the same as Zelma's granddaughter making the front page."

"Now I was thinking about sticking it down in the corner on the front page if nothing too exciting happened this next week." He took a little sip of coffee as if trying to conserve what was left. "You think anything exciting is going to happen this week, Deputy?"

"I hope not." Michael stood up and dropped some money on the table.

Hank stuffed the rest of his muffin in his mouth, grabbed up the clippings, and tagged after Michael. When he swallowed, he said, "You might make some people believe that, but not me. Weathermen like storms and policemen like knocking heads with bad guys."

"You've got it all wrong. Policemen like getting bad guys off the streets so all the regular folks are safe and happy."

"So if you like locking bad guys away, that means you have to like murders and robberies, because without something like that, there aren't any bad guys to get off the street."

"What do newspapermen like?" Michael asked.

"News, of course. A rare commodity in Hidden Springs, I must say."

"Then why are you here?" Michael looked back at Hank as he held the door open for him.

"I tell myself it's the challenge. You know, finding news where there is no news, and then every once in a while some nutcase tries to jump off a bridge and I get to take pictures of a hero."

"I'm no hero." Michael let go of the door. It banged into Hank's shoulder.

"You'll do till Superman shows up." Hank pushed on through the door and waved the papers in front of Michael's face. "Don't you want to read what the Eagleton papers had to say about you?"

"No." Michael headed down the street.

Hank trotted after him. "Just wait. Next time I make a hero, I'll pick somebody like, like . . ." Hank hesitated as if no likely candidate would come to mind until he noticed Paul Osgood checking parking meters down the street. "Like Paul. Now he'd appreciate being a hero even if he's a little short for the job."

Paul was at least ten feet away from them, but at the word "short," his head whipped around.

"He couldn't have heard me, could he?" Hank looked in the opposite direction from Paul, who was glaring at them. "I won't be able to park in my own driveway without getting a parking ticket."

Michael laughed, which caused a dark look to thunder across Paul's face.

"You're not helping." Hank frowned at Michael. "Now he thinks we're laughing at him. Uh-oh, here he comes. We were talking about Cindy's strawberry shortcake."

"That hasn't been on the menu for weeks."

"But we were wishing it was, okay?"

Hank looked so desperate, Michael took pity on him. "It would taste good with a scoop of ice cream on top."

"That's the way to play the game." Hank held up the articles and let them flap in the breeze. "That's all this other is too. Just a game. Play along a few days. Talk to the reporters, smile for the cameras, and endure it when the average Joe tells you how great you are. By next week everybody will have forgotten. That's why they call it being hero for a day. A week at the outside."

Paul was definitely in earshot now, and Hank switched seamlessly to the virtues of Cindy's shortcake, making sure to say shortcake every other word.

Paul gave him a look. "You're going to have a heart attack if you don't learn to control that appetite, Leland."

"Ah, life is full of forbidden pleasures for sure, Paul."

Paul looked at him suspiciously, as if he suspected some kind of double meaning in his words, but Hank looked as innocent as a four-year-old kid bringing a wilted bouquet of dandelions to his mother. Paul turned to Michael. "Well, Keane, I hear you were in the right place at the right time again." He tried to quit frowning, but the thin line of his lips didn't lose their downward tilt.

Paul Osgood had to force himself to give Michael the time of day. He disliked Michael, partly because Michael had once been a policeman in the big city before coming back to Hidden Springs to grab headlines that should have been Paul's, but mostly because Michael was tall. Paul was short. It was the tragedy of his existence. He believed if he were only a few inches taller, he would have been accepted at the police academy to train as a state policeman. Then he wouldn't be stuck working for the chief of police, who happened to also be his father-in-law. He was tired of writing parking tickets the judge tore up if folks complained.

Buck Garrett claimed it would take a lot more than an extra inch for Little Osgood to make the state police, but if the man wanted to believe it was a lack of height instead of brains, then maybe that was for the best.

Michael had finally talked to Buck early that morning. Buck had information about the recovered stolen vehicle. He hadn't even heard about the jumper. He rarely read the newspapers, but he promised to go by T.R.'s station out near the interstate to get the VIN number and run a check on the man's car.

Michael tried to call Alex a couple of times too, but had to settle with leaving a message on her voice mail. He never knew what to say on voice mail and ended up saying something idiotic like, "Hi, heard you called. Sorry I missed you. Hope you're winning." What he really wanted to say was, "Hidden Springs isn't so bad. Sheridan and Sheridan would look good on a shingle outside your uncle's office. Hidden Springs needs you. I need you."

She'd laugh at that. All of it, from the prospect of her ever giving up the big-city life to write wills for a bunch of country bumpkins, to him saying he needed her. But it's what he wanted to say nevertheless, and someday if he ever got up the nerve, he might even say it.

Now he forced himself to tune back in to the conversation Paul Osgood and Hank were having with more than the agreeable nod he was giving to Paul whenever he paused and looked his way. Paul was going on and on about the need to coordinate their services to the community. It was his latest attempt at reorganizing Hidden Springs to suit him better.

"You think maybe we should have a joint city-county government?" Hank baited him. He even pulled out his little notebook and stub of a pencil.

"Now I'm not sure you should quote me on this one just yet, Hank, but there might come a day when the city and county governments could better serve the town of Hidden Springs and Keane County by merging."

"And who would be in charge of such a combined police force? That might be a hard call to make."

"That's a no-brainer." Paul stretched up a little taller. "The police chief is always the head of those merged law enforcement agencies."

Hank looked thoughtful as he stuck the lead of his pencil against his tongue for a moment. "That might be a big job for Chief Sibley to take on so near retirement age and all."

"Well, of course, a younger man would need to be in charge," Paul said.

"Did you have anybody in mind?" Hank poised his pencil over his little notebook.

Michael decided he'd best take his leave before Sheriff Potter caught him fraternizing with the enemy. "I'll leave the two of you to work out the details."

As Michael walked down the street toward the courthouse, he almost felt sorry for Paul. Almost. But Paul was a hard person to feel much sympathy for, and the man should know by now to watch what he said to the editor of the *Hidden Springs Gazette*. If he didn't, he would after the next edition.

Betty Jean was sorting through the mail when he got back to the office. She said Lester was out patrolling around the school to get people used to slowing down before school started in August. Sheriff Potter was checking things out along the lake today, which meant he'd gone fishing.

"The hero rush over?" Michael asked.

"Pretty much, thank goodness." Betty Jean looked up to point to a message on his desk. "You did get a call from that doctor. What was his name?"

"Dr. Colson?"

"That sounds right." Betty Jean slit open another envelope with her letter opener. "Said to tell you the jumper had faked out security and jumped ship."

"You mean he broke out of their psychiatric ward? I thought those places were the same as jails."

"Prisoners break out of jails all the time," Betty Jean said. "I suspect it would be easier out of a hospital. They could just get an orderly's uniform and be gone. They do it on TV programs all the time."

"Has the guy called about his car?"

"Not here. Could be he hitched a ride to T.R.'s. I mean, Hidden Springs doesn't have that many places that tow cars. He could figure it out."

"We have the keys."

"So he has an extra key in his billfold or maybe in one of those little magnetic boxes stuck under his fender or something. Lots of people do that. And he doesn't want to get stuck with the towing bill." Betty Jean looked across at Michael. "What is it that you're worried about? If he decides to pitch himself off some other bridge, I doubt we'd even hear about it."

"I don't know, Betty Jean. But haven't you ever had a bad feeling? A feeling that something's not quite right, but you're not sure exactly what. That something you've done is going to come back to haunt you."

"You saved his life, Michael. That doesn't make you responsible for him the rest of yours."

"But what if he was a child molester?"

"A child molester? Where did that come from?"

"That's what that Dr. Colson said when I went up there

yesterday. I told him what the man said. How he told me I'd be sorry I didn't let him jump, and the doctor said maybe I'd saved a child molester. What kind of hero would that make me?"

Betty Jean screwed up her mouth and considered her answer for a moment. Finally she said, "One who is going to have worry lines from borrowing trouble."

9

The week passed. No more reporters called. New stories, new heroes grabbed the headlines. Nobody cared that the jumper had walked out of the hospital and disappeared. Nobody in Hidden Springs knew he existed a week ago, so there was no reason to put him on their worry list now.

Buck ran a check on the man's old car. The jumper bought it from a used car dealer in the south of the state a couple of years ago. Jackson's listed address was a post office box in a little town down that way. No lien showed on the title. The trail was even shorter on Jack Jackson, which Buck figured meant the man had grabbed a new name to escape bill collectors or to duck child support payments.

When Michael caught up with Buck early on Saturday morning at T.R.'s Station out by the interstate, they pulled parallel, window to window, to swap news while they drank T.R.'s thick coffee out of Styrofoam cups.

"T.R. must have got the axle grease and coffee mixed up this morning." Buck took another sip of the stuff and winced when he swallowed.

"You could probably get some fresh brew over at the Stop

and Go." Michael looked across the road at the shiny green-and-yellow station that had gone up last spring. The bright lights on the roof over the pumps stayed on sunshine or dark.

"The sight of that place turns my stomach." Buck's voice lowered to a near growl. "America's becoming a string of brand-name stores every stop. One big homogenized highway. Virginia, California, no difference. If T.R. and Billy Samuels decide to stay home and go fishing, this place will look like a thousand other exits, all golden arches and speedy-fill convenience. It's enough to make a man move to Alaska."

"They have golden arches up there too." Michael sipped his coffee. It was every bit as bad as Buck said.

"Don't spoil my dream of the wilderness, kid, but you're probably right. Bear burgers on the drive-through menu." Buck took another swallow of his coffee before dumping the rest out his window and crumpling his cup. "Small-town America is taking a nose dive." He pitched the cup onto his floorboard.

"Oh, I don't know. Hidden Springs is hanging in there about as small town as you can get." Michael gave up on his coffee too and put it in his cup holder. "With the help of Aunt Lindy."

"That's the pure truth. As long as Malinda Keane is breathing air, nobody's going to rubber-stamp Hidden Springs." Buck shot a look over at Michael before staring back at T.R.'s pumps again. "Plus a few heroics from her nephew to keep the blood pumping."

"Don't you start on me, Buck."

Buck laughed without looking back at Michael. "T.R. wants to know what to do with the car. Says he can't just let it set there forever. At least not unless he knows somebody's going to pay the storage fee."

"I told him to give the guy another couple of days to show up."

"He won't show up. You've done given him a fresh start, son. He's probably already applied for three new credit cards with some name he dug out of a trash bin out behind an apartment building up in Eagleton. He's gone, vamoosed, never to be heard from again."

"I hope you're right."

Buck's eyes settled on Michael. "What is it about this guy that bothers you?"

"I'm not sure." Michael turned to stare out his windshield a minute before he answered. He worked his fingers up and down on his steering wheel. "The look in his eyes, maybe."

"The man was within a desperate inch of meeting his Maker. That can take the lid off."

"Yeah, I know." Michael sighed and looked back over at Buck. "Betty Jean says I'm worrying this like a dog licking at a sore."

Buck made a face. "Our Betty Jean does have a way with words, but could be she's right. If you're going to be worrying something, worry about something that matters, like figuring out how we can get a decent cup of coffee without going over to the enemy." Buck glanced over at the Stop and Go as he put his car in gear. "I guess I'd better go find some tourists to slow down."

"Since when have you been on patrol?"

"We're running this big push this week. 'Slow down and live.'" Buck boomed out the last four words. "It won't slow them down, but it will up the take for the month. Anyway, I volunteered some overtime. Billie Jo's off to Baskin U. next month."

"Nice college."

"That's what Susan says, but the tuition's nice too. Nice and high. They take your kid, brainwash her into thinking everything you ever told her was hogwash, and bill you some gosh-awful amount like they're doing you a favor. I don't know what the world's coming to."

With that, Buck drove off to chase down cars with Baskin U. bumper stickers and Michael headed over to put in his weekend hours keeping the Keane mansion and grounds up to Aunt Lindy's standards. While the house wasn't really mansion size, it was old, so something was always in need of repair or paint.

Today Aunt Lindy had pulled out the shovels and hoes for their semiannual fight against the honeysuckle vines and wild rose briars that kept creeping into the back garden. As Michael hacked at the vines, he thought maybe he should have gone to Baskin U. and learned how to leave home.

He had left home for a few years, but Hidden Springs had called him back. He liked knowing everyone he met on the street, and he liked the fact that in a small town like Hidden Springs he had a real chance to do what all good lawmen wanted to do, and that was keep the peace in spite of what Hank had said about catching the bad guys. In the city he'd been a street cop, the one who tried to staunch the bleeding. The bandage was never big enough. For every bad guy taken off the street, three more popped up in his place. Sort of like dandelions.

Alex told him he was hiding out from the world, and fooling himself besides. Bad people were in every town, every walk of life, every situation. His problem, according to Alex, was he didn't have the courage to step out into the unknown and accept the challenge of life. He asked her once if she didn't think people lived in Hidden Springs, but she had an answer for that too. They just existed, put in their days, and clocked out at the end of their lives without leaving a trace of shadow behind.

That proved Alex didn't know much about small towns. Small towns were full of shadows. As Michael grubbed up the roots of a wild rose bush that had taken up residence in the back corner of the garden, he felt Keane shadows all around him. His grandfather had no doubt fought weed intruders in this very spot. His ancestors' shadows lay heavy over the town as well, from Jasper Keane, who founded the little town almost two hundred years ago, to Aunt Lindy, who devoted her life to keeping Hidden Springs on the map.

Michael could move to China and not get out from under those shadows, and the fact was he didn't want to. His roots spread out and clung to the ground here at Hidden Springs every bit as tenaciously as the wild rose he was yanking up bit by bit, all the while knowing that next summer he'd be out here grubbing up the same bush all over again. Some roots couldn't be killed.

Alex didn't have small-town roots. When she was a kid, she spent a few weeks every summer here with her uncle Reece, but roots take longer than that. She never put down roots anywhere else either. Her father, a high school basketball coach, moved on to bigger challenges every couple of years, until he finally settled into a coaching job at a small college on the outskirts of Atlanta. By then, Alex was in law school. To her, the idea of roots choked out ambition and made a person settle for mediocrity. She didn't think of Hidden Springs as being the slow lane, more like the exit ramp to a rest stop. A nice place to stop for a break now and again, but not somewhere to settle.

Michael gave the rose roots an extra hard jerk, and Aunt Lindy looked up from patiently unearthing dandelions. "You must be thinking about Alexandria."

Aunt Lindy had an uncanny ability to read his thoughts. She said it came from crawling inside his head during the weeks he'd been in a coma after the automobile wreck that killed his parents. Whatever it was, there were times when he was almost afraid to think around her. He stood up now, the fragments of roots in his hand, and met her eyes without saying anything. She smiled and dug her trowel into the ground to oust another dandelion.

"Wouldn't chemicals be easier?" He asked the same thing every time they fought the weed battle in the garden.

"The easy way is not always the best way, and you know chemicals kill the good along with the bad." She let an earthworm crawl up on her gloved hand. "My mother kept the weeds out without any such poisons. I surely can as well."

"Your mother had Uncle Eunice." Uncle Eunice had been his grandmother's bachelor brother who earned his keep by making the gardens the showcases they still were. Michael had grown up on stories about his tall, thin great-uncle who preferred the company of his hoe to that of other people. People laughed at his slow movements, the way his bones cracked and popped when he curled down to the ground to nurse a seedling, and how he could go for weeks saying little more than yes or no. No matter what stories they told, nobody denied his roses were the most beautiful in Hidden

Springs. Over the years he had developed a large pale yellow rose that still grew in the garden and that Aunt Lindy guarded diligently. To show how much she valued it, chemicals were part of the arsenal to keep it going.

"And I have you." Aunt Lindy smiled. She was also impossible to sidetrack. "Have you and Alexandria been talking?"

"She talked to Betty Jean. I talked to her voice mail."

"Rather unsatisfactory, I would say, throwing your voice out along some wire to perhaps languish unheard for days. Letters are surely better." Aunt Lindy dug around another dandelion. "She must have had a purpose for calling."

"I guess she saw the picture. Hank sold it to a dozen papers, last I heard."

"I hope he gave you a percentage."

"He said he'd tell Rebecca Ann to smile at me. Seems my picture is helping pay for her braces."

"Well, the child did need her teeth straightened, and Hank does struggle to keep on top of his bills, or so I'm told. I suppose that allows you to see an extra bonus in the story. The poor man you grabbed back from the brink has a second chance and Rebecca Ann gets a new smile." She unearthed another dandelion and laid it in the pile beside her. "Not to mention giving you an excuse to talk to Alexandria."

"I don't need an excuse to talk to Alex." Michael smoothed the ground back down where he'd ripped out the wild rose bush.

"Of course not."

He loved his Aunt Lindy, but sometimes she drove him crazy. For sure, he didn't want to get into a conversation about Alex with her. Aunt Lindy thought all he had to do was ask and Alex would forget her career in Washington,

DC, and come running to Hidden Springs. Why Aunt Lindy would think that, he had no idea. She knew Alex. Plus, she knew about being career minded. She was career minded. A devoted teacher for decades, seemingly happy with her single life. She had told him once that she had been in love when she was young, but her intended was killed in the service. Someday Michael needed to get her to tell him more about that, but right now he wanted to tiptoe away from talk about love and marriage. Better to change the subject.

"What about the jumper? Did he look like someone you'd seen before?" He didn't know why he hadn't asked her earlier. If this man had ever lived in Hidden Springs, she might remember.

Aunt Lindy paused her digging and looked up at Michael. "He could be one of my former students, but as much as I'd like to deny it, in forty years of faces, a few have escaped my memory. However, there was something familiar about his picture. So, as a matter of fact, I pulled out the annuals for the range of years I thought might be right, but there were no Jacksons I'd forgotten."

"He might not have been a Jackson then."

"An assumed name. I didn't consider that possibility. I'll look through the books again." Aunt Lindy stuck her trowel in the ground to go back to work on the weeds. "Although I don't know why it matters. He didn't commit any crime. There's really no need for either of us to attempt to track him down."

"His car's still at T.R.'s." Michael straightened up and stretched his back.

"And if he leaves it there forever, that's certainly his own business. Saving a man's life doesn't give you any claim over his future, you know."

"In some cultures, the person would have to follow you around till he could return the favor." He grabbed the grubbing hoe again and eyed the next invading bush.

"That could be a problem, but in this particular case, you say the man has simply chosen to disappear. Story over. Ended. On to a new chapter." Aunt Lindy was good at moving on. She loved the past, had spent a lot of her life making sure the past in Hidden Springs wasn't forgotten, but she didn't live there.

She said life wasn't like a math book where you had to have the formulas in the last chapter memorized before you could work on the next chapter. Life just kept rolling the same sort of problems by you over and over again, giving you chance after chance to finally figure out some answers. Of course, she was always quick to point out that there weren't always clear answers. Not like in math. Life was a process. A glimmer of truth discovered here and a speck of reason unearthed there were the best a person could hope for.

Now Aunt Lindy climbed slowly to her feet, grimacing a bit as she stood up. "Let's take a break for some refreshments." She pulled off her gardening gloves. "I made lemonade. Real lemons."

"Sounds good." Michael stuck his shovel in the ground and leaned the grubbing hoe against it.

As Aunt Lindy passed by him, she put her hand on his cheek briefly. "I'm not sure why this hero bit is bothering you so, Michael."

"It's not the hero part, I don't think. It's more that I feel like Old Blue."

"Old Blue?" Aunt Lindy frowned.

"That dog we had when I was kid that could hear a storm an hour before the rest of us and would tear up the screen door getting inside to hide under the bed."

"I remember that poor dog. You had to feel sorry for him, but he was a bother. As well as I recall, Old Blue often panicked even when the storms never edged close enough to give us more than a sprinkle of rain." She looked at Michael a long moment, her hand still on his cheek. "Do you hear thunder, Michael?"

"I feel it, Aunt Lindy."

"Well, don't let it drive you crazy like Old Blue. Just wait and see if the winds blow the storm your way before you get too concerned." She patted his cheek a couple of times. "You did the only thing you could do at the bridge. You couldn't very well let the man jump."

You'll wish you'd pushed me. The man's words rang in Michael's head, but he didn't say them aloud. Aunt Lindy was right. There wasn't much you could do about an imagined storm.

Monday morning the storm hit full force.

10

Betty Jean bemoaned the sorry life of a single girl whose phone hadn't rung all weekend as she slit open the envelopes on the weekend's accumulation of mail. The office mail varied little from week to week, so Betty Jean had no problem discussing her own lack of romance and quizzing Michael about his weekend as she scanned the letters and forms and sorted them into piles according to importance. Opening the mail and romantic fantasies were a Monday morning ritual.

"Wasn't the moon just perfect Saturday night?" Betty Jean sighed, glanced at the letter in her hand, and placed it in one of her piles. "Did you and Karen do something?"

"I told you Karen and I aren't dating anymore. I went fishing till dusk. Then watched some dumb movie on television. Guess I missed out on the moon."

"You are hopeless." Betty Jean picked up a manila envelope. "What did Karen preach about Sunday? Or did you even go to church?"

"I went to church. Karen preached on the Good Samaritan."

"Wonder where she got that idea?" Betty Jean looked up

at him as she ran her long, thin letter opener under the flap
of the brown envelope. "Maybe from some guy she knows
yanking a stranger back from the edge of a bridge?"

"Her sermon had nothing to do with me."

"Come on, Michael. It's not a bad thing to inspire—"
Betty Jean shrieked and dropped the papers she had pulled
out of the envelope. She jumped up from the desk, banging
her chair into the file cabinet behind her.

Michael looked up from the on-call schedule he was filling
out. "What's the matter?"

All the color drained out of Betty Jean's face and her lips
quivered. She stared at her desk as if vipers had spilled out
of the envelope and were slithering toward her. She threw a
wild look at Michael and pointed toward the papers.

Michael had never seen Betty Jean speechless. He might
have savored the moment except for the thunder sounding
louder in his ears. Even before he picked up the paper off her
desk, he knew the storm had hit.

A young girl stared up out of a crime-scene-style photograph. A trickle of blood traced a line from a blue-black hole
in her forehead down onto her small upturned nose. Brown
eyes that had stared death in the face were wide and fixed.
Brown hair with blonde streaks lay around her face like a
carefully arranged halo. Her dark red lipstick was smudged
where fingers had pushed her lips into an unnatural smile.
She was young, not more than sixteen, and very dead.

"Is it a joke?" Betty Jean found her voice. She took another
peek at the photos and shuddered.

"No joke." Michael had seen his share of corpses, people
dead from both natural and unnatural causes.

While he'd been in the city, he and his partner were sometimes the first policemen on the scene when a body was found or a crime reported. The hardest ones were kids like this who overdosed on drugs or got caught in a street shooting or let the wrong guy pick them up.

Pete, hardened from years as a Columbus beat cop, had called them throwaways. "Use them once and throw them away. No credit for returns."

Michael stared at the picture in his hand. He wanted to drop it. To walk out of the office and up the street where the Hidden Springs citizens would be going about their routines. Where things like this didn't happen.

"Who is she?" Betty Jean whispered.

"I don't know." The second page was a view of the whole body, laid out with her arms folded across her middle and her legs looking too white below black shorts. She was barefoot and her toenails painted a bright shade of turquoise stuck up in the air in a sad celebration of life. A teddy bear looked out from her pink T-shirt under the words *Somebody needs a hug*.

The picture shook in front of his eyes, and he willed his hand to stop trembling.

"Why did they send them to us?" Betty Jean asked.

"And who sent them?" Michael added, although the thunder sounding in his head had already answered both those questions. Still, maybe that wasn't it. It could be something official. A couple of crime photos sent to the wrong place.

"The envelope had your name on it." She reached past Michael toward the envelope.

"Don't touch it," Michael warned and dropped the picture on her desk. He should have thought of fingerprints and not touched the pictures at all.

Betty Jean jerked back her hand. After a moment, she flipped the envelope over with her letter opener. "No return address."

"How about the postmark?"

"Eagleton. Saturday."

Michael glanced at the envelope. The address had been printed out on a label. Michael scooted the rest of the mail out of the way and used Betty Jean's letter opener to spread the pages apart on her desk. The last page wasn't a picture but a message printed in large bold font.

I TOLD YOU YOU'D BE SORRY YOU DIDN'T PUSH ME. THIS GIRL IS DEAD BECAUSE OF YOU. WHAT KIND OF HERO DOES THAT MAKE YOU NOW?

Michael wanted to grab the letter and pictures and rip them to shreds. Make it all disappear, but destroying the pictures wouldn't destroy the facts. The fact was, this poor girl would never see another sunrise. Michael pulled in a shuddering breath and forced himself to think. "Did you hear the news this morning?"

"I keep my radio on that country music station that says they play the most music. I figure any news I need to know will come across the scanner here." Betty Jean was almost whispering as if afraid to speak loudly with the dead girl's face staring up at them. "Besides, people are always getting shot over in Eagleton."

"I didn't hear anything about a homicide this morning."

"Could be they haven't found the body yet. Can you tell anything about where the pictures were taken?"

Michael forced himself to look at the pictures again. The background was blurred, probably on purpose, so that the girl's body stood out in clear relief to the rest of the picture. "Looks like she's lying on a floor or it could be dirt."

"I'd say a floor. A tile floor." Betty Jean peeked over Michael's shoulder. "Maybe those big brown and white squares like in schools."

Michael looked closer. "You could be right."

"Whoever killed her must have put a pillow under her head. And look—she's only wearing one earring." Betty Jean pointed at the girl's ear.

"Maybe on purpose."

"And maybe she lost the other one in a struggle or something." Betty Jean leaned closer to the picture on the desk. "It looks like she has a hole in the other ear for an earring."

Michael stared at the teddy bear earring the girl must have matched to her T-shirt.

"You think she was a street kid?" Betty Jean asked.

"I don't know. Maybe. Probably a runaway who hadn't figured out the ropes yet."

"I think I'm going to cry." Betty Jean yanked a tissue out of the box on the corner of her desk.

"Go ahead. Everybody should have somebody cry for them." Michael covered the photos and letter with white paper from the copier beside Betty Jean's desk. It seemed the decent thing to do, and he could think better without the child's dead eyes staring up at him. Besides, somebody could come into the office on business or just to shoot the breeze after the weekend. It would be better if they didn't see this.

Betty Jean dabbed at her eyes and blew her nose. "Poor

thing. She looks like she should still be playing with dolls. Do you think anybody knows she's dead?"

"Somebody does."

"I didn't mean whoever did it." Betty Jean sounded a little shaky. "You really think it might be the jumper?"

"Looks that way," Michael said grimly. He yanked open a drawer in the file cabinet in the corner with so much force the whole cabinet fell over toward him. Michael pushed it back and stood there with his hands on the cool metal and ordered himself to stay calm. He couldn't think about a girl who would never grow up because of him. He needed to concentrate on finding the person responsible. "Where are those plastic evidence bags? I know I saw them here some-where a couple of months ago."

Betty Jean looked over at him. "Top shelf, right corner, under the extra coffee filters."

Michael found the size he needed and came back to her desk. She was still standing in the same place.

"I meant her family," she said. "Do you think they know?"

"I doubt it. They probably didn't even know where she was. You'd better check the missing persons files."

Betty Jean leaned closer to the picture of the girl's face and dabbed at her eyes. "Brown hair with blonde streaks from a bottle. Too much makeup. What do you think? Maybe fifteen."

"Hard to tell, but young. Very young." Michael tried to push the picture into the plastic evidence bag, but suddenly his hands were shaking so much, it was all he could do to hold the letter opener, much less use it to guide anything.

"Here." Betty Jean took the letter opener out of his hand. She found some tweezers in her desk drawer and efficiently slipped the pictures, letter, and envelope into separate plastic bags. She held them out toward Michael. "It's not your fault."

Michael didn't meet her eyes. Instead he stared at the bags. "Can you make copies of the pictures through the plastic, front and back? The envelope too."

She had just turned to the copier when Hank Leland stuck his head in the door. "Good morning," he started, but then picked up on the tension in the room. "Something's going on?" It was half question, half statement.

Betty Jean kept her back to Hank as she made the copies. Michael stepped around her desk toward the door to block Hank's entry. "Not much. Betty Jean saw a spider. I was sending him to his reward."

"I wouldn't think Betty Jean would have any problem dispatching her own spiders." Hank frowned a little and fingered his notebook in his pocket.

"This was the monster variety," Michael said.

"Well, you shouldn't have squashed it. I could have taken a picture of the creature and run it on the front page. It'd be the nearest thing to news I've found all morning."

"Slow morning in Hidden Springs?" Michael tried to keep his voice light, and then wondered why he was bothering to hide the pictures from Hank. He would know all about it before the paper went out Wednesday, at any rate. Pictures, Michael suddenly thought, that might be waiting in the editor's own mail pile. One computer-generated enlargement could easily become two. "Have you opened your mail yet this morning?"

The editor narrowed his eyes on Michael. "Why?"

"I don't know. Just wondering if people maybe sent you stories sometimes."

"News doesn't come in the mail. Not unless you count pictures of somebody's daughter running for Miss Hog Valley, USA, or something."

Behind them, Betty Jean made a strangled sound at the copier and her shoulders began shaking as she started crying.

"What's with her?" Hank asked.

"Bad weekend." Michael grabbed the tissue box off her desk and pushed it over in front of Betty Jean, who still had her back to them. "You okay?"

She nodded as she yanked a tissue out of the box and buried her face in it.

Hank started to step into the office, but Michael stopped him by taking his arm and turning him back toward the hall. "Sometimes a good cry helps."

"But don't you think she needs a hug or something?" Hank looked over his shoulder at Betty Jean, who let out a wail and started crying harder.

"We're just making it worse hanging around here." Michael felt an answering wail crowding his heart, but he clamped down on the feeling. "Come on. I'll walk you back to your office and watch you open your mail."

"Something's going on." There was no longer any question in his words.

"Could be." Michael shut the office door behind them and propelled Hank up the hall toward the double doors to the street.

"I'm not under arrest, am I?" Hank looked worried. "You didn't read me my rights."

"Do you have reason to be arrested?"

"I didn't think so, but then you're acting mighty strange this morning." Hank glanced back at the closed door to the sheriff's office, then planted his feet and refused to budge. "Okay, Mike, you tell me what's going on or I'm going to scream police brutality."

"Who would believe you? Or care." Michael studied the editor's face, which was set and determined. The only way he was going to get Hank to move was to pull his gun on him or tell him enough of the truth to get him curious. Michael opted for the truth. "All right, you win. Something weird came in the mail. I want to see if you got the same thing in your mail."

"Monster spiders?" Hank looked as if he couldn't decide whether the whole thing was a joke or if he should pull his notebook out of his pocket and start taking notes.

"Monsters, at any rate."

11

The editor's desk was loaded down with every imaginable type of paper, from newspaper clippings to cereal box coupons. Here and there the slick edge of a photograph stuck out among the letters, as though trying to come up for air. A wire tray on the corner of the desk held a foot-high stack of letters with envelopes clipped to them. A scarred-up softball served as a paperweight.

Michael stared at the desk. "How in the world do you ever know what's news and what's not?"

"If it's news, it tends to keep floating to the surface. Most of this is junk." Hank waved a hand at the mess. "Letters from 'concerned' but 'chicken to sign their names' citizens, wild threats to shoot the editor for this or that, requests for free advertisement, or 'how to make a million bucks working out of your home' offers. Every year or two, I shove it all off into a big trash can and start over."

"How about today's mail? Is it lost in there?" Michael gave the desk a dubious look.

"Nah, nothing goes into the slush pile till I look at it and date it. I wouldn't want something newsworthy to get past me." Hank turned to a computer desk behind him and reached for a pile of mail.

The corners of at least two clasp envelopes poked out of the pile of letters, magazines, and newspapers. "Don't touch it." Michael quickly moved around the desk to step between Hank and his mail.

Hank froze, his hand suspended in midair. "What is it? A letter bomb?"

Instead of answering, Michael asked, "Do you have a pair of gloves around here?"

"Gloves? Don't you think a bomb squad might be better?"

"This is serious, Hank."

"And a letter bomb isn't?" Hank asked, but he pulled open the bottom drawer of his desk and rummaged around to come up with two gloves, one black wool and one brown leather. "Not exactly a pair, but at least they aren't both rights or lefts. They do?"

Michael felt like an idiot in the clumsy gloves sorting through the envelopes. Maybe there wouldn't even be an envelope with pictures. He was trying to think of some kind of story to tell Hank to satisfy his curiosity when the camera flashed. Michael looked up as the editor clicked the shutter a second time.

"Proof." Hank lowered the camera. "Of a federal offense. Messing with someone else's mail. Don't you have to have some kind of warrant for that?"

"Don't need a warrant if you give me permission, and believe me, you do want to give me permission." Michael eased an envelope out of the pile. It bore a printed white label addressed to the editor of the *Hidden Springs Gazette*, no return address, and an Eagleton postmark. He held it out toward Hank. "You want the gloves?"

"No, go ahead. This way I'll have something on you and you'll have to give me the story. And it has to be some story if it's got Betty Jean crying and you breaking the law."

"I'm not breaking the law. I'm just helping a friend open his mail."

Michael glanced around for an empty spot without success. He pushed aside some papers on the desk and laid the envelope on the flat surface before pulling loose the flap. With care, he shook out the contents.

The photograph on top was different from the one the killer had sent to Michael. In it the girl was still alive, smiling, looking even younger than she had in death. Michael leaned down to study the picture, but he couldn't see any hint of fear in her sparkling brown eyes or the lines around her mouth. Her hair looked in need of a comb, but so did half the models in the magazines these days. She wore a matching set of teddy bear earrings.

Hank moved over behind Michael to look at the girl. "You know her?"

"No." Michael slid the second picture to the top. Behind him, Hank gasped. It was the close-up death shot of the girl's face, an exact copy of the one in the envelope addressed to Michael.

Michael laid it on the desk and looked at the words printed in all capitals on the last page.

IF IT HADN'T BEEN FOR YOUR HERO, HOPE MIGHT STILL BE LAUGHING. NOW ALL HOPE IS LOST. TIME TO WRITE A NEW STORY WITH A NEW ENDING.

"What is this, Michael? Some kind of sick joke?"

"If only." Michael shut his eyes, but the girl's image was imprinted on his brain. "He told me I'd be sorry, and I am. I surely am."

"Who? The man on the bridge?" Hank didn't seem able to grasp the facts. He gave the picture a closer look. "My gosh, she doesn't look much older than Rebecca."

Michael pulled in a breath and looked at Hank. "I need a bigger envelope I can put these in to take to Eagleton."

"Eagleton? Why Eagleton?"

"The postmark, and it's where Jackson was last seen. It's as good a place to start as any."

Hank held out an envelope, then pulled it back. "I hate myself, but I got to ask. Let me make copies. You know, just in case I need to print the picture to help find out who she is or something."

Michael let him make the copies and extras for his own file. He didn't know why. Once he turned it over to the Eagleton police, he would be out of it. A curiosity to the case perhaps, but not somebody to pull into the investigation. He'd dealt with the Eagleton police department before. A deputy sheriff from Hidden Springs didn't command much respect.

Michael tried to reach Buck Garrett before he headed out to Eagleton, but with no luck. Probably in the middle of handing out a ticket. Just as well. Buck couldn't make any of it different.

Michael called ahead and talked to a desk sergeant, but the man must have thought Michael was some prankster wasting his time. He gave him the "we'll be sure to check into it" line and hung up. But by the time Michael got to Eagleton, the department had received another call, a tip about where to locate "Hope." They sent a car around to check it out just in case, and by the time Michael got there, they had found the girl's body.

So when Michael showed up at the desk that guarded the door, a policewoman was waiting for him. With a face that looked like it might break if she smiled, she shoved a marked map at him and told him to ask for a Detective Whitt at the crime scene.

"What crime scene?" Michael asked.

"Don't know, don't care," the woman said shortly. "All I know is you're from Hidden Springs, so that means you're the hero and Detective Whitt said send you on out. I'm sending."

Things went downhill from there. While he was driving the interstate over to Eagleton with the pictures practically breathing on the seat beside him, he had nevertheless been able to still think it might not be true. The pictures could be some kind of cruel hoax. The movies these days proved what could be done with makeup or with those picture apps. With the right programs, a person who knew how to work with computers could probably print out faces pale as death.

But there'd been no makeup or doctored pictures. The body was discovered in a church basement in the neighborhood where the old part of town met the new part. Two streets over, office buildings reached toward the sky. Here in their shadow, the houses huddled together in fear of the next urban development plan.

Somehow the old building that housed the Abundant Hope Church had escaped the bulldozers through the years in spite of various congregations periodically abandoning the location for larger buildings out in the suburbs. The current congregation had started meeting there about a year ago.

Michael made his way through the police lines and found Detective Whitt questioning the pastor inside the church. Michael stood back, listening and waiting. The detective shot a look his way when he first walked up but quickly turned his attention back to the preacher, Reverend O'Banion, a round little man in blue jeans and a plaid shirt, who kept glancing at his pulpit as though he'd like to get behind it to have something to hold onto.

They had had services Sunday night, but nobody had gone down into the basement. The body hadn't been there during the morning services. At least the preacher didn't think so. He'd made his usual check of the building before he locked up after the morning service just in case somebody off the street slipped in unseen. Not that the congregation minded the street people coming in, he claimed. They welcomed them and tried to find them whatever help they might need when possible. But the fact was, not all the people out there had the proper respect for a church building and brought in alcohol, drugs, that sort of thing. The church could hardly sanction that.

When the preacher kept slipping off and away from whatever questions he asked, the detective obviously struggled to hold onto his patience. Detective Whitt was tall, probably taller than Michael, but he lost an inch or two with the way he slumped forward, as though he had too much to do to worry about fighting gravity too. He looked like the kind of man who either didn't have time for eating, or when there was time, preferred a liquid diet. It was plain the man had used up the best years of his life serving the citizens of Eagleton, who had just as surely never shown the first bit of appreciation. The people he had the most contact with were apt to run if they saw him coming. He appeared to be a man who would like making them run.

Reverend O'Banion rocked a little on the balls of his feet now as he went over it all again just in case he'd forgotten something on the first run-through. "So as I said, I took a peek at the basement yesterday, but I didn't actually go over in the kitchen area. Sometimes I do walk behind the counter down there, you know, to make sure nobody left the water running or whatever. But Mrs. O'Banion and I, we were eating with the Redmons, and I didn't want to hold up lunch, you see. So I suppose the poor child could have been there, but I'd have thought somebody would have been down there for a drink or something."

"Can you find out?" Detective Whitt asked. "Plus we will need the names and addresses of everybody who came to either of your services yesterday. Detective Chekowski will take down the information." Whitt made a motion with his head toward a young female detective who appeared by his side practically by magic at the sound of her name. She took the pastor in hand and freed Whitt to turn his attention to Michael. "Keane?"

Michael nodded.

"They tell me you got pictures in the mail. Bring them with you?" When Michael held up the envelope, Whitt went on. "Okay. They should be about through collecting down there. Let's go see if she's the one."

"Any reason to believe she is?" Michael followed the detective down the steps to the basement area. Over the gardenia smell of air fresheners that had been set at intervals to combat the musty smell of the basement, Michael noted the sweet, peculiar odor of death.

"Yeah." The detective looked back over his shoulder at Michael as he stepped onto the concrete floor. "You."

"Me?" Something about the man's voice put Michael on guard.

"Yeah, you're the hero, aren't you? The hero of Hidden Springs. The jerk who called this in said you'd have pictures."

"So you have his voice on tape?"

"Don't get excited. He used some kind of computer-generated voice. Nothing we could ever use for identification. Now, stand still here and don't touch anything while I find out how much longer the nitpickers are going to be. Not that fingerprints are going to do us much good. I hope the Abundant Hope Church members don't mind getting their fingers inked." Whitt took a couple of steps and then turned back to Michael. "What do you think, Keane? Has our sicko got a sense of humor?"

"Not much funny about killing little girls." A shudder wanted to work through Michael, but he held it off.

"Maybe not for you and me, but this guy definitely thinks he's pretty cute." Whitt's mouth twisted into what might have been a smile. "Abundant Hope Church. He didn't chance on this place by accident, but we'll see who laughs last."

Michael stood where he was told to stand and watched Whitt confer with the man from the medical examiner's office. It was always easy to pick the coroner out at a scene like this. He was the only man in the room without that strange pinched look around his mouth. While Michael watched, he pulled out a pack of gum and offered Whitt a piece. Whitt shook his head, and the man unwrapped a piece and folded it three times before he popped it in his mouth. He lounged against the counter as if he had all day, and in truth, his charge wasn't going anywhere.

Michael surveyed the rest of the men and women scurrying around the basement. It was one big open area with tables covered with white paper runners and metal folding chairs now pushed willy-nilly out of the way by the police. A couple of the blue artificial flower arrangements in the middle of each of the tables had fallen over. Behind the gray counter that served as a kind of room divider, an old refrigerator and stove stood against the concrete walls. A coffeepot rested upside down on a towel beside the sink in the middle of the counter. The fingerprinters had been through and left a film of fingerprinting dust on everything. A woman stood at the far end of the counter, sorting and labeling plastic evidence bags.

A corner of a black cover sheet stuck out from behind the counter, but Michael couldn't see any part of the girl from his spot by the stairs. The body could have been there when the church met Sunday. The old tile flooring matched that in the picture. The killer might have expected the body to be found before his pictures made it to Hidden Springs. The envelope had to have been mailed on Saturday at the latest, which meant the girl likely was killed on Friday.

The coroner's report would pinpoint a time of death and determine whether she was killed here or just dumped here because of the name of the place. Had there been forced entry? Michael could think of a lot of questions to ask, but he kept his mouth shut. Nobody owed him any answers. He might have given the murderer the chance to kill again, but that didn't make it his case.

The technicians gathered up their equipment and Whitt beckoned to Michael. The detective pulled on some plastic gloves and muttered, "I hate putting on these things. Nothing good ever happens when you or anybody around you puts on plastic gloves."

"You're spot-on there." The coroner laughed as he knelt down beside the body and pulled back the plastic sheet.

"That the one in your pictures?" Whitt asked Michael.

Her skin had darkened and purple streaked out around the wound in her head now. Her eyes were still open, but they'd lost the shine they'd had in the photograph.

"That's her." Michael was glad when the coroner dropped the sheet back over the girl's face.

"Well, let's have a look." Whitt pulled the pages out of the envelope. He laid them all out in a row, not taking them out of their protective plastic bags. "How come there are two envelopes?"

"This bunch came to the sheriff's office in this envelope." Michael pointed without touching them. "The others went to the local editor."

"Is he planning to run them?"

"The *Gazette* only comes out once a week on Wednesday."

"Wish we could say the same up here. Would make life simpler, wouldn't it, Harold?"

"You can say that again. The hounds are probably outside by now. A little yellow police line draws them like ants to a picnic." The coroner stood up. "Can I load her up now?"

"Have at it," Whitt said.

The man left to get his gurney. Michael watched him go up the stairs and wondered if Whitt had planned it that way so they would be alone in the basement.

"You ever see the girl before, Keane?"

"No. Have you made any kind of ID?"

"She wasn't wearing a name tag, if that's what you mean."

"You think her name might really be Hope?" Michael stared down at the body on the floor.

"I doubt it, but you never know. This guy might be just cute enough to hunt down a Hope. He makes me think he might be the hunting type, and that he's not bagged his limit yet. What do you think?" Whitt's eyes burned into Michael in the bare-bulb light of the basement.

"I think you need to talk to Dr. Colson at Eagleton General. This Jackson walked out of there on Thursday, but the doctor had him under his care for a couple of days. He might have some information that might help you. Me, all I know is I should have let him jump."

12

Michael followed Detective Whitt back to the Eagleton police station, where Whitt commandeered an empty office while Chekowski, as anxious to please as a lap dog, hurried to fetch coffee. Michael had yet to catch her smiling, but the generous cut of her mouth and a trace of dimples hinted at a stunner smile. From her clear blue eyes to the curves her dark suit couldn't hide, Chekowski looked more like a beauty queen than a homicide detective, which was why Michael doubted he'd see her flash any kind of smile with Detective Whitt around to see it.

"Where exactly is Hidden Springs?" Whitt leaned back in the chair behind the desk and began flipping a pen through his fingers.

"Not far from Eagle Lake," Michael said.

"Nice lake. I've been there, but I don't remember a town."

"The name is on the exit sign, but sort of as a footnote. Tourists don't pay much attention since they're looking for the lake, not Hidden Springs. Besides, most people heading for Hidden Springs already know the way."

Chekowski brought in three Styrofoam cups of coffee and handed them around. Whitt stirred two packets of sugar in his. "Sounds like you think this Jackson was a hometown boy." Whitt looked up.

As Michael started to answer, Whitt interrupted to set a recorder on the desk between them. "You don't mind, do you?"

It wouldn't matter if he did. Whitt was trying to play up the fellow-officer, good-buddy feeling, but it wasn't working. Michael felt more like some lowlife pulled in off the street. Somebody they suspected of knowing more than he was willing to admit about the whole thing.

Michael's eyes slid from the recorder to Chekowski in the chair beside him with her pen poised over a small notebook and back to Whitt who continued to lace the pen through his fingers.

He might not like Whitt's attitude, but that was no reason not to answer his questions. "I haven't found anybody who says they knew him, but I figure he must have been there before some time or other."

"What makes you think that?"

"Because he knew about the bridge."

"Couldn't he have just happened upon it?" Chekowski asked.

Michael looked at her, surprised not by the question, but that she'd spoken up at all. Whitt's pen went still between his fingers for just a second before he began twirling it again. "Good question, Chekowski."

The young woman's cheeks burned as she dropped her eyes back to her notebook.

"He could have." Michael directed his answer toward her,

but she didn't look up. "But I got the feeling this was something he'd been planning, and most folks don't leave much to chance when they plan their own deaths."

"So you think this Jackson did that?" Whitt kept his eyes on the pen he was twirling. "Made this plan to come jump off your bridge and end it all in Eagle River?"

"It seemed that way to me."

"And then you come along and play the hero and give him another chance?"

The detective didn't say it, but Michael heard the echo in his words. Another chance to off little girls. "He looked harmless enough. Just some poor guy down on his luck."

"That's one of the bummer parts of being a cop. The worst killers can look the same as you and me." Whitt stopped twirling the pen for a minute and picked up the plastic sleeve containing the picture of the girl alive and laughing. "She doesn't look worried about anything bad here. More like she's on some kind of picnic with not the least inkling that she's the basket of goodies. What do you think, Deputy?"

"I don't think she looks frightened, but definitely excited."

Whitt studied the picture a minute. "Yeah, but if I had to wager a guess, I'd say not high on alcohol or drugs. More thrilled like she just got off a roller coaster or knows she's got a winning lottery ticket in her pocket." Whitt put the picture down and began with the pen again. "Okay. Let's start from the top. Tell me everything you remember from the minute you spotted him on the bridge."

So Michael went over it all again and then answered Whitt's questions at the end. Chekowski took notes and once or twice looked tempted to ask a question but bit the corner of her lower lip and kept silent.

The tape clicked off, and Whitt flipped it over to the other side. He let it record the silence in the room for a minute before he asked, "Now why was it you chased this suicide wannabe to Eagleton?"

Any illusion that they were colleagues had long fled the room as Michael began to feel more and more as if the detective was trying to somehow unbalance him and get him to confess to something, though what Michael couldn't imagine. It was already obvious he'd saved a killer. What more could Whitt want him to say?

Michael shifted in his chair and thought about telling Whitt to just rewind his tape and listen to his first answer again. Instead he swallowed his irritation and went through it again. "It bothered me. What the jumper said about me wishing I'd pushed him. I thought if his doctor would allow me to speak to him, I could figure out whether or not what he said meant anything."

"But the shrink wouldn't let you talk to him?"

"Right. I told you that already. The doctor felt Jackson wasn't in stable enough mental condition to talk to anyone."

"This doctor. Colson, wasn't it? At Eagleton General?" When Michael nodded, Whitt glanced over at his partner.

"Got it." Chekowski scribbled down the information.

Whitt switched off the recorder and stood up. "Well, you've been a big help, Mike." He leaned over the desk to offer his hand to Michael. "Give your telephone number to Chekowski here. We'll keep you informed."

The woman turned to a fresh page in her notebook and

handed it to Michael, who jotted down the sheriff office's number. He looked back at Whitt. "Do you think he might kill again?"

"Who knows?" Whitt shrugged. "If I could predict the criminal mind, I'd write a book and be on the daytime talk show circuit getting rich instead of stirring through the slime on the bottom of the food chain, trying to get a lead."

Chekowski walked out with Michael as if she had the unspoken assignment to be sure he left the building. Outside on the street, she touched his arm to delay him walking away. "Don't mind Aaron. He can be a pain, but he closes out a lot of cases."

"How long have you been working with him?"

"Long enough to know when to keep my mouth shut, but I forget sometimes. He has to be top dog, and that's the way it should be. He's very good at what he does."

"And what's that?" Michael asked.

Chekowski looked surprised by the question. "Coming up with leads. Making arrests. I mean, most homicides are by known-to-the-victim people where you take a look around and arrest the person holding a smoking gun or so random you could look forever and never find a reason to it."

"And which one do you think Hope is?"

"We don't know that Hope is her name," Chekowski protested. Then as if she felt her protest had been too strong, she explained, "Aaron says you can't think about the victim as a person with a mama at home worrying about her little girl's choice of boyfriends or a kid brother she promised to take to the park on Sunday afternoon or you'll be too busy crying to ever figure anything out. Until we know her real name, she's homicide number thirty-three."

She sounded like Michael's old partner in the city. "Then when you know her name?"

"It doesn't make that much difference. It's just another piece of the puzzle that might help us find the name that matters more. Her killer's name."

"Good hunting." Michael turned away.

"Hold on a minute, Deputy." She waited till Michael looked back around at her. "I don't guess you could get your editor to squash that story Wednesday. You know, the 'hero saves a killer' bit."

"I'll talk to him. He's a decent enough guy, but he likes selling newspapers. And headlines like that sell newspapers even in little towns like ours."

"Yeah. You'll be wasting your breath." She fanned herself with her notebook. The sun was beating down on them there on the sidewalk. "I guess the best we can hope for is no more envelopes in the mail."

He was in his car ready to get on the interstate when he realized he didn't want to go back to Hidden Springs. What was he going to do there besides sit around and wait for that next set of pictures? And unless Aaron Whitt was able to pull rabbits out of hats, another set was going to show up in the mail. That terrible certainty settled inside Michael like a heavy stone.

He had to do something to stop it, but what? He hadn't exactly been invited into the investigation. No, it was go back to your little town and let the big dogs take care of the mess you made by grabbing some psycho back from the edge.

Michael drove past the entrance to the interstate. Instead he made a left turn, then a right, and a few miles later was in the parking garage beside Eagleton General before he really let himself think about what he was doing. What would it hurt if he talked to the doctor again? He could surely think up some reason that might sound halfway official. Maybe he could question the nurses who gave Jackson his medicine or the aides who brought him his food. If he came up with the right questions to ask, he might get a clue as to where to look next.

Michael was still wondering exactly what questions those might be and how he would explain the fact that he was asking them, when he spotted Detectives Whitt and Chekowski striding across the parking structure toward the elevator.

Whitt hadn't wasted any time taking Michael's advice, but then in a homicide investigation, the first twenty-four hours were critical. Every day after that increased the odds in the killer's favor until after a year, the killer was usually sitting free on his pile of bones. Not that the police quit looking for the perpetrator. Homicides were never filed away, but cold cases where the leads had dried up got pushed off the front burner by new crime investigations.

After Whitt and Chekowski disappeared through the hospital entrance, Michael started his car and drove slowly back out to the street. He was not only out of his jurisdiction, he was out of his league. Facts Whitt would be sure to forcefully remind him of if he caught Michael stepping on the trail anywhere.

Still, he needed to do something, talk to somebody. There was always Aunt Lindy. She had a clear-eyed view of most things, but what did she know about psychos? Who knew anything about psychos? Michael thought of the doctor again, but even though he'd like to talk to him, maybe even look over his records of Jackson's treatment, Michael couldn't think of any way to make that happen without Whitt's cooperation. And Whitt wasn't the type to consult.

Besides, even if he did talk to Dr. Colson, he might not learn anything. Just because the doctor treated mental problems didn't make him an expert on the criminally insane. That was the kind of person Michael needed to talk to. Someone who might help him predict the killer's next move. An expert on serial killers.

Alex popped into his mind. While that wasn't unusual lately, this time as he started to shove her aside to keep from being distracted, he realized she might know a psycho expert. As far as Michael knew, she had never defended a serial killer, but he was confident her firm, which had at least twenty-five names down the side of their letterhead, had experts lined up for every potential contingency. She'd be able to give him a name.

He waited until he was close to the interstate to call. After waiting impatiently through her recorded message, he asked her to meet him at Wayland, West Virginia, a halfway point to Washington and about four hours for each of them. When Alex first started working in DC and was struggling to get her foot in the door of the elevator that went up to the floor with the private offices, she met him at Wayland once a month or so. She needed to talk to someone she could count on always being on her side, even when he didn't exactly agree with her.

That had been a few years ago, while he was working in Columbus and she still thought he'd do something that mattered instead of hibernating in Hidden Springs. She was glad when he quit the Columbus job, had actually let out a cheer when he told her he'd given notice. She wanted him to get on with the FBI or go back to school. He could even study law like she had. That would open up all kinds of opportunities, propel him up to the big time. He listened to her dreams for him and had to laugh. Later, he was never sure which had made her angrier—the fact that he had quit the Columbus force to go back to Hidden Springs or the laugh.

He sometimes thought about chasing the big time just so he might have a chance to catch Alex, but he didn't even like to fish with artificial lures. He liked using crickets, grasshoppers, mealy worms. He couldn't pretend to be something he wasn't.

Halfway to Wayland, he called the office.

"Where are you?" Betty Jean demanded.

"Just crossed over into West Virginia," Michael said.

"I can't believe this." Silence hummed on the phone for a minute before she let out a tired sigh. "You picked a fine time to run away from home."

"I'll be back tomorrow. Something going on you can't handle?"

"Everything's going on I can't handle." Betty Jean's voice went up an octave. "Hank has called me fifteen times to see if you've gotten back. What am I supposed to tell him?"

"That I've taken the rest of the day off and I'll talk to him tomorrow. He doesn't have to have a headline till he goes to press."

"I wish you'd taken him with you. He's driving me crazy."

"Thanks, but no thanks."

"Then what am I supposed to tell Uncle Al? I thought I was going to have to call Dr. Hadley to come with the ambulance when he saw those pictures."

"You could have not shown him," Michael said.

"I thought about that, but he is the sheriff. He needed to

know, and anyway, I figured Hank would jump him about what was going on since you'd disappeared on the wind. You're going to have a hard time making up for this."

"I'll bring doughnuts in the morning."

"It'll take more than doughnuts. Besides, you know I'm on a diet." Betty Jean was always on a diet.

"Carrot sticks then," Michael said.

"I don't think anything can make up for this."

"I know."

"Okay. Well, at least you did call." She blew out another long sigh. "Did they know anything about the pictures up in Eagleton?"

"They found her body."

"Where?"

"In a church. The Abundant Hope Church."

"Abundant Hope," Betty Jean echoed. "That's almost too much, isn't it?" When Michael didn't answer she went on. "I guess you want me to call your aunt for you."

"You're an angel."

"I'm not going all the way out to the lake to feed your dog. Not by myself. Not after those pictures today."

"I fed him this morning. He'll be all right until I get home," Michael said. "Anything else I need to know?"

"That doctor called you again. What was his name?" On the other end of the line, Betty Jean shuffled through some papers.

"Colson?"

"Yeah. He's the one treating the jumper, isn't he?"

"Right. The Eagleton police were questioning him this afternoon. When did he call?"

"A half hour or so ago. Left a number, but said you'd have

116

to call him tomorrow, that he was going to be out of his office the rest of the day."

"I guess I don't need the number then. Anybody else?" He tried to say it casually, but Betty Jean could read his mind even with a hundred miles between them.

"Yeah, she called. Said there's no way she can meet you tonight. She said she tried your cell, but you didn't answer."

"Guess I was in a dead spot." That might have been true, but then he couldn't be sure since he'd turned his phone off. He knew she wouldn't come if she could talk to him on the phone. So he made sure she couldn't. "She told me to tell you she'd keep trying to call you. I told her you were probably already on the way."

"What'd she say to that?"

"Oh, I don't remember. Some general 'men do the craziest things' remarks. Gave you a number to call if you called back in. Her cell phone, I think." Betty Jean rattled off some numbers.

"Right. I have that already, but thanks, Betty Jean. I promise I'll be back tomorrow. If another envelope comes, don't open it before I get there."

"Another envelope? You're just trying to scare me, aren't you, Michael?" Her voice sounded squeaky in his ear.

"There probably won't be another one, but just in case."

"Okay. And Michael."

"Yeah?"

"I hope she shows."

13

He tried the cell phone number, but when it went straight to her messages, he didn't bother leaving a message. Instead he held down the off button on his phone again. Back out on the interstate, he told himself he was crazy to pass up the next exit and drive on east as though he actually expected to find Alex waiting for him at the old Cherry Blossom Inn. In fact, he couldn't even be sure he'd find the Cherry Blossom Inn. They'd last met there over two years ago. Plenty of time for it to give way to a Motel 6.

Michael had never thought of himself as impulsive. He thought things out, did the sensible thing, and didn't expect miracles.

"Why not?" Alex used to ask him. "You're practically a walking miracle yourself. Think about it. You were in a coma for weeks and everybody but your Aunt Lindy gave you up for dead and here you are walking around practically in your right mind."

"I didn't say I didn't believe in miracles. I said I didn't expect them," he told her.

Now here he was driving away from the afternoon sun

as if he did expect a miracle to happen. Aunt Lindy liked to call him an optimistic realist. Maybe she was right. He never shied away from the facts. He liked being sure of the facts and had been, ever since he came back into the knowing world after the wreck that left dark spaces littering his memory. With Aunt Lindy's help, he managed to fill in some of the blanks over the years, but not all of them. While it might not matter all that much who his best friend had been in fifth grade, the fact he didn't know, that he couldn't remember, made him feel something like a stranger to himself.

Once when Michael told Alex how those lost memories bothered him, she laughed and told him she could fill in the blank on that fifth grade best friend. She was his best friend when he was in the fifth grade. She had always been his best friend and she would always be his best friend.

That was what he was counting on as he turned in to the Cherry Blossom Inn. He was relieved to see the building looked the same. He parked his Hidden Springs sheriff's car near the road where she couldn't miss it and looked at his watch. He'd wait an hour, then turn his phone back on. He wasn't ready to hear the messages proving how foolish he was to be sitting there waiting for her. He wanted to believe she would come. The waiting wasn't hard. He was used to waiting. Even in Hidden Springs, a police officer spent a lot of hours waiting and watching.

Across the street, cars threaded through a fast-food restaurant's drive-thru window the way the events of the last week ran through his mind. Funny how something that seemed good could turn bad so quickly. Michael hadn't been caught up in the hero bit. Heroes ran into burning buildings or jumped into shark-infested waters to pull people to safety. Catching the jumper teetering and yanking him back from the edge hadn't been heroic. Lucky, maybe. Or perhaps, as things turned out, not so lucky.

Still, in spite of the way the man's words had echoed ominously inside Michael's head all weekend, Michael had felt good about giving somebody's son or father a second chance. As it turned out, the second chance he'd given him had been to kill.

Two girls, maybe thirteen or fourteen, came out of the restaurant across the street carrying ice cream cones and laughing. Wet ponytails feathered out over the towels draped around their necks, and wet spots darkened the blue knit shorts they'd pulled on over their almost identical neon orange swimsuits. The taller girl had a trace of that white stuff across the bridge of her nose to protect it from the sun. As they walked away down the street, Michael had the urge to pull out and trail along behind them to make sure they reached their destination safely.

He gripped the steering wheel until his knuckles went white as the before and after photos of Hope flashed in his mind. She should be walking down a street somewhere, licking ice cream and going home to a mother who would yell at her for throwing her wet suit on the floor. But instead Hope had ventured out into the world and met a monster.

Michael shut his eyes and rubbed his forehead hard with the tips of his fingers. If only he could shut out Hope's image and do like Chekowski said. Change her into nothing more than a number on somebody's case list. It would be easier not to think about her begging the monster to let her live, but her last panicked screams echoed in his imagination. And the monster had enjoyed the sound. A monster who would be dead but for him.

Michael blew out a long breath and looked at his watch. Fifty-three minutes had slipped away with the sun that was disappearing in the west, and his stomach was letting him know he'd skipped lunch. He picked up his phone and stared at it. If he turned it on, it would tell him where Alex was. After a couple of minutes, he slipped the phone into his shirt pocket and kept waiting.

Out on the street, people driving by spotted his bubble lights and braked to match the speed limit. Some of them stepped on the gas again when they read the logo on his car.

Thirteen minutes past Michael's final deadline for giving up on Alex showing, the black sports car turned into the parking lot and slid up beside his, a sleek panther next to a spotted hyena. The tinted window glided down and Alex peered out at him. "Well, Michael, did you get them to hold our favorite table?"

He always forgot just how gorgeous she was between the times he saw her. He'd think he remembered, think he had her pictured exactly in his mind, but then she'd show up and blast all those past images to smithereens. A few strands of dark hair escaped the twist on the back of her head to curl around her face. Eyes just a shade darker than her blue jacket smiled over at him. When she stepped out of the car to stretch after the drive, her skirt inched up to show a lot of thigh. Nothing about her outfit was flashy. Instead, it was quietly elegant down to her small gold earrings. Her firm believed in conservative dress. She was what put the zing in whatever she wore.

"I hate these long drives." She gracefully smoothed her skirt back to its mid-thigh length.

Michael made himself stop staring at her before he did something stupid like tell her how beautiful she was. "Nice car," he said.

She laughed a little as she clicked a button on her key ring to lock the doors and set the alarm. "It's a cop car magnet. See, it's even cozied up next to one here in the parking lot."

"Maybe it thinks that will keep it safe."

"I don't think many people around here will worry about the Hidden Springs police force."

"Then they don't know the deputy there."

She smiled and tucked her hand under his elbow. "They will if they see him. It appears you didn't have time to change out of your uniform either."

"I like yours better." The touch of her hand was enough to make his heart start beating faster.

"I'd be a lot happier in blue jeans."

"I'm glad to hear you're just a country girl at heart."

Walking into the inn together, they made as odd a pair as the two cars out front. Nothing matched about them. She drove in the fast lane; he poked along in the slow. She liked Chinese; he liked Mexican. She liked tennis. He liked baseball. She liked philosophy. He had an obsession for Civil War histories. To her, the law was something to be used to her and her clients' advantage. To him, the law was something to be respected and enforced. Yet somehow they had no problem being easy with each other, even if it had been months since they'd last gotten together.

Maybe she really had been his best friend in the fifth grade, but he had the suspicion that even then he'd been in love with her and afraid to admit it for fear it might spoil their friendship.

A young girl, who looked as if her sixteenth birthday might have been yesterday and this was her first day on the job, let them sit at the table Alex pointed out to her, gave them menus, and promised a server would find them even if none of the other tables in that section of the restaurant were being seated right now. Michael slipped the girl a five-dollar bill, and she flashed him a smile that slammed the picture of Hope, excited and smiling, front and center in his mind again. He was glad Alex had her eyes on the young girl moving away from their table instead of on him.

"Do you think you should find the owners and arrest them for violating the child labor laws?"

He pushed thoughts of Hope away. He was going to tell Alex about her, but not yet. He managed a smile. "You're just trying to drum up business. You'd be handing them your card before I could get the handcuffs on." Coming up with reasons for him to arrest people they saw was a game they'd been playing ever since he'd first pinned on a badge.

"I need some way to turn this trip into billable hours. Of course, the depositions I reviewed on the way down here should make for a few billable hours." She opened the menu.

"I guess your client is innocent as always."

"At least until proven guilty." She looked at him. "We can agree on that, can't we?"

"Every person is entitled to his or her day in court, but do you guys have to find so many ways to get around the law?" He didn't pick up his menu. He preferred looking at her.

"We don't get 'around' it. We use it, and you'd want us to if you were the client."

"And wouldn't want you to if I was the victim."

"Sometimes our clients are the victims."

He let her have the last word. "Whichever way, I pity the poor opposing attorney. You look great."

She smoothed back a loose strand of hair. "Nobody can look great after a day in court and a four-hour drive right in the middle of three cities' rush hours."

"You do."

"You always were a great liar." She touched his hand lightly and turned her eyes back to the menu. "What used to be good?"

"The blackened chicken or the steak fajitas."

"Maybe a salad." Alex didn't look up. "And don't I remember that they have pie to die for?"

They gave their order to the tired middle-aged waitress who found them. A frown lurked under her "I can't afford to blow a tip" smile. As she took the menus, she checked their hands for signs of wedding rings, and by the time she brought their drinks, she'd forgiven them for making her walk too far.

"I hope you brought a lot of cash for a tip," Alex said.

"No doubt it will cost me six months' worth of my expense account."

"You have an expense account?" She raised her eyebrows at him. "Uncle Reece said Keane County was coming into the modern era. Next thing I know, you'll be saying Lester is on the take."

"A dedicated deputy sheriff like Lester Stucker would never be on the take." He wanted to reach across and capture her hand but he didn't. "But the place is growing. Lots of lawyer work."

"I'm sure. Uncle Reece has probably updated three wills in the last month and done two deed searches, one estate probate, maybe an adoption. Probably not a divorce. I mean, we are talking about Hidden Springs." Her eyes danced with amusement.

"People get divorced in Hidden Springs same as anywhere else." He sat still and watched her, hardly able to believe she was right across the table from him.

"Nobody I know, I hope."

"Some of us would have to get married before we could worry about getting divorced."

She rearranged the salt and pepper shakers between them. "Oh, is that what this is all about? Somebody getting married?" She looked up at him, the smile gone from her eyes. "Are best wishes in order for you and your preacher friend? Karen, isn't it?"

Michael laughed. "Not likely. I've been gun-shy ever since I asked this girl to marry me when I was fourteen or fifteen and she said no."

"I don't remember saying no." She leaned back, her smile dazzling now. "The trouble is, you went out and banged your head and forgot you asked."

"But you told me I did. Some years later."

"Hearsay. Not permissible in the court of love." A faint blush colored her cheeks.

He couldn't stop himself. He reached over and captured her hand. "What is permissible?"

"It's hard to say. It all depends on the kind of judge you draw. Fairytale romantic or 'this is your life' practical."

Alex pulled her hand away as the waitress approached with their orders, and Michael retreated. One of these days he was going to ask. He just hadn't figured out the right way yet. Besides, if he never actually asked, then she couldn't actually say no. That way he could keep believing that maybe someday they would find a way to be together.

While they ate, she talked about some of her recent cases. One had netted her clients a million-dollar settlement. Another hadn't gone as well. She kept away from actual names and skirted sensitive information, but she had a way of making the courtroom scenes come to life.

Michael listened to her talk, drinking in her presence. He'd needed to see her. Asking her to come had little to do with getting an expert contact. He could have done that over the phone in three minutes. He needed someone to talk to who would see the issue clearly. Yet here he sat, letting her do all the talking.

She savored every bite of her lemon meringue pie. "Almost as good as the one Aunt Adele used to make." She put down her fork after the last bite and gave him a long considering look. "But as delicious as that was, I'm guessing you must have had some other reason to command my presence."

"I didn't command. I just asked." Michael paused a second before he added, "And hoped."

"You knew I'd come. How could I turn down Hidden Springs' own hero, after all?"

The word "hero" stabbed through him, brought forth the pictures in his mind, and robbed some of the pleasure of the night. He looked around. They were the only customers left in the restaurant, and their waitress was hovering in the background while the little hostess upended chairs on the tables in the front section.

"I think they're rolling up the carpets." He peered at the check and tossed down double the amount. "Let's go find a bench out in the garden."

126

Shadows played across the garden paths as the heavily leaved trees blocked out most of the light from the streetlamps. When they found a secluded bench, he wiped the dew off it with his handkerchief. The summer night wrapped warm arms around them and gave off the faint fragrance of roses from somewhere in the garden. It didn't seem the best place to talk of murder, but he told the whole story from beginning to end.

She stopped him three or four times with a quick question or two. When he was through, she was quiet for a long minute. At last she said, "What could you have done differently, Michael?"

"I don't know. But because of me that girl is dead."

Alex put her hand on his cheek and turned his face toward her. In the dim light, he could still see the shine of her eyes. "No, not because of you. Because of him."

"Maybe so, but what can I do, Alex? He's going to send me more pictures."

For once in her life, Alex didn't have an answer.

14

By the time he got home to his log house by the lake, it was that deep of night when even Aunt Lindy might see monsters in the shadows under the trees. Since monsters had been stalking Michael all day, armies of them swarmed in the darkness around him now.

He smiled at the thought. Armies of ghosts maybe, soldiers from a forgotten Civil War battle still marching across this ground toward their destinies or maybe an army of bats from a hidden cave across the lake, but hardly an army of monsters. Monsters were loners, intent on their own path of destruction without thought or regard for any other monster. And one monster at a time was plenty, whether you were the chaser or the one being chased.

Jasper jumped up on the side of the car and whined at the window.

"Sorry I'm so late, buddy." Michael pushed open the door to rub Jasper's head. The dome light flashed on, then off as Michael climbed out and let the door shut. With the light gone, the black lab almost disappeared into the night except for the glitter of his eyes.

Usually Jasper pushed closer to make sure Michael didn't forget he liked his chest scratched, but tonight his hackles were raised. He jerked away as though Michael's hand on his fur might keep him from hearing what needed to be heard. Michael straightened up, his own hackles rising on the back of his neck as he too listened.

Lake water lapped gently against the shoreline down behind the house. A jet droned across the sky. The ever-present interstate traffic sounded in the distance. Sometimes in the winter when a snowstorm slowed or stopped traffic, Michael would stand out in the middle of the night and soak in the silence the way it was before the road was built. But now, even in the dark hours of the early morning, cars and trucks rolled steadily through the countryside. Michael couldn't hear anything that might upset Jasper. No dog barking in the distance. Not even the sound of a hoot owl. Beside him, Jasper must have disagreed as a growl rumbled in his chest.

Michael put his hand on the dog's back and murmured, "Easy, boy."

The growl died, but the dog stayed tense and ready. Michael heard a whisper of movement somewhere behind him, but when he spun around, he could see nothing except fibers of darkness so thick it looked like a piece of cloth.

As he moved away from his car toward the lake, his eyes slowly adjusted to the night and shapes began to form in front of him. The dogwood tree. The bird feeder swinging from its pole. The wooden picnic table where he cleaned fish. His rowboat turned upside down next to the lake. Nothing out of the ordinary, and in fact whatever had upset Jasper seemed to be gone. The dog pushed against Michael, his tail wagging once more.

Michael took his hand off his gun and scratched Jasper behind the ears. "What was it, boy? A fox sneaking too close to your bone stash?"

Jasper licked his hand, and Michael let out a slow breath while the night settled quietly around him without the strange menacing feel that had been there moments ago. Even so, he kept listening so hard his ears tingled as he climbed the porch steps. The second step squeaked the same as always under his weight. Normally it was a comfortable, homey sound, but now he tensed and froze in place for a second, his heart pounding. No monster charged out of the dark. Michael reined in his imagination and quickly went up the other two steps and across the porch.

As he pushed open the door, the thought crossed his mind that maybe he should consider locking up the house. He never had. It hadn't seemed necessary in this isolated place where the only people who came out this way were people he knew and trusted. But tonight monsters were lurking.

When Michael let Jasper in ahead of him, the dog made a reassuring beeline to the closet where the dog food was stored. Michael stood a moment in the dark, oddly reluctant to surrender his night vision to the light. In the kitchen the faucet dripped. He made his mind reach back to the morning before the pictures, before Whitt and Chekowski, before Alex, and was sure he'd given the faucet the necessary extra-tight push to stop the leak before he left for work.

Someone had been in the house, but that wasn't cause for worry or even unusual. Reece Sheridan sometimes fished off his dock. He might have come in for a drink or to wash his hands, or Aunt Lindy might have stocked his refrigerator with carrot sticks, cauliflower, and assorted healthy green things she feared he wouldn't buy himself. And the kids on the high school baseball team had standing permission to use his rowboat to build up their muscles before next season. It didn't have to be a monster, but somehow monster scent was in the air.

Across the room Jasper whined, but it was just a "hurry up with the food" kind of whine. Michael switched on the lights. Everything was the way he'd left it. A new biography of Stonewall Jackson lay facedown across the couch arm, open and ready for the next chance he had to read. An empty glass sat next to his gun cleaning kit on the coffee table where he'd left it late Sunday night. The smell of the oil lingered in the air. He didn't mind the smell, which was a good thing since it took a lot of cleaning to keep his antique guns in firing condition. He took a quick look at his gun cabinet. Still locked, the old guns lined up behind the glass same as always. A thief would have gone for those first.

In the kitchen area of the room, a few dirty dishes cluttered the sink, which proved without a doubt Aunt Lindy hadn't been there. Unwashed dishes drew Aunt Lindy like a four-alarm fire drew firemen. The usual clutter of junk mail was scattered on one end of the oak kitchen table, along with last week's *Gazette*, which he still hadn't read. The picture was facedown, but the word "hero" in the headline was easy to see.

Jasper walked back across the room to nudge Michael's hand and then hurried back to the closet, his toenails clicking against the wood flooring.

"Okay, boy. I get the message." After Michael poured out Jasper's feed, he gave the hot water faucet a hard push to stop the leak.

Then he checked out the rest of the house. It didn't take long. The log house had only two bedrooms and a bath besides the front living area. The towels in the bathroom were dry in spite of how he'd left them stuffed in clumps over the towel rod. In the spare bedroom the dust on the bedside table was undisturbed. The digital clock flashed a red twelve where he'd obviously forgotten to set it after the last thunderstorm had knocked out the electricity for a while.

His own bedroom was in its usual disarray with the dark green striped comforter pulled up on the bed but not quite covering the pillows and a pile of dirty clothes spilling out of the bottom of the closet. Yesterday morning when he left the house, he planned to do laundry after work. He glanced at his watch. Almost twenty hours ago. It seemed even longer. Days.

Out in the kitchen, Jasper crunched his dog food and the clock on the wall above the television clicked off the minutes till dawn. Nothing was out of place. He might not have given the faucet a firm enough push before he left. It was just the pictures of Hope flashing in his head that brought the monster scent.

The red light on the answering machine on the table by the couch flashed busily. Probably Alex telling him he was crazy and she wasn't coming.

Michael went to the front door and turned the lock, then did the same on the kitchen door that opened out to the deck on the lake side of the house. Jasper stopped licking his empty bowl and padded behind him back to the bedroom, where Michael shrugged off his uniform shirt and draped it across a chair. In the doorway, the dog growled. The growl turned to a flurry of barks that bounced off the walls.

"Quiet, boy," Michael ordered. Then he laughed when the dog stalked stiff-legged over to sniff the dirty clothes on the floor. "You're as bad as I am tonight. Both of us seeing monsters."

The dog worked his nose across the pile. Finally after one final bark, he decided the clothes were harmless enough and followed Michael back out to the front room to plop down on the braided rug by the couch.

Michael pushed the play button on his machine. The first message was a hang-up, probably Aunt Lindy, who refused to talk to machines. Michael fast-forwarded to the next message. Karen asked him if he'd forgotten his promise to go with her to look for a new computer in Eagleton that afternoon. Of course, he had.

After a little pause as if she almost expected an answer, she went on, "I suppose something came up, but I wanted to be sure you weren't just running late before I left. I tried your cell, but you didn't answer. I'll talk with you tomorrow."

She didn't sound upset. Their friendship—comfortable, convenient, quiet—had stalled on the edge of being anything more than that. She wouldn't be angry at him for forgetting. Not even if she found out he drove four hours to see Alex instead of keeping his promise to her. While everybody else in Hidden Springs might still think romance had a chance between them, Karen knew better and wasn't upset in the least by that.

Michael pushed the button again and Alex's voice filled the room. "I hope you're not on the interstate headed this way, because there's no way I can come. Absolutely no way. Not unless an earthquake hits the courtroom and makes the judge postpone my case due to rubble blocking the bench.

I'm really sorry, Michael. I know you wouldn't have asked if it wasn't important, so give me a call. Maybe we can talk it out over the phone."

The next message an hour later was also from her. "This is crazy, Michael. I know we promised to always be there for one another, but I just can't come. Not tonight. You won't file a breach of promise suit, will you?"

Michael smiled, wondering how old they'd been when they made that promise, but glad she remembered it even if he didn't. He replayed it just so her voice would linger in the room a bit longer.

Jasper raised his head off his paws and whined.

"Yeah, me too, pal. Me too," Michael said.

Michael pushed the button to let the next message play. "Deputy Keane." A man's voice. Jasper lost interest and dropped his head back to his paws. "Dr. Colson speaking. It's 5:03 Monday p.m. Your office staff was kind enough to supply me with your home number when I told her how imperative it was I speak with you as soon as possible about our Mr. Jackson."

Michael wondered why the doctor was calling him and not Detective Whitt, but he wrote down the number the doctor repeated twice before urging, "Please call as soon as you come in no matter the hour."

The doctor would have to wait. In spite of his words, nobody wanted a call at this time of night. Rather, morning.

Michael resisted the impulse to back up the messages to hear Alex's voice again. He'd seen her. She'd come. He didn't need her recorded voice when he had that memory.

He went back to the bedroom and shucked his shoes and the rest of his uniform, leaving the gun within reach on the table by his alarm clock. He stared at the gun a moment before he turned the light off. What was he afraid of? Water snakes when he was swimming. Forgetting who he was. Aunt Lindy dying. Alex marrying a high-profile lawyer. Monsters without faces.

But this monster had a face. Michael had the urge to turn the light back on and go look at Jackson's face in the picture on the front of the *Gazette*. Instead he pushed it all out of his mind and slept.

Four hours later he was up, loading the washer while he called Betty Jean at the office to let her know he'd be an hour or two late and to remind her not to open the mail till he got there.

"You don't really think there'll be more pictures, do you?" she asked in a small voice that didn't even sound like Betty Jean.

"I don't know."

A small silence fell between them then before she said, "Did she come?"

"She came."

"I'm glad." She sounded more like herself. "That doctor called again."

"Yeah, I got his message last night."

"I'm talking about this morning. The phone was ringing when I unlocked the door."

"Did he say what he wanted?"

"You. Said he needed to talk to you. That it was urgent. Acted like he thought I hadn't given you the message from yesterday." Now she sounded huffy.

"I'll call him when I get in to the office, but I'm not sure Whitt will appreciate it."

"Whitt? Who's Whitt?"

"Eagleton's finest and smartest."

"I hope so. I hope he has this nut behind bars already."

"I can agree with you there." Michael turned the dials on the washer and let the water rush in on top of his clothes.

On the other end of the line, Betty Jean heard the water. "It's the pits not having a woman to do your laundry for you."

Michael smiled. "Or a man to do yours."

"That's not what I want a man for." She laughed and hung up.

A half hour later when Michael transferred the wet clothes to the dryer, he spotted something shiny in the bottom of the washer. When he fished it out, a sharp post stuck his finger. He never wore a tie clip. Maybe Aunt Lindy had lost one of her stick pins down here sometime.

He turned it over in his hand. He shut his eyes, shook his head a little, and looked again, sure his eyes were playing tricks on him. Hoping his eyes were playing tricks on him.

But the earring was a teddy bear, a friendly pink-and-yellow teddy bear.

15

As soon as Michael stepped in the back door of the court-house, Hank jumped him. "What'd you find out? Was it her? Can I print?"

Hank didn't wait for answers. "I've got to print. What can it hurt if I print? The poor little girl can't get any deader because it's in the paper, can she?"

"No." Michael moved past Hank up the hallway.

Hank hustled around in front of Michael to keep him from going in the sheriff's office. "Hold on just a minute. You're going to have to say more than that, Michael. You can't leave me hanging on this one."

Michael resisted the urge to push past Hank and made himself look at the editor. He tried not to think of the teddy bear earring in his pocket, but that was like not thinking about the rain while standing in the middle of a stormy deluge. The monster had been in his house, maybe sat in his chairs, ate his food, drank his water, but Jackson was no Goldilocks easily scared off with a growl.

"You look awful." Hank peered at Michael's face.

"Didn't get much sleep," Michael said.

"I can understand that." Hank shifted from one foot to the other. "Not that any of this is your fault or anything. You couldn't know the jumper was a psycho."

"You didn't get any new pictures, did you?"

"No, did you?" Hank looked worried, but Michael wasn't sure if it was because he was afraid he'd get more pictures or that he wouldn't.

"I don't know. I just got here."

"Yeah, running sort of late, aren't you?" Hank looked at his watch, then back at Michael. "You'll tell me if you get more pictures, won't you?"

"I'll tell you." There was no need to keep Hank in the dark. He was part of it already. He'd seen the pictures.

"Whitt wouldn't tell me anything," Hank said.

"Detective Whitt questioned you?"

"Actually I called up there to try to, you know, flesh out the story." Hank looked uncomfortable. "I knew you'd tell me whatever you found out and all, but a good reporter can't just sit on his hands. I'd have driven up there, but Perry's out of the office cutting hay and so I had to knock up the new ads for the run tonight. Murders might sell papers, but ads pay the bills. I told Perry I hired him to do ads on Mondays, but he says he has to get his hay up when his hay is ready."

"So you called." Michael stuck in his words to keep Hank from going off on a tangent about how Perry needed to decide whether he wanted to be a newspaperman or stay a farmer.

"Yeah. I figured I wouldn't get past the front desk, but they put me right through to this Whitt. Obviously he already had my name from you. Said he was glad I called. That he wanted to go over everything again, just so he'd be clear on exactly what happened. Said that sometimes newsmen noticed things other people didn't and what I saw might give him a new perspective on things." Hank fingered his notebook in his shirt pocket as if he'd like to pull it out and jot something down, but he let it stay in there.

"That makes sense." Michael could feel Hank's eyes on him, but Michael stared down the hall at the big penny scale that had been there in that spot ever since he could remember. He'd seen a penny scale just like it one time in a museum, but there were ropes around it so no one could step up on it. Hidden Springs citizens still quoted their weights from the penny scale over the doctor's scales, maybe because it was usually five pounds lighter.

"Nothing makes sense." Hank's voice went up. "He said I might have to come to Eagleton to make a statement and that I should be careful what I publish so as not to make things worse. How could things get any worse?"

"More dead girls." Michael finally looked back at Hank. "So what are you going to do?"

"He asked me if I had copies of the pictures." Hank took out a handkerchief and wiped his forehead. The courthouse air conditioning had never done much to cool off the hallway. "He wasn't too happy when I said I did. He said you should have confiscated them. Not just the pictures but the copies too. I didn't tell him you let me make them."

"You could have. It wouldn't have bothered me."

Hank wiped his face again. "I got to print it, Michael. I mean it was dumped in my lap. I can't sit on it. The big-town papers are already sniffing around. There's something about a body being found in a church basement in the papers this morning." He yanked a clipping out of his pocket and waved it at Michael. "Whitt asked me, tried to order me, not to run anything about it, but I got to, Michael. You understand that, don't you?"

"It's not your usual small-town story."

"You're right about that." Hank wiped his forehead again and stuffed his handkerchief back in his pocket. "But it's a story with Hidden Springs connections. I've got to run it."

"Then be ready for whatever happens next."

"You think he's going to kill again?" Hank finally pulled out his notebook and pen.

Michael looked at the little notebook without a word.

Hank dropped it back in his pocket. "Off the record then."

"I've got a bad feeling that he might unless Whitt's some kind of miracle detective." Simply saying the words sent a sick chill through Michael. "This Jackson is slick."

Hank frowned as he fingered the top of his notebook. "That's the part about all this that doesn't fit. I didn't get that picture at all of Jackson out on the bridge. He seemed more like a mess-up of the first order. You think he has multiple personalities?"

"Who knows? Maybe you can ask that doctor up at Eagleton General."

"That's an idea." Hank pulled out the notebook again and jotted down a couple of words. "Some of those shrinks like seeing their names in the paper. Free advertisement." He looked up at Michael. "Anything else?"

"Nope." He certainly wasn't going to tell the editor about the earring in his pocket. Whitt was the one he had to tell. Not Hank.

"Then I guess it's to work for both of us. But remember—" Hank pointed his pencil at Michael—"you promise to let me know if something else happens."

140

"You'll know." Michael was relieved when Hank headed on up the hall toward the front doors.

In the office, the mail, unopened, was neatly stacked on the corner of Betty Jean's desk. It was probably the first time in the three years they'd been working together that she'd followed his orders explicitly.

She looked up from the computer. "Did you call that Dr. Colson?"

"Not yet. I told you I'd call him when I got here."

"Fine." She pointed at him. "But don't try leaving here until you call him. He's driving me bananas."

"Maybe he needs new patients."

"Very funny."

"Sorry." Michael meant it. It was no time to make jokes. "I'll call him as soon as we look at the mail. Where's the sheriff?"

"Grandma Potter's got pneumonia. He went over to the nursing home to check on her. Said he might not be in at all, that there wasn't anything he could do about this other stuff anyway. That he was sure you could handle whatever came up." Betty Jean's eyes narrowed on him. "Of course he hasn't seen you this morning. You okay?"

"Not enough sleep." Michael sat down in his chair.

"I hope she looks better than you do today."

"She always looks better than I do."

"Oh, to be an Alexandria." Betty Jean sighed a little.

"She's not married either."

"Not because no one has ever asked her, I'll bet." Betty Jean barely hesitated before asking, "Have you?"

Michael pretended not to understand. "What? Been married?"

"Stop trying to avoid the question. Have you asked her?"

"It's none of your business, but as a matter of fact, Alex said I did when I was fourteen or fifteen. I don't remember it."

"Not since then?"

"No, Betty Jean. Not since then." Michael tried to change the subject. "Let's get at this mail."

"Chicken." Betty Jean made a face at him as she picked up her letter opener, gingerly slit open the only manila envelope. A brochure about a weapon seminar spilled out. After she got past that envelope, she moved quickly through the routine letters. When she had opened the last one, she heaved a sigh of relief and pushed away from her desk. "I need a break. I'm going outside and smoke a cigarette."

"You don't smoke."

"Okay, so I'll go watch Stella smoke hers. The law says I can have a break." The phone rang before she got to the door. She didn't slow down as she looked back at him. "Your turn."

Michael picked up the phone and tried to listen patiently as Madeline Sanders complained that Lester had used his lights and siren to pull her over.

"There was absolutely no need for him to use his siren. None at all," she said. "Made me feel like some sort of criminal. I stopped as soon as I saw his lights, even though I couldn't have been going much over the speed limit. You need to do something about him."

The woman's words were only a small distraction, like a fly buzzing his head while he was crawling through a rattlesnake pit. He should have called Whitt as soon as he saw the earring instead of just pulling the door of his house shut and locking it. Whitt might want to send a team down to take fingerprints or look for footprints. In a way he was concealing evidence, but evidence of what? That Jackson had been in his house? That Jackson had planted the earring in his clothes? That had happened. The evidence was in his pocket. But why?

In his ear Madeline Sanders had paused as she waited for some kind of confirmation her complaint had been noted. He jumped into the silence before she could start through her tirade again and promised to talk to Lester.

He hung up and immediately forgot about Madeline Sanders. He had to tell Whitt about the earring, and now with Betty Jean out of the office was a good time. Once he got that over with, he would try to reach Dr. Colson to see what he wanted. Michael reached for the phone, but before he could pick it up, it rang.

Bill Lassiter was out in his front yard over on Elm Street, waving a gun around and threatening to shoot his neighbor's cocker spaniel. Michael slammed down the phone. Bill was in his eighties and hadn't been exactly in his right mind for the last year, but most of the time it was just a matter of taking him home when he got lost downtown.

He found Betty Jean talking to Stella in the county clerk's office. "Call Sarah Jane at the bank."

"Oh dear, has old Bill gone out without his trousers again?" Stella gave Michael an up-and-down look that said she might like seeing Michael without his.

"Nope. He's found his gun."

"Loaded?" Betty Jean asked.

"I guess I'll find out." Michael headed out the door.

"Don't you go out there and get shot, Michael," Betty Jean called after him. "Not until you call that doctor."

On Elm Street, Bill Lassiter staggered around his yard,

waving the gun first at one target and then another. A fluffy blond cocker scooted around behind a hedge between the yards, stopping at every break in the bushes to bark at the old man. The dog's owner, Guy Crimshaw, kept popping out his front door to call the dog, then popping back inside when Bill swung the gun his way.

The crisis had caught Guy in nothing but a pair of jogging shorts, which was pretty much a joke since Guy had never been jogging in his life. His large round belly was glistening with sweat as he stuck his head out the door to call his dog. "Here, Baby. Come to Daddy."

Michael could hear a siren wailing on Main Street and figured Betty Jean must have called Lester to back him up. Sometimes she had a mean streak. Michael wondered how hard it would be to cut the wires to Lester's siren.

Of course, he might not have to worry about it. Old Bill might decide he was a better target than a yapping dog that wouldn't sit still long enough for him to sight down the gun barrel.

"How you doing, Bill?" Michael called from the edge of the yard as if the old fellow was sitting in his chair on the porch. All around him, Michael could sense people watching out doors and windows as Bill swung around to focus on him. The old man was tall and so skinny that he must be forgetting to eat. His green shirt hung off his shoulders and flapped loosely around him, and a creased old belt gathered his pants around his waist. A few months back, before he forgot everything, he had enjoyed telling folks he was half the man he used to be. Literally. This morning, he was wearing one houseshoe, and Michael guessed at his problem with the dog.

"Ornery dog ate my shoe," the old man said. Behind him, Guy Crimshaw scurried off his porch to grab his dog.

Bill heard him and started to swing his gun that way. Just then Lester pulled up, siren screaming and lights twirling, and Bill forgot about the dog. "What's he doing out here? Don't he know folks can't think straight with all that noise going on?"

"Oh, you know Lester." Michael kept his voice low and calm. "He likes being a deputy."

"That boy never did have much sense." The old man spat on the ground.

"Could be you're right." Michael stepped up beside Bill and put his arm around the old man's shoulders. "You look tired. Let me take that for you."

The old man stared at the gun in his hand as if he'd never seen it. "Now where did that come from?" He looked up at Michael. "You didn't give it to me, did you?"

"I don't think so, but I'll hold it for you." Michael took the gun out of his hand. "Let's go look for your shoe."

The old man glanced down at his feet. "Well, look at that. I have lost one of my shoes now, haven't I?"

Sarah Jane screeched her car to a halt right behind Lester. She jumped out and ran toward her father and Michael. "I'm so sorry." She looked close to tears. "I had no idea he still had that."

"I'll put it in your car so you can put it somewhere safe."

"Right. Thank you. I'll make sure Dad doesn't get it again." She moved up beside her father and raised her voice. "Are you okay, Dad?"

Michael unloaded the gun before he laid it in the floorboard of Sarah Jane's car. He stared at the two bullets in his hand and pulled in a deep breath of hot summer air, glad he could still feel the breeze against his face. Old Bill might not even remember how to pull the trigger, but then again, he might.

Michael pulled in another breath and dropped the bullets into his pocket. That made him remember the teddy bear earring. He'd have to deal with that, but first he had to handle the chaotic scene in front of him. Lester had cut his siren, but his flashing lights were drawing people out of their houses to see what was going on. Guy Crimshaw yanked a yellow T-shirt down over his belly as he bore down on Michael. At least he'd left the dog inside.

"Aren't you going to arrest him, Deputy?" Guy's face was a splotchy red. Beads of sweat rolled down his nose.

"I don't think I need to do that." Michael held a hand out toward Guy to try to calm him down.

"But he could have killed somebody."

"He didn't." Michael looked back over to where Sarah Jane had her arm around her father, leading him back in the house. "He's just an old man."

"Who's lost his mind."

"He has forgotten a lot of things." Michael settled his eyes on Guy. "How long have you two been neighbors?"

"We moved here seventeen years ago." Guy jerked up the bottom of his T-shirt to wipe off his face. "Okay, so maybe I don't want him to go to jail, but something needs to be done. For his own safety."

"I'll talk to Sarah Jane."

"You didn't give him the gun back, did you?"

"No, of course not. You don't have to worry about that." Michael kept his voice low-key. "But you might try to keep your dog in your yard. I'm guessing it must have grabbed Bill's houseshoe and that's what got Bill upset."

"Baby does like chewing up shoes." Guy found a dry strip on his shirttail and wiped his face off again. The splotches were fading. "Can't you tell Lester to turn off those lights, for heaven's sake?"

Michael motioned to Lester, who was coming toward them, to kill the lights. He turned back reluctantly to his car. Guy was still talking. "I didn't mean to jump on you, Mike. But I was watching television, and they flashed this special report on there about that cute little news girl on WKKT and then I hear a gun go off outside."

"What about her?"

"You haven't heard? Somebody shot her dead."

Michael had to push out the next question. "What was her name?"

"Kim something. You know, that one who came out here and did that hero interview with you."

16

Hank Leland slammed on his brakes and screeched to a stop beside Michael's cruiser. "Did I miss something?"

"Just old Bill Lassiter trying to shoot the dog next door."

"Glad I missed that. I'm not quite ready to get shot on the trail of a story." Hank got a funny look on his face. "You hear about Kim Barbour?"

"Guy Crimshaw told me a few minutes ago. Said the report came across the television. What do you know?" Michael hadn't really wrapped his mind around what Kim Barbour being dead might mean. He needed to see the report for himself. To know more about how she died.

"Just that she was shot." Hank hesitated. "You don't think it has anything to do with this other?"

Michael wanted to believe it didn't, but a sick feeling in the pit of his stomach was making that hard. "I don't know."

"This is not fun anymore, Michael. I like a good story, but I never wanted to be the media contact for a psycho." Hank ran a hand through his thinning hair.

Michael kept his eyes steady on the editor. "Then don't print it."

"I can't sit on a story like that. I'm a newspaperman. It's my job to report the news whether I like the news or not." He gripped the steering wheel and barely seemed to notice when Michael turned away to get in his cruiser.

All the way back to the office, Michael tried to think of reasons the reporter's death couldn't be related to Hope's. Psychos had patterns. What could connect a young kid like Hope with an up-and-coming reporter? He didn't like the only answer that came to mind. Michael Keane as hero of the day was taking a steep nose dive. And the teddy bear earring burned against his leg in his pocket.

No special delivery envelope was waiting at the office. Betty Jean turned pale when he told her about the reporter, but she only said Dr. Colson had called again. And Detective Whitt.

Michael called Whitt first, but couldn't get through to him or Chekowski. The murder of an attractive TV reporter no doubt had the entire homicide department on its ear and out digging for suspects. He hung up and dialed the doctor. A receptionist said Dr. Colson had left the hospital, but she gave Michael the doctor's digital pager number.

Michael dialed the pager number, entered the office number, and sat back to wait. Betty Jean was clicking the keys on her computer, but Michael didn't bother to make any pretense of working. He studied the door into the hall and thought about going to Alaska. It was one of those things he planned to do someday. Maybe he should let someday be now. The fishing was probably good this time of the year. Aunt Lindy would be so busy getting ready for the start of school she'd hardly notice he was gone, and as for Alex, he might as well be in Alaska already. Maybe if he disappeared from the scene, so would Jackson.

Dr. Colson didn't think so when he called a few minutes later. The doctor bombarded him with questions. Had he heard from Jackson? Did he know the dead girl? How had he felt when he saw the pictures? Did he feel guilty?

Michael was beginning to wonder if the man planned to bill him for a counseling session. At last Michael interrupted the doctor's questions to bluntly ask, "Why did you call me?"

"As you reminded me when you came to the hospital, it's my duty to help the law enforcement officials as much as possible whenever something tragic happens that involves a patient I've treated."

"It's not my case. You need to talk to Detective Whitt with the Eagleton Police Department."

"I did speak with the detective previously, and I must admit I found him to be not only arrogant, but extremely rude. His obsessive need to control everything around him made any kind of open communication impossible." A note of irritation slipped into the doctor's voice as his complaints about Whitt picked up speed. "I would have suggested therapy, but I didn't feel he'd be amenable to the idea. Nor was he ready to listen to any theories I would have been more than willing to explore with him in regard to Mr. Jackson. That was a shame since we are all on the same team."

"Theories? What sort of theories?" Michael picked up a pencil in case he wanted to jot down a note about what the doctor said.

"First off, that Jackson may not be following an archetypal pattern with his victims."

"Victims?" Michael drew a dark box on the paper in front of him.

"Surely you've heard about Kim Barbour."

"I heard, but nothing to prove connection with the other murder."

"You're avoiding reality, Michael."

For some reason Michael didn't like the doctor using his first name, but he didn't know why. Everybody used first names anymore. "Okay, Doctor. What is reality?"

"Reality." The doctor sounded impatient with Michael's question. "I fear answering that might take longer than either one of us has, but you of all people as a policeman surely know that facts must be faced. Jackson killed the first girl and found a way to inform you of the deed, or so I surmise. I think it was your local editor who may have mentioned something about a picture in the mail when I spoke with him yesterday. Whatever it was, that was a warning. Perhaps even a plea for you to find him and stop him as he had planned to stop himself by jumping from the bridge. Then when you didn't catch him, he moved on to more desperate means to get your attention, targeting someone he knows you know."

"I didn't know Kim Barbour." Michael pressed the pencil lead so hard against the paper, it broke.

"Perhaps not intimately, but he may have seen her interviewing you on the news. What you have to remember is that Jackson is mentally ill. He is operating on a whole different level than a sane person. A killing level."

"So if he's trying to get my attention for whatever sick reason by murdering these girls, then if I vacate the scene, perhaps he'll lose his incentive to kill." Michael could almost feel the cool wind of Alaska on his face. Maybe he could take Jasper with him and they could hole up in a cabin in the northern backwoods and learn to dogsled.

151

"You're selling our Mr. Jackson short. He wouldn't quit. He'd become more focused on his intent."

"Focused?"

Betty Jean looked up at the sound of Michael's voice and said something, but Michael was concentrating on the doctor's words. She turned back to her computer.

"He'd target someone whose death would be sure to bring you back on the scene."

"Why doesn't he just jump off another bridge? I wouldn't stop him again." Michael picked up another pencil and began connecting dark lines on the paper again.

"I suppose not." The doctor made a sound that might have been a laugh. "Unfortunately the deranged mind is rarely that logical. That might make sense to you or to me, but who knows what Mr. Jackson is thinking?" The doctor paused a moment before adding, "Or planning."

"Look, Dr. Colson, nothing would make me happier than seeing Jackson behind bars, but Detective Whitt is the man you need to talk to. He's handling the case." Michael was ready to end this counseling session.

"Oh, you can be sure I will attempt to share my thoughts with the detective before Jackson strikes again, but I would be remiss not to warn you of the danger to your loved ones. Your wife? A daughter perhaps? Especially in light of this young newswoman's death."

"What do you mean?"

"Just that Jackson is getting more personal."

"I still have no reason to believe Kim Barbour's death has anything to do with Jackson or me."

"You may not have any reason to believe it, but you do believe it." The doctor paused, but when Michael didn't say anything, he went on. "As a matter of fact, I talked with Ms. Barbour myself early yesterday. She wanted to know how she might contact Jackson to do a follow-up on her hero story. To see if he was grateful. I think we can assume not, right?"

Michael forced his hand to relax on the phone and didn't respond.

Silence hummed on the line a moment before the doctor continued, his voice taking on a doleful sound. "She didn't know about Jackson murdering that poor child, and I couldn't very well tell her since Detective Whitt was quite adamant in demanding I not share that information with anyone as yet. But the fact that Jackson had walked out of the hospital— I think she used the word 'escaped'—mesmerized her. I'm sure if Jackson had called her, she would have arranged a meeting with him without hesitation. Even knowing about the dead girl might have made no difference. Young people never seriously consider the prospect of death."

"I advise you to report your talk with Ms. Barbour to the Eagleton police right away." Michael used his best official tone.

"Don't worry, Deputy. I know the rules. What you need to remember is that Jackson is operating without rules." The man disconnected the call without bothering to say goodbye.

Michael put the phone down.

"What did the doctor want?" Betty Jean kept her eyes on her computer screen. "He know something that might help catch his guy?"

"Not really. I guess he was anxious to report in now rather than be accused of not cooperating in the investigation later." Michael stared down at the dark squares he'd drawn while talking to the psychologist. "Plus he said he wanted to warn me."

"Warn you?" Betty Jean swiveled her chair around toward

him. "Does he honestly believe Jackson is killing people to get your attention? Sorry, but I couldn't help but overhear."

"That was his theory." Michael massaged his forehead. Could the day get any worse?

Betty Jean was silent for a moment as she frowned at him. "Do you think he could be right?"

"I don't know. It seems crazy to think so, but I don't know. Right now I don't know anything." Except he did know the killer had planted Hope's earring in his house. The earring he had in his pocket and still hadn't reported. The day was going to get worse when Whitt returned his call. "Nobody from the Eagleton police called, did they?"

"No." Betty Jean turned back to her computer. "Hank did, but he was screaming in my ear. So I hung up on him."

"Screaming?" Michael's stomach flipped. "About what?"

"I couldn't make it out. Something about Rebecca Ann. I figured he'd call back and I'd let him yell in your ear."

The front door of the courthouse crashed open. Michael had barely gotten out from behind his desk when Hank ran into the office and slung a plastic grocery bag with an envelope inside it at Michael.

Michael dropped the sack on his desk and caught Hank by the shoulders. The man's face was beet red, his glasses were fogging over, and his whole body was shuddering.

"Take a deep breath," Michael ordered.

Betty Jean pushed a chair toward Hank. "Should I call the paramedics?" She actually sounded concerned.

"I'm not having a heart attack." Hank gasped for breath. "At least I don't think so." He put his hands over his heart.

Michael pushed him down into the chair. "What's happened?"

Hank motioned toward the brown envelope that had slipped out of the sack. "That."

Michael looked at the envelope with dread. The front was blank, no address or name. Michael raised it up with a pen. The seal had been torn open. "I told you not to open any envelopes."

"I didn't open it." Without warning, Hank put his face in his hands and began to weep.

"I'm calling Dr. Hadley." Betty Jean reached for the phone. "He may not be having a heart attack, but he's having something."

Hank didn't seem to hear her as he looked up at Michael, his face lined with despair as he said, "I didn't, but Rebecca Ann did."

17

Betty Jean put down the phone and pulled a couple of tissues out of the box on her desk before handing the box to Hank, who snatched out a handful to mop up his face. Michael took one of the pink tissues and lifted the envelope to slide the pictures out far enough to get a look at them. Kim Barbour, the light gone from her eyes and her face frozen in terror, stared back at him.

Michael let the pictures slide back out of sight in the envelope. He wished he could slide them out of sight in his mind as easily, but the image of the woman's face burned in front of his eyes the way a too-bright burst of light lingered on the back of your eyelids.

"All right, Hank, tell us what happened." Michael put a steadying hand on Hank's shoulder. "How did Rebecca Ann get these pictures?"

It took a while but finally Hank got out his story. Rebecca Ann had been walking home from a friend's house. The friend had a pool. Rebecca Ann went over there most every day. She was watching the yards for this neighborhood cat that sometimes came out for her to pet it and didn't even know the car was beside her until the driver spoke her name.

"I've told her not to talk to strangers, but I've never harped on it. It didn't seem that important here in Hidden Springs. There aren't any strangers. Strange people maybe, but no strangers." Hank pulled out another tissue and blew his nose loudly.

"Was it Jackson?" Michael asked.

"Who else could it be?" Hank added the tissue to the pile on the desk beside him. "She said she didn't know the guy, but Rebecca Ann doesn't pay much attention to the paper, so she might not have recognized him anyway. I was too upset to ask her much of anything. I told them—her and Barbara—to lock the door and not open it to anybody while I brought these to you."

"Did the man in the car try to grab her or anything like that?"

"No, he just handed her the envelope and told her to give it to me. Said she could look at it first if she wanted to, and then he drove off." Hank swallowed hard and rubbed his hands up and down his thighs.

"So she looked." The death picture of Kim Barbour was back in front of Michael's eyes. Not something a kid should see.

"She looked." A tear slipped down Hank's cheek.

"Did you ask her about the car?"

"She thinks it was blue, some beat-up old model. Sounded like the car Jackson drove to the bridge." Hank swiped the tear off his cheek and spoke in a steadier voice.

"T.R. was supposed to call if anybody came for the car."

Michael turned away from Hank and dialed the service station's number.

Jackson's car had been there when T.R. closed up last night and gone when he got to the station that morning. He aimed to call Michael, but Holly Baxter called in a panic with a dead battery because she was going to be late to work. He was sorry, but he let calling about the car slip his mind. Besides, the guy stuck a hundred-dollar bill in an envelope on the door and that about paid the storage and towing charges. So he didn't really have any complaint against the guy, who did him a favor getting the junker out of his way.

On the way to Hank's house, Michael asked, "Rebecca Ann real upset?"

"Some, but not like Barbara. Not like me." Hank stared out the windshield. "Rebecca Ann hasn't ever really seen a dead person not already fixed up for a funeral, but she's all the time watching those scary movies with blood splashing everywhere. Maybe that's how she thought this was. Something pretend no matter how real it looked. But this." Hank hesitated as if searching for the right word. "Well, this isn't pretend. Barbara already had the suitcases out from under the bed when I left."

"Maybe they should go visit her folks down in Georgia for a while." Michael kept his eyes on the street. Everything looked the same. The red salsa flowers bloomed bright as ever in the half barrels on the street corners. Gordon Evermon, the president of the Hidden Springs Bank, was out washing the bank's entrance door the way he did almost every day. He said he liked seeing what the weather was like on the other side of the glass. A bunch of kids in baseball uniforms were coming out of the Hidden Springs Grill, carrying soft drinks and chips. Bill Wharton and Sanders White stood in front of the drugstore, catching up on the news. It looked like any other Tuesday afternoon. The town gave no notice of the fact that evil had come to call. That evil might yet be riding its streets.

"You don't think she's in any real danger, do you?" Hank asked.

"He knew her name and where she lived." There was no need pretending.

"You're scaring me, Mike."

"Good."

"Barbara says all this is my fault. That I'd do anything for a story." Hank dropped his head in his hands as if his thoughts were too heavy. "If she goes, she might not come back."

"She's scared. Once she has time to think about it, she'll see you didn't have any way of knowing he'd get personal."

Hank looked over at Michael. "He's laughing at us, Mike."

"What makes you think that?" Michael kept his eyes on the road and forced himself to relax his grip on the steering wheel.

"I don't know. It's almost like I can hear him."

"Get hold of yourself, Hank. Things are already strange enough." Michael kept his voice calm, even though he knew what Hank meant. Monster laughter was in the air.

A few minutes later, inside Hank's home, things got stranger. Rebecca Ann looked at the picture of Jackson in the paper and, without a second's hesitation, shook her head. "That's not him."

Hank stared down at the paper as though to make sure he had the right one. "Take another look, honey." He poked the picture of Jackson. "This man right here. His hair might be different, but the eyes would be the same."

"He had on sunglasses," Rebecca Ann said. "Those mirror kind you can't see through."

"Well, the nose then or the shape of his face," Hank said.

Rebecca Ann looked from her father to the picture again. She was thirteen, but baby fat still plumped her flushed cheeks. Michael could tell she wanted to say whatever her father wanted her to say, but that she didn't know how to say anything but the truth. "I didn't look at him real close." She peered at the picture, then shrugged a little. "It was just some old guy with a beard. The man in that picture doesn't have a beard."

Hank yanked his pencil out of his pocket and drew a messy beard on the man's picture in the paper. "How about now?"

"I don't know. Maybe."

"Maybe?" Hank tapped his pencil on the man's picture. "Take a better look."

"I'm looking, Daddy." Tears floated up into Rebecca Ann's eyes. "I don't know whether it was him or not."

Michael put his hand on Hank's shoulder. "Easy, Hank. She's doing her best."

Hank stared up at him. "But it has to be him."

"Let me talk to her." Michael stooped down to eye level with Rebecca Ann. The tears were still there and she was struggling to keep her lips pressed together over the braces on her teeth. "Forget the picture, Rebecca Ann. Just describe him the way you remember him looking."

She wiped the corners of her mouth with the back of her hand as she thought about it. "I didn't pay much attention except for the sunglasses. I could see my reflection in them, one of me in each lens."

"Did you notice his hair? What color it was?" Michael asked.

"He had on some kind of hat. Like a fishing hat or something. I think it was dark green." Rebecca Ann sighed. "He was just some old guy I didn't know. When he gave me the envelope, I figured it was wedding pictures or something for Dad to put in the paper."

"So did he hand you the pictures and drive off?" Michael asked.

"No. He kind of acted strange. He waved the envelope out the window at me, but then when I tried to take it, he held on like he wasn't going to give it to me after all. Then all of a sudden he let go and leaned out the window to tap me on the forehead and tell me not to forget." Rebecca Ann frowned. "The weirdest thing, he had on gloves."

Behind them, Barbara gasped, but Michael kept his eyes on Rebecca Ann. "Gloves?"

"Yeah. I mean it was really hot today and he had on these black gloves. Like Daddy's leather gloves he wears in the winter. I didn't notice them till he reached out to touch me. I didn't like that. I mean, grownups are always patting you on the head and stuff, but this was different." Rebecca Ann shuddered a little.

Hank hovered behind her as though unsure of whether to comfort his wife or grab Rebecca Ann in a hug. Michael ignored him and kept his eyes on Rebecca Ann. "Why?"

"I don't know. The gloves maybe. The sunglasses. I don't know. It just creeped me out. Anyway, when I jerked back away from him, I tripped on the edge of the sidewalk and fell down."

"Then what happened?" Michael asked.

"That was creepy too. He laughed—you know, like he thought it was funny that I fell down. Then he waved and drove off."

"Did you notice his license plate?"

"Uh-uh. I dropped my swimming goggles and stuff when I fell, and by the time I got it picked up, he was gone. So I came on home and got something to drink."

"You weren't curious about the pictures?"

Rebecca Ann shrugged. "Not really. I turned on the TV and sort of forgot about them. I mean, the guy was weird, but when I go out with Dad, we're always running into weird people. Mama says you have to be weird to live in Hidden Springs to begin with." Rebecca Ann glanced behind her at her mother.

Barbara Leland sat up too straight on the couch, twisting a tissue into shreds. She hadn't said anything since Michael got there, but she looked ready to spring to her child's defense at the first wrong word.

"But you did look at them." Michael kept his voice soft.

"Obviously," Rebecca Ann said, then blushed. "Sorry, I didn't mean to be smart."

"That's okay. I guess that was obvious." Michael gave her a little smile. "Just tell me what you did."

"Mom saw the envelope and asked what it was. I told her they were probably wedding pictures, but when I pulled them out, they weren't." Rebecca Ann peeked back at her mother again and then stared down at her hands. "Mom got real upset."

"So she called your dad?"

"Actually I called him. I thought he might be able to calm Mom down, but he went totally berserk. Even worse than Mom. You'd have thought it was me in the pictures."

Behind her, Barbara moaned and covered her face with her hands. Hank lost his indecision and wrapped his arms around Rebecca Ann. "Don't say things like that, honey."

She pushed her father away. "Stop it, Dad. You're squishing me."

Hank stepped back reluctantly, but kept one hand on her arm.

Rebecca Ann looked past him to Michael. "It was that reporter on TV, wasn't it? The one who came out here and interviewed you after you kept that man from jumping off the bridge." She didn't wait for an answer. "I saw something on TV about her. She was really pretty in the pictures they showed of her."

"She was," Michael said.

"But why did you think it was the guy on the bridge that gave me the pictures?"

"Because of some other things that came in the mail," Michael said.

"Other pictures?" Rebecca Ann asked.

"Yes."

"Of somebody dead?"

"Yes." There was nothing for it but to tell her the truth.

"You think the guy that took the pictures did that to her?"

"Seems the reasonable thing to think," Michael answered.

"Was he the guy who gave me the pictures?" Rebecca Ann shivered and wiped the corners of her mouth again.

"I don't know," Michael admitted.

18

There was a lot he didn't know. He left Hank hovering over his daughter and drove around town looking for the blue Oldsmobile. The man was surely long gone, but Michael needed to do something while he waited for Whitt and company to arrive from Eagleton. He wasn't looking forward to Eagleton's finest taking over Hidden Springs. Maybe that's why he hadn't been more insistent about getting through to Whitt about the teddy bear earring still in his pocket.

Kim Barbour had been wearing gold earrings in the picture he'd seen, but if Jackson tried to plant something of hers in his house, at least he'd have to break a lock or window this time. Somehow Michael didn't think that was going to happen. The killer didn't seem to be following a specific pattern, but Michael had no doubt the man had a plan. A plan that included Hidden Springs.

The town was quiet except for the roar of lawn mowers chewing up grass. On Court Street, a few kids kicked around a ball. At the elementary school some high school boys were shooting basketballs in spite of the heat curling up from the blacktop court.

Nothing was out of order. Michael knew every car he passed and every face he saw on the street.

He tried to empty his mind of thoughts of a monster stalking his town and think about the situation logically. Jackson or whoever was driving Jackson's car had to have gotten to Hidden Springs some way. No buses delivered people to Hidden Springs. A hitchhiker or walker drew a lot of attention out on the interstate, and a stranger on foot in Hidden Springs was rare enough that, often as not, a shopkeeper would call the police just in case the person was up to no good.

So it was probable the man had driven to Hidden Springs or someone had brought him. Psychos were loners. They didn't work in pairs. So what could explain Rebecca Ann saying the man who gave her the pictures didn't look like Jackson's picture?

Who but Jackson would even know his car was here in Hidden Springs or have a key? Of course, a car could be hot-wired easily enough. And Jackson could have intentionally disguised himself with the hat, beard, and mirror glasses. The winter gloves might have simply been to be sure none of his fingerprints were on the envelope.

Betty Jean radioed him that Detective Whitt was in town and headed to the Leland house.

"Okay, I'm on my way back over there," Michael told her.

"You didn't spot him—?"

Michael cut off her question. "Remember the town has ears."

"Yeah, okay, but did you?"

"No such luck. But track down Buck and bring him up to date. He could be patrolling out at the interstate."

"Sure thing, Michael. Then I'm locking up. I've got Bunco

tonight at my house, and dust is an inch thick on my lamp tables. Plus, the girls will be disappointed if I don't bake my lemon squares."

"The sheriff come in?"

"I tried to get hold of him, but they've taken Grandma Potter to the hospital in Eagleton. He's probably over there. I called, but she wasn't in a room yet. I could page him, but what good would that do except get his blood pressure up. I'll call him and fill him in later."

"All right. Just be sure to get Buck before you leave." Michael clicked off the radio. Buck probably wouldn't turn up anything, but at least he'd be on the lookout.

At the Leland house, Michael introduced everybody, then leaned back against the doorjamb while the others gathered around the round glass-top kitchen table. Rebecca Ann stared through the glass at her feet as she went through her story again.

Whitt let her tell it all and then asked his questions. Did she know exactly what time it was? Had she ever seen the man before? Was anybody else around who might have seen the man talking to her?

Chekowski took notes, and when Rebecca Ann told Whitt the man didn't much look like the one in the paper, Chekowski looked up and suggested a police artist. Whitt ignored her. Instead he fastened his eyes on Hank. "I think you can rest easy that your daughter is in no danger, Mr. Leland."

"That's easy for you to say." Barbara Leland spoke up, a tremble evident in her voice. "She's not your daughter. We're not staying here to take that chance."

Whitt leveled his eyes on her. "Ma'am, if the man intended to hurt your daughter, he could have done so today. He simply used her as a messenger."

Barbara didn't shy away from Whitt's stare. "We're going. Tonight. To my parents' house in Georgia."

"Whatever you think best, ma'am. All of you going?" Whitt looked at Hank.

"I've got a paper to put out," Hank said.

"Nothing stops the news." Whitt's lips turned up into something resembling a smile as he reached into his shirt pocket to pull out a business card. He handed it across the table to Barbara. "If your daughter remembers anything else, give me a call."

"Don't you think she should talk to your police artist first? Before they leave." Michael spoke up for the first time. Chekowski kept her eyes on her notebook.

Whitt narrowed his eyes on Michael. "I don't think that will be necessary, Deputy, since we already know what the perpetrator looks like. We have photos on hand."

Michael clamped his lips together and kept quiet, but Hank didn't let it go. "But, Detective, she's not positive it was the same guy."

"Mr. Leland, your daughter's description clearly indicates the perp had disguised his appearance. A sketch of a disguise is next to useless." Whitt chopped his hand through the air as though to close the matter. He settled his eyes on Rebecca Ann, who looked close to tears. His voice softened. "Rebecca, you've been a big help, but we don't have any more questions now. If you think of anything else, you tell your mama and she'll call me, okay?"

She nodded.

Whitt smiled at her, as human as Michael had seen him look. "And don't you worry. We're not going to let anybody hurt you."

Whitt and Chekowski followed Michael back to the courthouse to check out the pictures he'd left there. All the offices had long since closed, and Whitt shifted from one foot to the other impatiently while Michael unlocked the back door to the courthouse and then the sheriff's office.

Beside him, Chekowski was taking in the silent building with an expression near to wonder. "Doesn't anybody break the law down here after hours?" she asked.

"We have a dispatcher over in the police chief's office. Something happens, she knows where to find us." Michael pushed open the door to the sheriff's office and flicked on the lights. "We don't have a lot of crime down here during or after hours."

"Lucky you," Chekowski said.

"Sounds boring," Whitt said.

"Yeah." Michael pointed out the envelope still on his desk where Hank had thrown it.

Whitt was all business again. "Who opened it?"

"Rebecca Ann. Then she showed her mother and father."

"Did you look at them?" Whitt pulled a pair of plastic gloves out of his pocket and slid them on before picking up the envelope.

"I slid one out enough to see what it was. I didn't touch them." Michael didn't like Whitt's attitude, but he couldn't do a lot about it. No doubt he would like it even less after he showed him the earring in his pocket.

"Is there a letter?" Whitt asked.

"I don't know. I told you I didn't take the pictures out of the envelope."

Whitt dumped the envelope on the desk and spread out the pictures. Different girl, but shots eerily similar to the first set. One showed the young reporter, alive, looking intense but not frightened, and then the one Michael had seen earlier where she looked terrified. In the posed shots of the girl after she was dead, her head and hands were positioned exactly the same as Hope's. But there was no sign of a bullet hole in Kim Barbour's head.

"Same weapon?" Michael asked.

Whitt kept his eyes on the pictures without answering. Chekowski, for once not totally tuned in to Whitt, spoke up. "Same type. They'll have to do the lab work before we know if it was the same gun. Of course, this shot was different. The fatal wound appeared to be under the ribs and up through the heart. At least it was quick." The woman suddenly became aware of Whitt's eyes on her. Color pinked her cheeks as she dropped her eyes to her feet. "Sorry, sir."

Whitt sighed and looked back down at the pictures. "A little different MO but same killer. Widely dissimilar victims. Barbour wasn't nameless. Far from it. And she wasn't found in a church."

"The radio said her body was found in her car in front of the television station," Michael said.

"Only a fool believes everything on the news." Whitt didn't bother to let Michael know what, if any, part of the news could be believed. He scooted around the pictures. "Here's the letter."

Michael wanted to move close enough to read the killer's words, but he stayed where he was on the far side of the desk. Best watch from a distance and do his best to not blow up at Whitt.

He could almost hear Aunt Lindy's voice in his head giving him reasons to tamp down his anger. *A man who can't control his temper is at the mercy of his emotions. Angry people lose arguments nine times out of ten. Seeing red keeps a person from thinking clearly.* He believed all that was right, but the red haze kept growing around Whitt's head anyway.

Whitt looked up and locked eyes with Michael. "The letter's to you, Deputy." Slowly he turned the page around and pushed it across the desk. Michael moved closer to read it. Chekowski stepped up beside him and took a picture of the letter.

SHE THOUGHT YOU WERE A HERO AND THAT SO WOULD I. I WONDER WHAT SHE WOULD THINK NOW IF SHE HADN'T HAD TO DIE. ARE WE HAVING FUN YET, MR. HERO? YOU SHOULD HAVE LET MY NIGHTMARE END. THEN HOPE AND KIM WOULDN'T HAVE HAD TO LIVE THEIRS. WHO'S DREAMING NEXT?

The all-capital letters were plain block, extra-dark font. Michael stared at the letter until the words seemed to lift up off the page and attack his eyes. The last sentence struck terror in his heart. Who would be next?

"He didn't waste any time between victims." At last Michael looked up from the letter.

"He's a go-getter for sure." Whitt leaned back in Michael's desk chair and surveyed the office. His eyes landed on the coffeemaker. "Any chance for some coffee?"

"Sure." Michael measured out the coffee and wondered how he was going to bring up the earring.

He'd waited too long. It was going to strike Whitt as odd.

It struck Michael as odd. So odd that he thought about just letting the earring stay in his pocket. Whitt was already looking at him as if the nightmare was his fault, that he'd set things in motion just by being country bumpkin enough to keep the poor schmuck from jumping. Hero of the day. Monster of the decade. More like lifetime.

The coffee machine gurgled. What was it Hank had said? That the poor Joe on the bridge hadn't looked like monster material. But then how many psycho killers had Hank actually met? About as many as Michael.

Behind him, Chekowski read her notes of Rebecca Ann's story out loud to Whitt. Michael listened with half an ear while he rummaged around in the cabinet under the coffeepot for Styrofoam cups. Betty Jean kept them hidden because she said if the cups were in plain sight, every Tom, Dick, and Harry in town would be lining up for free coffee. She had no intention of stealing Cindy's business at the Grill.

He finally found five or six of the cups stuck in behind Betty Jean's stash of tissue boxes.

Michael asked about sugar or creamer and sat their coffee in front of them. He didn't waste any more time wondering about the earring in his pocket. Every fact in an investigation could prove helpful in catching the perpetrator, and he wanted to catch this man. Besides, he had no reason to feel like a kid who'd just put a dent in the fender of his dad's new truck and was afraid to drive it home.

Michael pulled the plastic bag holding the earring out of his pocket and placed it on his desk in front of Whitt.

Chekowski spoke first. "Victim one's other earring."

19

"What's going on here, Keane?" Whitt frowned up at Michael. "You lift this from the crime scene yesterday?"

The red exploded in front of Michael. He put both hands flat on the desk—his desk—and stared at Whitt. "It's time we got a few things straight, Detective Whitt. I may be a small-town deputy but that doesn't make me dumb."

"Being a deputy doesn't." Whitt leaned forward in the chair and locked eyes with Michael. "Tampering with evidence does."

Chekowski circled them. "I think everybody needs to calm down."

Michael kept his eyes on Whitt. "I don't tamper with evidence. I bag it and label it and give it to the officer in charge. Now do you want to know where I found it or do you want to keep on trying to prove who's got the biggest nightstick?"

Whitt rose up out of the chair until his face was inches from Michael's. "No contest there, Deputy. You keep messing with me and you won't even have a nightstick."

"All right, guys, get a grip." Chekowski put a hand on Michael's shoulder and pushed him back. "While you're yelling at each other, this psycho could be zeroing in on victim three."

Michael slowly straightened up and took a deep breath. Chekowski was right. Nothing could be accomplished by butting heads with Whitt. What he needed to remember were the killer's words. *Who's dreaming next?* The guy had been to Hidden Springs. Was he picking out a victim here? Thank God, not Rebecca Ann.

"Sorry, Detective. I got out of line," Michael said.

"You got that right. It happens again, I'll slap you behind bars so fast you won't know what hit you."

"Aaron," Chekowski started, but after a swift look from Whitt, she didn't say anything else.

Michael tried counting to ten, but only made it to five. "On what charges? Last I heard it wasn't against the law to stop a suicide."

"Maybe not, but there's obstructing justice and concealing evidence." Whitt sat back down in Michael's chair, leaned back, and put his long fingers together in a tent shape as he stared at Michael, almost as if he were waiting, even hoping, for another outburst.

But the anger drained out of Michael. He was exhausted, and all he wanted to do was get this man out of his chair, out of his office, and out of his life. He kept his voice level. "No evidence has been concealed. At least by me. I called you, left a message, and didn't get a return call. So there it is in front of you now. I found it in the bottom of my washing machine this morning and put it in that bag. I would have shipped it over to you, but then things went haywire around here."

"Your washing machine?" Whitt motioned to Chekowski

to pull out her notebook. "You want to explain to us how that could have happened?"

"The only way it could have happened. Jackson must have come into my house and planted it in a pile of dirty clothes in the middle of my bedroom floor." Michael sat down in the chair Hank had collapsed into earlier and waited for the next question.

"Break and entry?" Chekowski asked.

"Doors weren't locked." Michael glanced over at her. She had pulled Betty Jean's chair out away from the desk and was scribbling in her notebook propped on her knee.

"You always leave your doors unlocked, Deputy?" Whitt asked.

"I live out on the lake. It's a very remote spot. Nobody comes down that way unless they're coming to see me, and I have an open-door policy for my friends who fish there. There's never been any need to lock the doors before."

"What a place," Chekowski muttered over her notes.

Whitt stuck to business. "Nothing missing? Out of place?"

"No. My dog was acting funny when I got home last night, but I didn't see anything out of the ordinary."

"Acting funny? What do you mean?"

"Growling, hackles up, barking at shadows. The way he does if there's a coyote or fox around."

"Or a stranger?" Whitt asked.

"Or a stranger," Michael said.

"So what time was this? Eight? Nine last night?"

"Three-forty-five a.m. when I went inside and checked my messages."

Whitt raised his eyebrows a little. "Sort of late for a working day, wasn't it, Deputy?"

"I met a friend in Wayland, West Virginia, last night for dinner."

"Wayland? That has to be three hours or more from here, right?"

"About four if you drive the speed limit."

"And did you drive the speed limit?" Whitt settled back in the chair, making it squeak.

"Not always."

"Anybody know you went? That is, besides this friend you met?"

"Betty Jean Atkins. She works in the office here."

Whitt leaned forward to prop his elbows on the desk. "Okay, now let's see if I've got this straight. You find out this miscreant you so heroically kept from jumping just murdered a poor innocent child of a girl and you take off for a town a few hundred miles away. Not your typical law officer response to crime."

"The murder wasn't my case." Michael met Whitt's stare straight on. "I had been told expressly not to get involved in any way with the investigation by the detective in charge."

"Okay, you made your point." Whitt picked a pen up off the desk and leaned back again. He twirled the pen through his fingers. "So you go home. It's almost 4:00 a.m. Your dog's nervous. How about you? You nervous?"

"I thought it might be more than a coyote, but when I went inside and nothing was out of order except my sink was dripping, then I decided my imagination was running away with me."

"Your sink was dripping?" Chekowski looked up from her notes.

"Right. That's how I can usually tell if somebody's been

there fishing. They come in and wash their hands and don't know they need to give the sink tap an extra shove to keep it from dripping."

"Any of your friends say they were there yesterday?" Whitt asked.

"I haven't had a chance to find that out. I'll check around tomorrow."

"So nothing messed with except your sink," Whitt went on. "So what did you do then?"

"Checked my phone messages and went to bed."

"Any messages?"

"Yes. One about a date I'd forgotten. Two from my friend saying she wasn't sure she would be able to meet me in Wayland, and one from that Dr. Colson who treated Jackson at the hospital, and one hang-up."

The doctor's name got Whitt's attention. "Why was Colson calling you?"

"When I called him back today, he said something about wanting to help the law enforcement agencies as much as he could. I told him to call you, but he claimed you didn't seem interested in his theories."

"Is that right? What kind of theories?" Whitt asked.

"Something about how Jackson wasn't following any typical patterns with his choice of victims."

"Typical patterns." Whitt made a sound of disgust and shook his head. "Save me from amateur detectives, but I guess I'd better hear it all. Go on."

"He thought Jackson was trying to get my attention with the murders. That perhaps Jackson might be hoping in some sick way that I'd catch him and stop him since it appeared the killer was getting personal with me."

"You didn't tell him about the killer's letters to you, did you?" Whitt's voice was strained as he leaned forward again and glared at Michael.

"I didn't tell him anything." Michael kept his voice level. "He was the one doing the talking."

"Hmph." Whitt sat back in the chair. "Sounds like the doc was chock-full of information. I don't remember him being that talkative to us, do you, Chekowski?" Whitt glanced at his assistant.

"No, sir. He claimed to be extremely busy and offered to reserve an appointment for us the next day."

Michael tamped down on the urge to smile as he recalled Colson's analysis of Whitt. Rude and arrogant fit. You didn't need to be a psychologist to figure that out.

"The twerp." Whitt snorted. "I told him he'd make time to talk to us right then. He did, but he clammed up. Claimed doctor-patient confidentiality. Then he calls you up and spills his guts. When was it you talked to him?"

"This afternoon. Right before Hank showed up with the pictures." Michael pointed toward the envelope.

"He tell you anything other than his half-baked theories?" Whitt asked.

"Mostly he asked questions about how it felt to save a murderer."

"Cheered you right up, I guess," Chekowski said.

"He's probably writing a book." Whitt rubbed his hand across his eyes. The man looked tired. "Everybody wants to read books about pretty girls getting killed. If they were out there seeing those dead girls, they wouldn't want to read about it, would they, Chekowski?"

"No sir."

Whitt took a drink of coffee and got back on track. He stared across the desk at Michael. "Anything else you need to tell us?"

"There is one more thing. Dr. Colson said Kim Barbour had called him to see if he could help her locate Jackson to do an interview. She knew Jackson had left the hospital. It was his opinion that Ms. Barbour would have agreed to meet Jackson if he contacted her. I stressed the importance of him reporting their conversation to you right away, which he said he would. That he knew the rules."

"Make a note to call this shrink, Chekowski." Whitt took another gulp of his coffee, sat back, and began twirling the pen again. "Okay, Deputy, let's see if I've got this straight. You got home at 3:45, got the heebie-jeebies, didn't find anything amiss in the house, listened to your messages, and hit the sack. Right?"

"After I fed Jasper."

"Jasper?"

"My dog."

"Right, the dog. You said your friend left messages about not meeting you. She show?"

"Late, but she came."

"Close friend?" Whitt's eyebrows went up as he started twirling the pen again.

Michael wanted to tell him it was none of his business, but decided to get it over with. "Alexandria Sheridan, the niece of Reece Sheridan, a lawyer here in town. I've known her since we were kids."

Whitt ruminated on that a moment as though he wanted to ask more about Michael's late-night trip, but instead he got back to business. "Okay. So you get up this morning, can't find any clean shorts, and throw some clothes in the washer before you come to work. Right?"

"Pretty close."

"And then?" The pen slipped out of his hands and dropped on the desk with a clatter. He picked it up and began tapping the end on the metal desk.

"I pulled the clothes out of the washer to put in the dryer and noticed something shiny down in the bottom of the washer. It was the earring."

"Did you recognize it?"

"I knew it matched the one in the victim's ear, if that's what you mean."

"So why didn't you call the department?" Whitt asked.

"I already told you that I did, but you weren't in. I left a message. Then I heard the news about Kim Barbour, and Hank comes in with the pictures. The earring didn't seem to be first priority after that."

"You better let me prioritize the information and determine what's important and what's not."

"There it is." Michael pointed at the plastic bag holding the earring. "Prioritize away."

Whitt's lips turned up in a small smile. "Your doors locked now, Deputy?"

"Locked, but nobody would be close enough to hear if a window was smashed."

Whitt stood up. "At least you can feel comfortable. I don't think this miscreant offs guys. Just females."

"I don't think we can be sure what Jackson might do," Michael said.

Whitt picked up the plastic bag containing the teddy bear

earring. "Except get personal with you." Whitt settled his eyes on Michael. "I can agree with the doctor on that."

"What do you mean, Detective?"

"I mean that if you have any special women in your life, it could be you should send them off to Atlanta or wherever with little Rebecca and her mama."

"I didn't know Hope and barely knew this reporter."

Whitt glanced at the envelope that contained the pictures and the letter to Michael. "Maybe not, but this sweetheart would still be drawing breath right now if she hadn't interviewed the hero of Hidden Springs. We both know that, don't we, Deputy Keane?"

20

"We'll catch him." Chekowski touched Michael's arm before she followed Whitt out the door.

At the sight of her sympathetic smile, a nightmare image of her face in one of the killer's pictures flashed through Michael's head. Who knew what Jackson would do next? He listened to their footsteps going out of the building and actually considered calling Dr. Colson to see if he could guess the killer's next move to give them an edge. But Colson didn't really know anything. He was just guessing too. Michael would do better finding out if Alex had come up with an expert for him to call. She hadn't called, but maybe she'd left him a message.

An icy feeling gripped his heart. Jackson could have listened to his messages when he planted the earring, and if so, he'd know about Alex. Whitt's warning echoed in his ears. All the women Michael knew and loved might be in danger.

Names started flashing through his head as he clicked off the coffeepot, turned out the lights, and locked the office door. Alex. Karen. Betty Jean. Aunt Lindy.

Michael couldn't bear the thought of any of them being

in danger because of him. He fingered the butt of his gun as he walked toward the back door, his footsteps ringing in the empty silence of the courthouse. If Jackson appeared in front of him right then, he could shoot him without hesitation. What kind of hero was that?

A very frightened hero. That was what. He could put his own life on the line if he had to, had done so before in the line of duty, but he wasn't ready to shove his loved ones out there on the firing line. He didn't even want them close enough to worry about a stray bullet. And now this murderer might have any one of them directly in his sights.

Panic gripped Michael as he stepped out onto the street. He glanced around as if the killer might be in the shadows behind the courthouse. Then he wished he really was there. That was better than thinking about him stalking Alex on the streets of Washington, DC, or watching Karen's house over on Madison Drive.

Michael crammed a lid on his panic and paid attention to what was around him. The sun had already slid out of sight behind the First Christian Church on the corner of Main and Church Street. Crickets called to each other out on the courthouse lawn, and a mockingbird was singing a goodnight melody. A few cars passed by out in front of the courthouse, but back here, the road was empty.

Michael's car was the only one left in the parking lot. Hidden Springs had closed down for the night. As Michael pulled out of the parking lot, he noticed Hank's van behind the newspaper office. The *Hidden Springs Gazette* was due out the next day, and it looked as if Hank intended to get the news out in spite of everything. Michael slowed as he went past the newspaper office. He wondered if Hank was writing headlines about Jackson giving Rebecca Ann the pictures.

He pressed on the gas and went on down the street. He couldn't worry about tomorrow's headlines. He needed to find a way to build a wall around his own loved ones. He figured Betty Jean was safe enough. As safe as Chekowski anyway. There wasn't any reason for Michael to upend her Bunco party. Even a deranged killer like Jackson would have to think twice before taking on a houseful of women. He'd check with her later after the party broke up.

Next he made himself think about the message Karen left on his machine. Not her name, so Jackson might not know who she was. The man couldn't very well go around asking folks in Hidden Springs about Michael's friends. People might recognize him from last week's issue of the *Gazette*. Then again, Rebecca Ann hadn't been sure the man she saw was Jackson. Could somebody be helping Jackson? That didn't seem probable, but it was best not to take anything for granted. Michael would drive by Karen's house on the way home.

Then there was Alex. Alex had said her first name, which meant Jackson could have found her phone number in Michael's phone book. The area code would let him know Alex was in Washington, DC, but exactly where might not be easy. Still, he did have the number. He might call her, somehow involve her, if she wasn't warned.

Michael pulled over and dug his phone out of his pocket, relieved to see the battery still showed some green. He'd forgotten to charge it up. Not the first time. Betty Jean kept telling him that someday he was going to have to embrace the modern world of technology, but out at the lake, the cell phone barely got a signal, which made using it there nearly impossible. That didn't bother him. There were times he liked being unconnected. Now was not one of them. He wanted to hear Alex's voice. To know she was all right.

He did hear her voice. Recorded. Saying she was busy. When wasn't she busy?

The phone beeped in his ear and Michael left his message. "Alex, it's me. Don't answer any number you don't know. None. Call me when you get home no matter what time. If I don't hear from you, I'll be on the road, heading up there, and how would it look for Hidden Springs' finest to crash your trial? No joke. Call me."

Henry Hardesty braked his car to a stop beside Michael's car and Henry's wife, Bertie, rolled down her window. "Henry wants to know if anything's wrong, Michael. You're usually gone by this time of the day."

"Just running late tonight." Michael got out of his car to talk to them. "But thanks for asking."

Henry had been retired for years, but when Michael was growing up, he was a city policeman and a familiar sight, checking the parking meters or directing traffic at school events. Now he patrolled Main Street a couple of times every night to make sure the town was quiet. Bertie rode shotgun. In the summer, they always ended up at the Dairy Bar for an ice cream cone before heading home.

The ice cream cones were rounding out Bertie's face, but Henry was as skinny as ever, the skin drawn tightly over his high cheekbones. He shot a look at Michael with as much of a smile as ever showed on his face. "I'm here to help if I can."

"I know." Michael smiled back at him. "You see anything out of the way on your rounds tonight?"

"Nope. Town's all tucked in for bed and that's where me and the missus is headed. After the ice cream."

"No strange cars or anything?" Michael asked.

"Nope. Bertie waved at every one of them, knew where most of them were headed."

Bertie's round cheeks turned a pretty shade of pink. "Now, Henry, you make me sound like an old busybody."

"Nope. Just a girl in the know." Henry shifted his car into drive. "We'd better move along, Michael. Dark's coming on fast and the Dairy Bar might close up on us."

Michael waved as they pulled away. Bertie waved back, but Henry kept his eyes straight ahead as he rolled on toward the stoplight. It was Bertie's job to wave, his to drive. The old man couldn't see so well anymore. Some townsfolk said Bertie rode with him to tell him when the stoplights were red, but so far he'd managed not to hit anybody.

Michael watched the taillights disappear before he got back into his cruiser. Karen was always telling him he couldn't personally see to the safety of the whole town any more than she could follow her church members around to make sure they didn't fall into some sinful situation. That a person couldn't play God. That position was already taken. Rather capably.

Karen was always sensible. Calm and sensible. Then again, Karen might not be all that calm when he warned her about Jackson.

He certainly wasn't feeling very calm and sensible himself. Especially when he thought about the one woman Jackson would know for sure was connected to him after reading the story in the *Gazette*. Aunt Lindy.

She had an old friend who lived in Boston. He started up

the car. Maybe he could convince her it was a good time for a visit.

But a few minutes later when he stepped into her kitchen and suggested Boston, Aunt Lindy stared at him as though he'd suggested she book a flight to the moon.

"Whatever are you talking about, Michael? I'm not going to Boston." She gave him a puzzled frown. "I have things to do here. You know school starts in a few weeks. Have you forgotten that?"

"You could retire."

Aunt Lindy looked totally perplexed by his words. "I could have retired for the last ten years, but I did not retire. I do not plan to retire this year. The Lord willing, I aim to introduce a whole group of new students to the necessity and wonder of math. Even if, from all indications, the classes coming up appear to be the worst bunch of prospects in all my teaching years."

If Michael's panic hadn't been boiling under the lid he had shoved down on it, he might have smiled. In the forty-plus years that Aunt Lindy had been teaching math at Hidden Springs High, she had never claimed a good bunch of prospective learners at the beginning of a school year. Not even when he was in the group. Maybe especially not then.

Aunt Lindy sipped a neat spoonful of tomato soup and broke off a bit of the grilled cheese sandwich she was having for supper. She had insisted on fixing Michael the same when he showed up while she was heating the soup.

"This can just be a snack," she said when he told her not to bother. "Eating alone all the time gets old. Food's better shared."

So he sat down across from her and ate. His stomach

grabbed at it eagerly, reminding him he hadn't eaten since morning.

Aunt Lindy was still frowning. She didn't like things she couldn't figure out. "Exactly why are you suggesting I visit Martha right now?"

"You need a break? The weather should be nice up there, not as hot as here? Martha would love to see you?"

Aunt Lindy's frown got deeper. "Why don't you try the truth, Michael?"

Michael finished off his sandwich, sat back in his chair, and studied Aunt Lindy. She was a thin, spry little woman who didn't worry with makeup or fancy hairstyles. Being pretty took more than cosmetics, she liked to say, and she hadn't worried about being pretty since she was thirteen. But nobody ever really noticed the wrinkles in her skin or the nose that was a bit too large for the rest of her features. They just got swallowed up in her eyes that seemed able to see everything there was to see about you.

To Michael she was bossy, demanding, hard to please, and the bedrock of his existence. It was impossible to hide anything from her. She knew him too well.

Not that she tried to smother him. She never had. But she was the reason he had settled into place here in Hidden Springs. She didn't demand it. Told him to go wherever he was happy. He had gone, lived in the big city for a few years, wasn't happy, and came home. Was happy, or at least most of the time before Tuesday last when he grabbed Jackson back from the edge.

Nobody could be happy living a nightmare, no matter the scene around him.

Aunt Lindy ate the last of her sandwich and brushed her

lips with a cloth napkin. She refused to buy paper napkins. She believed in certain standards a person should live by, and convenience didn't figure into those standards. She fixed her gaze on Michael. "It's the jumper, isn't it?"

So he told her the whole thing, starting with the girl in the Abundant Hope Church and ending with Rebecca Ann opening the package that contained the pictures of Kim Barbour. He didn't leave out anything. Not even the earring. She needed to know the danger was real and present.

She listened without interrupting once, which had to be a first. When Michael ran out of words, she blinked her eyes and set her mouth. "I understand why you are concerned, but I'm still not going to Boston. However, I will hunt up your father's revolver to keep by the bed to make you feel better about me being alone here."

"That doesn't make me feel much better." Michael leaned toward her and tried to think of words to convince her.

"Don't act as if I'm not capable of using it to protect myself if the occasion arises. You surely remember when we had that rat invasion before I got Grimalkin." Her eyes narrowed on Michael as if daring him to deny she was a crack shot. At the sound of her name, the gray-and-white cat suddenly appeared from who knows where to glare at Michael too.

Michael refused to be intimidated. "That was years ago."

"Some things a person doesn't forget how to do. My hand is still steady." Aunt Lindy held her hand out over the table. There wasn't the slightest tremor.

"Rats and people are not the same. When faced with someone out to do you harm, you need more than steady hands."

"Are you questioning my nerve, Michael?" She looked as if that thought amused her.

Michael backed down with a sigh. "Just don't shoot me if I show up in the middle of the night."

"Now you're questioning my good sense." She did smile this time as she leaned down to stroke Grimalkin once, head to tail. The cat, pacified by her touch, sat down and began licking a paw to wash her face.

"Never, Aunt Lindy, but this guy scares me. I don't like to think about what he might do next." He reached across the table to touch her arm.

"As well I can understand, but it is unlikely he would choose an old lady after picking young ones, isn't it? Don't these types of killers follow patterns?"

"Sometimes, but we have no idea what pattern this monster is following. We don't even know who he is."

Aunt Lindy stood up, stepped around the cat, and picked a yearbook up off the counter. "I've been saving this to show you when you came by. If I'd known the jumper was a suspected killer, I would have called."

She opened the yearbook to a page of sophomore class pictures. "I think I found your jumper. Jackie Johnson, class of '93."

Michael peered at the boy staring up out of the small square. If that was the jumper, he'd changed a lot. But Aunt Lindy was good with faces. "Do you remember him?"

"Actually, I do. A harmless enough boy. A bit slow. Sort of a loner who invited ridicule from some of the other students, perhaps because he was a newcomer to Hidden Springs. Not a hometown boy. His family lived here for maybe three years. His father was worthless, best I recall, and Jackie wasn't anyone you expected to excel in anything. Tried to cheat on tests sometimes. Got caught every time. He was the sort of

189

boy who would have you feeling sorry for him one day and then he'd pull something so brainless the next that you'd be ready to send him to the principal's office. He seemed determined to mess up."

"Mess-up kid to mess-up adult. That's how both Hank and I pegged him out on the bridge. And now these murders with everything neat and arranged and carried out perfectly."

Aunt Lindy came around the table to peer over Michael's shoulder at the picture as if trying to see the man the boy had become. After staring at the picture for a long moment, she said, "Are you positive you have the right suspect?"

21

Michael left Aunt Lindy in her sitting room, working on her lesson book, her cat curled at her feet. She looked like she could be the model for a Norman Rockwell *Saturday Evening Post* cover, except for his father's gun beside her on the lamp table. Seeing the gun there didn't make Michael feel any better.

He had no choice but to go home, load up Jasper, and come back. She insisted that wasn't necessary, but when he said he wanted to be in town in case something else happened, she didn't argue. She simply said, "You'll have to tie Dog outside."

Aunt Lindy never called Jasper by name. She hadn't found it amusing when Michael named his dog after their Keane ancestor.

He looked in the rearview mirror at Aunt Lindy's house as he headed down the street. Everything looked peaceful, the same as always, but he still wished she had agreed to ride with him. He needed to protect her. He needed to protect them all. Aunt Lindy, Alex, Karen, even Betty Jean. He was the reason they could be in danger.

Karen was next on his list. She came to the door in faded red warm-ups, her reading glasses propped on top of her head. Her long blonde hair was yanked back and captured in one of those evil-looking clips. She hesitated a half second before she pulled open the door and invited him in.

"Working on a devotional." She waved a hand at a couple of Bibles and study books on her coffee table. A new laptop she must have bought the night before was open and humming on the couch. "You remember I told you I was starting an online devotional blog."

"Oh." He didn't remember, but that hardly mattered right now. "Sorry to interrupt, but this is important."

Her pastor nature kicked in then and she focused on him. "What's wrong?"

"We better sit down."

"Sure." Without a glance at the screen, she shut her computer and placed it on the table beside the Bibles. She motioned him toward the couch and then sat sideways beside him to watch his face while he went through the story again about Jackson. When he warned her she could be in danger, her steady brown eyes widened a bit.

When he was through, she closed her eyes a moment and Michael knew she was praying. He thought he should be doing the same. Praying that he'd wake up from this nightmare. But he didn't. He just sat there and waited.

"What are you suggesting I do, Michael?" she asked when she opened her eyes.

"Go visit your mother in Florida."

"There's an elders' meeting in the morning and then my Bible study group tomorrow night." Her gaze drifted to the open Bibles.

"Call the elders of the church. Tell them to fill in for you."

"But my members expect me to be the one there if they need something. I can't just take off without a good reason."

"What better reason do you need than staying alive?"

Karen studied his face a long moment. "You're trying to frighten me."

"Yes, I am, Karen, but I don't know what else to do but tell you what could happen." He leaned toward her. He had to make her see that she might be in danger. "I want to say he wouldn't come after you, but I can't be sure. Nobody can be sure what Jackson might do next."

"How many other women are you telling to leave town?"

"What do you mean?" Karen had never shown the first indication of jealousy. Not even back when they were still dating and Alex would show up on the scene to make Michael forget Karen and everything else.

She didn't appear to be jealous now, merely concerned. "From what you've told me, it wouldn't have to be a very direct connection. You didn't even know the first girl and the reporter only interviewed you. Any old girlfriend or acquaintance might become a target."

"I know." Michael dropped his face into his hands. She was right. He wasn't going to be able to clear the whole town of the females he knew. He massaged his forehead and tried to think. "I don't want anybody else to die. Not because of me."

"You're not responsible, Michael. Not for any of this. You're a victim, not the villain." Karen moved closer to him on the couch to rub her hand up and down his back. "You want to stay in town tonight? There's that cot in my office over at the church."

He raised his head to look at her. She was calm as ever,

already laying the problem at the Lord's feet in prayer. "No, I'm going to Aunt Lindy's as soon as I go get Jasper."

Karen looked surprised. "You think she might be in danger too?"

"I don't know, Karen. I just don't know." He stood up. He needed to hurry. That gun on the table beside Aunt Lindy's chair was nothing but false security. It would be useless against a killer like Jackson.

Karen got to her feet too. "All right, Michael. I'll contact the elders in the morning. I've been planning to drive down to South Carolina and check on my sister. She called tonight to say the doctor thinks her baby might come anytime now. Mother can't make it up from Florida until next week, and Janet is nervous there by herself when Bryan is at work. She'll be thrilled for me to come and you'll have one less female to worry about until you catch this guy."

"Thank you, Karen. Until then, keep all your doors and windows locked." He looked around at the windows. Every blind was closed and the drapes pulled.

"I always keep my doors locked."

"You do?" Michael looked back at Karen.

"Don't look so insulted." Karen smiled and patted his cheek. "I didn't grow up in Hidden Springs. Besides, some people think preachers should have an open-door policy to everybody."

"I thought you did. You're always counseling somebody or praying for them."

"It's part of my calling to help those in trouble, but I like to see who's at the door before I swing it open. The Lord not only gave me a heart, he gave me a brain. A woman living alone has to be sensible."

"You sound like Aunt Lindy."

"I'll take that as a compliment." She gave him a little push toward the door. "Now go on and get Jasper so you can get back to do guard duty over Malinda. I promise to call 911 at the first rattle of the doorknob."

He hesitated at the door. "You could spend the night at Aunt Lindy's too. She has lots of extra bedrooms."

She looked up at him. "This has really got you spooked."

"Yes." He met her eyes.

"I'll pray for you. And that everybody here in Hidden Springs will be safe."

"That's good, but sometimes prayers need feet. Remember how the Lord gave you that brain." He pointed toward her head.

She shut her eyes for a few seconds, then sighed. "Could be you're right. Maybe I will pack up my computer and hit the road to Janet's tonight. I'd rather drive at night anyway. My church people will understand."

Michael felt a rush of relief. "Call me when you get on the road and out of Hidden Springs."

Karen was right, Michael thought as he pulled away from her house. Jackson did have him spooked to where he couldn't think straight. He checked the rearview mirror, but no car was following him. Still he drove around the block and past Karen's house again. Light edged out around the blinds, but inside she'd be packing. Not because she was spooked like him but because she wanted to be with her sister. Whatever the reason, he didn't care. Not as long as she got out of Hidden Springs. Jackson couldn't possibly know about her sister in South Carolina.

Maybe he was panicking. Maybe she wasn't in any real

danger. Michael fervently hoped that was so. Actually, the neighborhood looked peaceful with everybody shut inside their air-conditioned houses. Here and there, he spotted the flash of a television screen through a window. Things had changed since he was a kid when, on a hot night like this, half the town would be on their porches slapping at mosquitoes while the kids played hide-and-seek in the dark or made up ghost stories to see how scared they could get. When had kids quit doing that sort of thing?

But tonight he was glad everybody was inside behind closed doors. Maybe locked doors. Could be the whole town had started locking up their doors. After that murder at the courthouse last year, there was a run on locks at the hardware store. Even though that murderer had been caught, perhaps, like Karen, people decided better safe than sorry. Weren't his own doors locked now?

The Bunco party was breaking up when he got to Betty Jean's house. Several of the women gave him curious looks when he passed them on the front walk.

"Why, hello, Mike." Stella Pinkston stopped in front of him. "If I'd known you were coming by, I'd have stayed to help Betty Jean clean up."

Michael stepped to the side to give her plenty of room to move past him. "I'm sure she would have appreciated the help." Mike gave her a bland smile. "Tell Ralph hello for me." He hoped the mention of her husband's name would slow her flirting down a little.

"If you're riding with me, you'll have to come on, Stella," Trudi Heightchew called back as she opened her car door. Trudi smiled over the top of the car at Michael. "Nice to see you, Michael. I'd love to stay and chitchat, but I've got to pick up the kids at Mom's. I'm about an hour past her limit already. She's probably ready to lock the boys in a closet by now."

Michael laughed. "Guess you'd better go rescue them."

"Rescue Mom, don't you mean?" Trudi waved and slid under the steering wheel to start the motor.

Michael was relieved when Stella's high heels clattered on down the sidewalk to Trudi's car. She let her skirt ride up on her thigh when she stepped into the car, but he pretended not to notice.

When Michael tapped on Betty Jean's open front door, she looked up from stuffing paper plates in a trash bag. "Michael. What are you doing here?"

"You rushed out so fast this afternoon, I forgot to tell you something." Michael smiled as another of Betty Jean's guests gave her a hug and waved at him on the way out the door. He looked around. "Is that the last one?"

"The last what?" Betty Jean laughed. "What's the matter? All these women in one place making you edgy? You do look sort of nervous."

"Just worried I might mess up your good reputation."

"Right. We all believe that." Betty Jean twisted the top of the trash bag closed and squeezed out the extra air before she fastened it with a twist tie. "Actually, my reputation probably soared to new heights with you showing up at this time of night. But we know you haven't really come courting or anything." She dropped the bag and stared at him with wide eyes. "Not more pictures already?"

"Not yet. This guy appears to be enjoying the whole thing, but surely it'll take him longer than a day to find his next victim. At least, we can hope so."

"If he's enjoying it, why would he be so ready to jump off a bridge to stop himself?" She folded up one of the chairs. "Since you're here, make yourself useful and help me put up the tables and chairs."

Michael folded up a card table and leaned it against the wall. He stared at it a minute, thinking about Betty Jean's question. "I don't know. Could be he's a multiple personality or something. I should have asked that Dr. Colson if he thought that could be true. I don't know anything about psycho killers."

"All I know is what you see in movies. You can always tell the bad guys there because they have scary eyes. Did Jackson have scary eyes?"

"He looked a little strange, but then again, he intended to kill himself." Michael folded up the other table. "I wish we'd had to drag the river for his body."

"Quit beating yourself over the head. You couldn't know he was a psycho." Betty Jean handed him the last chair to stack with the others. "You just need to catch him now. And tell me why you're here. You didn't come by to discuss cases with me, now did you?"

"Well, that's not the only reason." Michael picked up the high school annual he'd brought with him and pointed out the picture of Jackie Johnson. "Aunt Lindy thinks this is Jackson. What do you think?"

Betty Jean took the book and stepped closer to the lamp to study the picture. "Class of '93. Could be the right age. Looks like his hair is brown, so that fits. Can't tell about the eyes, weird or otherwise, but the chin and nose are sort of the same." She looked up at Michael. "You think the Eagleton police have one of those age-progression computer programs? That could nail it for sure."

"Who knows whether Whitt would try that or not, but you can send the picture over tomorrow. Plus, you might check to see if there are other shots of him in clubs or sports teams, whatever."

Betty Jean stared back down at the picture. "It could be him. Did your Aunt Lindy remember him?" She jumped in front of his answer. "That's a dumb question. I'm sure she did. Miss Keane remembers all her students."

"Yeah, she said he was a loner. Pretty much a kid who messed up most of the time."

"Hmm. I think my cousin, Laverne, was in this class." Betty Jean flipped a couple of pages over. "Yep, there she is. She was class secretary when she was a senior and used to try to keep up with everybody for reunions and stuff. She might have a line on this guy. You know, where he went from here. Last I heard she was setting up a page on the internet for Hidden Springs High. Said she'd heard from some of the kids who'd moved away. Maybe he was one of them."

"You think so?" That sounded way too easy.

"Well, probably not, but it's worth a shot." Betty Jean looked at the clock on her mantel. "Too late to call tonight, but I'll call first thing in the morning. I can check out some things on the computer tonight. Don't guess anybody got a fingerprint?"

"I suppose we could have before his car disappeared."

"But you didn't." Betty Jean breathed out a sigh. "You think the hospital would have something? They might fingerprint psychiatric patients."

"I don't think so. But then, I've never been in the psychiatric unit."

"Yet." Betty Jean grinned over at him.

"A little therapy might help me get a handle on things. Karen told me I was spooked."

Betty Jean raised her eyebrows. "You've been to your Aunt Lindy's and to Karen's and now here. You doing poor lonesome women rounds?"

"I wish that was all." Michael reached for one of the folding chairs, opened it back up, and sat down. "Sit down a minute."

"Why am I not liking the look on your face?" Betty Jean dropped down on the couch facing Michael. "What aren't you telling me?"

"You remember about how I said Dr. Colson called to warn me that Jackson might be trying to get my attention. Whitt said the same thing. About Jackson targeting me. Not the girls he's killed, but me."

"You're still breathing. Dead-on-your-feet tired, but breathing."

Michael leaned a little closer to her. "Whitt thinks the guy might pick somebody I know for his next victim."

"But you know everybody in Hidden Springs. No strangers here."

"You hit the nail on the head. Guess that won't make it too hard for Jackson to find a new target."

Betty Jean jerked up straighter on the couch. "You think I might be a target?"

"I don't know, Betty Jean. But I think it would be wise for you not to take any chances. Nobody knows what this guy might do next."

Betty Jean sprang to her feet as if her couch had suddenly sprouted spikes. "You stay right here and don't go anywhere. Not till I pack a few things and then you can follow me over to Mom and Dad's house. They'll be in bed, but I'll just wake them up."

"At last. Somebody sensible," Michael called after her as she headed down the hall toward her bedroom.

She yelled back, "Karen wasn't worried?"

"More concerned that I was acting so strange than about herself."

"She hadn't seen the pictures." Betty Jean stuck her head out the bedroom door. "You don't honestly think Miss Keane is in danger, do you? Don't these kinds of killers follow patterns? Like this crazy would pick all pretty young things." Betty Jean made a sound somewhere between a giggle and a hiccup. "Guess that would leave me out too."

"The first child victim and then the reporter Kim Barbour didn't have all that much in common."

"You have a point there." Betty Jean disappeared into her bedroom. "I know I'll forget something."

She kept talking, but Michael couldn't tell what she was saying over water running. He got up, folded the chair again, and put it back with the others. Then he carried the garbage bag she'd left in the middle of the living room floor out to the kitchen.

"Oh, thanks." Betty Jean dropped her suitcase in the living room and came into the kitchen to grab a box of cereal out of the cabinet. "Mom will make me eat eggs and bacon if I don't take this, and there would go my diet for the rest of the week. Tonight was bad enough. Those lemon squares are rich. Still a couple of pieces over there on the cabinet if you want them."

Michael held his hand palm out in refusal. "Thanks, but I'll pass."

"Okay, that'll make Dad happy. I'll take them to him. He

doesn't worry about his waistline." Betty Jean wrapped up the leftover cake and stuffed it, along with the cereal, into a grocery bag. "That's everything but Sandy."

"Where is the furry terror?"

"The utility room. Some of the girls threaten not to come to my house if I don't put him up. I don't know what they think he's going to do to them."

"Shred their stockings maybe." Michael looked around to see if he needed to take evasive action. Sandy was not a friendly cat.

"Nobody wears stockings in this weather. Besides, he's not that bad." Betty Jean dipped some cat food out of a sack in the cabinet and filled the dishes by the refrigerator before she cracked the door to the utility room. A fluffy black-and-white cat stalked out into the kitchen, twitching his tail back and forth. He gave Michael a haughty glance but totally ignored Betty Jean.

"Come on, Sandy sweetie. I gave you extra food." Betty Jean leaned down to stroke the cat, but he dodged her touch. "Just my luck to get a cat with an attitude."

"Don't give me that. You love it. You probably spike his fur for him."

"Only when I'm having company." Betty Jean straightened up. "You spending the night at Aunt Lindy's or on Karen's couch?"

"Aunt Lindy's. Karen decided to pack up and drive to her sister's house."

"Now?" Betty Jean glanced at the clock again.

"Said she liked driving at night. Guess she decided that would be better than me insisting she come camp out at Aunt Lindy's house."

"Probably afraid Miss Keane would slip poison in her morning coffee."

Michael scowled at Betty Jean. "Aunt Lindy likes Karen."

"I'm sure she does, but you know your aunt is in the Alex camp."

"I've told you a dozen times Karen and I are friends. That's all and there is no Alex camp." Michael kept the scowl on his face even though he liked the idea of an Alex camp.

"But Miss Keane wants there to be." Betty Jean flicked on the light over the sink and turned off the ceiling light. She gave him a curious look. "Did you ask Alex to marry you last night? That was only last night you drove halfway across the country to see her, wasn't it? It's beginning to seem like days ago."

"Tell me about it." Michael was bone-tired. He should have asked Betty Jean to make him some coffee, but no time for that now. "And what I did or didn't ask Alex is none of your business. But she was supposed to call today and leave me a message. Did she?"

"You mean like yes or no?" Betty Jean gave him a sideways glance.

"No, Betty Jean. Like a name of an expert on how psychotic killers think."

"Now that would be a creepy job." Betty Jean shivered. "But no. No messages from Alex. Just that Dr. Colson."

"He didn't call again after I talked to him today, did he?"

"I don't know. There were so many calls, I lost track of who called when." She unplugged the laptop on the counter and stuck it into a padded bag.

"Whitt says the doctor is probably writing a book, so if he calls again, be careful what you tell him. You might see your name in print."

"Don't worry about that. I'm not telling him anything." Betty Jean looked around. "Okay. I'm ready. Be a gentleman and carry my suitcase out while I lock up."

Mike picked up the suitcase. "Do you always lock your doors?"

"Well, yeah. I'm a female. I live alone. Bumps in the night scare me." She switched off the lamp, then switched it back on as if the dark might be scaring her now. She looked over at Michael and almost smiled as she picked up her keys. "Don't look so disappointed, Michael. Bad things happen everywhere. After last year, you of all people should know that. You're going to have to face facts. There are bad people in this world, even in little towns like Hidden Springs."

"I guess you're right."

"I'm always right, remember?" She did smile then as she led the way out the door. "You know, that doctor isn't the only one to think about writing a book. I've thought about doing that myself. I could write about all the crazy things that go on at the sheriff's office. It would probably end up a bestseller."

"I hope you remember to change the names to protect the innocent."

She laughed. "There are no innocents. Just people who haven't gotten caught yet."

"We can hope this guy is one we catch tomorrow."

"I can agree with that." She watched as he loaded her suitcase in her car. "You are going to follow me over to Mom and Dad's, right?"

"I am."

Her parents' house was dark when she pulled up in front of it. Michael stopped behind her and got out to lift her suitcase out of the car.

She put her computer bag strap over her shoulder and reached for the handle of her suitcase. "It's got wheels, so I'll take it from here. Don't want to scare my folks silly. Bad enough me showing up at the door this time of the night, but I'll make up something. That my toilet's backed up or the electricity went off. Just make sure you don't drive off until you see me inside the door."

"Got it." He turned back to his cruiser.

"And Michael?" She waited for him to look back at her. Her eyes glittered in the dark. "Be careful."

"You just worry about you. I'll be fine."

"Weren't you the one who said nobody knew what this guy might do next?"

22

When Michael stopped the car in front of his log house, Jasper met him the same as he had the night before. And like the night before, Michael got what Whitt had called the heebie-jeebies. Maybe it was Betty Jean's warning. Maybe it was a lack of sleep or those images of Hope and Kim Barbour burned into his mind. But the dark pushed in on him like a black trash bag blowing against his face. Over the sound of his heart thumping in his ears came the rustling of monster feet closing in on him.

With a hand on Jasper's head, Michael breathed in and out slowly. Time to get control of himself. Jackson wouldn't chance coming back out here again tonight. Of course, the man had no way of knowing Michael had found the earring. For all Jackson knew, Michael might leave his dirty clothes on the floor for days without washing them. If the man wanted to be sure Michael found the earring, he would have left it in plain sight on the table or maybe in an envelope with Michael's name scrawled across the front.

Why had the man planted the thing in his house anyway? To show Michael he wasn't safe in his own home? If that was his purpose, why hadn't he written a warning on the bathroom mirror or ransacked the house? Why hide an earring in one of his pockets?

Michael pushed away the questions he had no way of answering and surveyed the yard between him and the house. He didn't spot anything that might be reason for alarm. Jasper shoved his nose up against Michael's hand and wagged his tail. Not one hair was raised on his haunches.

Karen had him pegged. He was spooked. Jumping at shadows. Even so, the thought of what could be in those shadows made him pull his gun out of the holster. He felt a little foolish creeping up his own porch steps and sliding along the wall to peek around the side of the house, but better foolish than dead.

On the south side of the house, the lake glittered serenely in the soft light of the half moon. Nothing out of the ordinary except a nasty odor. Jasper must have found a dead fish. Funny that he couldn't smell anything on Jasper. That was a good thing. Aunt Lindy wouldn't be happy about a dog that smelled like rotten fish tied among her roses.

When he tried to turn the doorknob, he remembered the door was locked. He dug into his pocket for the key while watching for something to move in the darkness. But nothing was out there. At least nothing he could see.

Inside everything was the way he'd left it. The sink faucet wasn't dripping. His clothes were wrinkling in the dryer. Remnants of cornflakes were crusted on the dish in the sink. All was still and peaceful. All except Michael.

Stock-still in the middle of the house, he listened as though he might hear the echo of any intruders. A cricket chirped out on the porch. The clock on the kitchen wall made that peculiar battery-powered click that replaced the ticking of a spring-wound clock. Jasper's tail swept back and forth against the floor where the dog sat and waited for his supper.

"You're right, boy. Time for me to quit imagining monsters going bump in the night." Michael filled Jasper's dish with kibble. "Here you go, but you better not get sick on the way to Aunt Lindy's."

He left the dog crunching his food and checked out the bedrooms. Nothing disturbed there. Back in the front room the light flashed on his answering machine. He hit the button to listen to the new messages.

First, a kid named Shane asked if he and his buddies could go fishing off Michael's dock on Friday. "I promise no booze and no girls. Just a few of us guys, okay? We might spend the night if we can find a couple of tents to borrow. You don't have one, do you?"

They probably wanted him to supply the bait too. A smile tugged at Michael's lips and for a moment this day seemed like any other ordinary day without worries. Then the next voice came on.

"Dr. Phillip Colson here, Deputy Keane. I wanted to thank you for talking with me earlier today. I'm wondering if you've heard anything more from our patient or perhaps I should say your suspect. At any rate, our Mr. Jackson. I did as you suggested, or should I say ordered, and attempted to contact Detective Whitt, but he was out of the office. In any case, I truly doubt my brief chat with that poor young reporter could be of any help to his investigation. Do call me if you think I can be of any additional help or if you yourself need someone to explore your feelings about all this. I'm sure you've been under a great deal of stress the last few days. If you're concerned about my fee, I often pro-rate my charges based on an individual's ability to pay."

Michael's smile vanished. The doctor was beginning to get on his nerves with his psychoanalyzing. Maybe Whitt was right and the man was planning to get rich off the story.

Finally, the next voice was Alex, obviously before his panic call a few hours ago. She sounded the same as always. "And you say I'm never home. I tried your cell, but as usual, you didn't pick up. I've got two names for you." Michael grabbed a pencil and jotted down the names and numbers. "I hope they can help. Try me later. I might be home around nine."

Michael looked at the clock. Ten thirty. She was probably already out again, but she should have called him again after hearing his message. He pushed the message button again to hear the mechanical voice say no more messages.

He dialed her home phone number from memory. Her answering machine picked up on the second ring. He waited through her greeting and the beeps. "I'm serious about this, Alex. You don't call me, I'm coming."

He hung up and called her cell. It went straight to voice mail without ringing. He left the same message there.

Then he pulled Whitt's card out of his pocket and dialed the number. After a couple of transfers, he got Chekowski. "Aaron's gone for the day, and I was on my way out. But I can get in touch with him if I need to. Something else happen?"

"No murders, if that's what you mean. But I may have a line on Jackson. A picture in an old high school annual. Could be him. Could not be. We'll get the information to you first thing in the morning."

"So you think he might have gone to school there. Family still in the area now?" Chekowski asked.

Michael could almost see her pulling out her notebook. "No, they were only here a few years while Jackson was in high school. Actually, Jackie Johnson is the name in the annual. We'll try to get a line on the parents' names and a current address."

"You really think it might be the same guy?" Chekowski sounded doubtful. "What would that make him now? Forty something?"

"Right."

"Probably a long shot, but we'll check it out. We check everything out." Chekowski sighed. "So far all we've found are dead ends. Everything still calm and serene in Solla Sollew?"

"Solla Sollew?"

"You know. Dr. Seuss. Solla Sollew—where they never have troubles or at least very few." Chekowski laughed. "You must not have kids if you don't know Dr. Seuss stories."

"You have kids?"

"Not yet, but I intend to someday. Until that someday, I borrow my sister's kids now and again to stay in practice on Dr. Seuss books. His stories take a nimble tongue."

"I see, I think."

"The perfect mindset for Dr. Seuss. But how about it? Things okay down there?"

"I guess you could say so. Things seem peaceful tonight."

"I hope they stay that way for you and for us too. This perp is way too good at what he does and way too fast at picking out targets." Every trace of laughter was gone from her voice now. "Watch your back, Deputy."

That was all he had been doing, Michael thought as he hit the off button on the phone. He started to put the phone back on the base, but then stuck it in his belt instead. He didn't want to miss Alex's call while he looked for Jasper's yard chain, which he seemed to remember leaving on the back deck a couple of weeks ago.

He didn't chain the dog often. Nothing out there Jasper could hurt except an occasional unwary possum. He never roamed far from the house. He was always waiting in the yard when Michael got home. But who knew what the dog did during the day? Michael imagined him swimming in the lake, sleeping in the sun, chasing squirrels—then again, he might have a whole pack of coyote girlfriends.

Michael touched the dog's head. "You better be careful. Those wild women can get you in trouble."

Jasper wagged his tail as he padded out on the deck behind Michael. The bad odor was worse here. Maybe Jasper and his wild girlfriends had downed a deer and dragged it up in the yard. But then dead fish could stink up the place too.

He surveyed the yard, but the night was too dark to see if anything was out there. He'd have to make time during the day to check it out and get rid of whatever it was.

Michael ran his hand down Jasper's back again, then sniffed his hand. Nothing but dog odor. Whatever it was, Jasper must be staying away from it. Not normal behavior for a country dog. Michael found the chain on the deck railing and retreated inside.

He had his duffel bag packed and ready to go out the door when the phone finally rang. He hit the answer button. "Hello."

"All right, you've got my full attention. What's going on?" Alex's voice was brisk, all business.

"Is that the way you talk to clients?" Michael asked.

"Not at all. I'm much sweeter to them. As long as they pay their bills."

"You're all heart, Sheridan. How much is this call costing me?"

"We'll work out something." Her voice was softer with the hint of a smile. "Fact is, your message sounded like it was time to be serious. So out with it. The bad news first. Then the good."

"Nothing but bad news. Jackson killed the reporter who interviewed me after that stupid hero story came out in the *Gazette*."

"You know Jackson killed her?" The lawyer voice again.

"I don't know anything." Michael rubbed his eyes. "But the killer—and who else but Jackson—brought pictures of her to Hidden Springs. The same poses as the first girl."

"Wait a minute. Brought pictures? What do you mean brought pictures? They weren't mailed like the others?"

He could practically hear her mind clicking. "Okay, where do you want me to start, Counselor?"

"Are you in trouble?"

"Why, Counselor, you sound like you care."

"I got three hours' sleep last night and may have lost a case in court this morning. All because an old friend yelled help."

"Yeah, thanks, Alex." It was time to cut the small talk and get straight to facts. "I am in trouble. This nut I pulled back from the edge is offing girls and sending me letters and pictures to let me know if it wasn't for me they'd still be smiling and laughing."

"All right. Let's try to make some sense of all this."

"Nothing makes sense."

"Wait a second. Let me set my phone to record what we're saying."

Some beeps sounded in Michael's ear. "Why?"

"Because you can miss some important things the first time you listen to somebody's story."

"Recorders make me nervous."

"Then pretend you don't know it's on," Alex said shortly. "Besides, you sound plenty nervous already, recorder or no recorder. So start over. Why are you in trouble?"

"I told you. This psycho is killing women and I can't catch him and I don't know who he might go after next."

"You actually think he killed the reporter because she interviewed you?" Alex sounded a little incredulous.

"That's what his letter said. Whitt, remember, I told you about him."

"He's the Eagleton detective who made you feel like small potatoes."

"More like no potatoes, though that's not important. Anyway, he thinks the killer is targeting me. Not his victims. Me. That he's killing people to get at me."

Alex was silent a moment. "So you broadcast a warning to all the women in your life. How could he even know about me?"

"He was in my house last night. He could have been here when you called and heard you leave your message. I have caller ID and your name and number is listed in a book right by the phone."

"Whole name?"

"No, only Alex."

"That's good. He might think I'm a guy."

"Not if he was here when you called and heard you. You don't sound like a guy."

"Now you're making me nervous, Michael." Her voice sounded tight.

Michael imagined Alex with the phone pressed hard against her ear. She'd be shoving her dark hair back away from her face, as if that would make her hear better. He wished he could really see her. "You didn't get any weird phone calls then?"

"Only from you. How do you know he was in your house?"

"It's a long story."

"You talk. I'll listen. Don't leave anything out, whether you think it's important or not." She was all business again.

Michael perched on the arm of the couch while he considered the best place to start. Across the room, the curtains were only half closed over the window, and Michael suddenly felt on display. He couldn't remember ever worrying about whether the drapes were open or shut, but now he got up and pulled them tightly together. He sat back down, ready to tell her anything she wanted to know except how he kept feeling monsters in the dark around him.

23

Michael talked and Alex listened, inserting a quick question now and again to clarify something. Finally he got it all told. "That covers it. The earring. What little I know about Kim Barbour's murder. Rebecca Ann getting the pictures. Jackson's car disappearing from T.R.'s. Whitt and his sidekick, Chekowski. Me going around scaring women."

He hoped that last would lighten the mood, but it didn't work. It was too true.

The only sound from the other end of the line was Alex tapping her pen on a table or her desk. When the silence went on so long that it started whining in his ear, Michael asked, "Well, Counselor, surely you have questions."

"There are always questions. We'll start with the most important one." Alex hesitated a bare second. "Where were you when Hope was killed?"

"What?" That was the last question Michael expected her to ask.

"I want to know where you were when that first young girl was killed. Friday night, wasn't it? Or has the coroner established a different time of death?"

"Whitt isn't likely to share the findings of the medical examiner with me, but it almost had to be Friday night."

"You haven't answered my first question. Where were you Friday night?"

Michael pulled in a deep breath and forced himself to relax his grip on the phone. "What difference does that make? I didn't even know that girl existed until I saw those pictures that came in the mail."

"Just answer the question, forever more." Alex's voice was clipped, impatient.

"All right." He didn't like the question, but he had asked for her help. He shut his eyes to think back to Friday. It seemed ages ago. "I went by Aunt Lindy's around dinnertime, maybe six thirty. Then I came home, went fishing for a while, and cleaned my guns."

"Guns? As in plural?" Alex didn't give him time to answer. "Oh, you mean your Civil War toys."

"My Civil War antique guns," Michael corrected. Alex liked to needle him about his gun collection, but tonight he just went through the motions of pretending to care. None of that seemed to matter much when she was asking him if he had an alibi for murder.

"Nobody with you? No girlfriend there to help you clean the fish you caught? Spending the night?" She kept her voice light, but it was obvious she was deadly serious.

"Nope. All alone." He wanted to pretend they weren't talking murder alibis. "If I didn't know better, I'd think you were jealous, Sheridan."

"Not jealous. Envious." Alex went along with him, perhaps giving him time to wrap his mind around the reason for her question.

He wondered if she used that tactic on her clients. Pressuring for answers, then letting up. He pushed that thought away. He was a friend. Not a client. "Envious? That's hard to believe."

"I don't know why. It all sounds so peaceful." Her exaggerated sigh came across the line. "I had to not only buy dinner for the obnoxious client of the year, but also hold his hand and tell him how the firm absolutely refuses to allow him to go to jail. I'm beginning to hope I was lying. If it wasn't for what it would do to the reputation of the firm, I'd wash my hands of the whole mess and hand him over to the prosecution in one of those extra-large gift bags."

"That bad, huh?" Michael wished she were sitting beside him holding his hand. "You could always hang out your shingle here in Hidden Springs."

"I may have to show up down there to keep a certain old friend out of jail." Her voice was serious again.

"What are you talking about?" Michael stared toward his window. A sliver of dark night showed at the bottom of the drawn drapes.

"Come on, Michael, you're a cop. Think like one. That man planted evidence on you. He didn't hide that earring there to scare you. He put it there to incriminate you, and now you've just told me you don't have alibi one for the time of death."

Michael's mouth was suddenly so dry he could hardly get out the words. "That's nuts, Alex."

Her voice went soft, almost a caress across the miles. "I know that, Michael. I do. But this man, this Jackson, Johnson, whatever his name, is mentally disturbed. You've got to try to think like he's thinking."

"I don't want to think like he's thinking. I want to find him and stop him."

"He has the advantage on you there. He's already found you." Alex paused a couple of seconds. "You do have your gun loaded, don't you?"

"Yes. And where I can reach it. But Whitt doesn't think Jackson will come after me personally. Just that he might pick someone connected to me somehow."

"He won't show up in DC." Alex sounded as if she were trying to convince herself as much as Michael.

"He couldn't find you. Not with just your telephone number." Michael hated the doubt in his voice. "Could he?"

"Maybe. It's not listed, but if a person knows what he's doing, he can track things down on the internet." She was silent a minute with the pen tapping on the desk again. "You think this guy has that much on the ball? To be able to do that?"

"I wouldn't have thought so. That's the weird thing about all this. Out there on the bridge he looked like nothing more than a run-of-the mill bum down on his luck and tired of it all. He was ready to pitch himself in the river rather than face whatever scrape he was in. But no, I didn't peg him as too smart or at all dangerous to anybody but himself."

"Unfortunately, you can't always tell by looking. About the dangerous part."

"Yeah." Michael stood up and walked into the kitchen and back. He needed to be moving. "You ever defended any murderers? Clients you knew were guilty?"

"The firm handles all sorts of cases." Her voice sounded a little stiff, as though he'd stepped on her toes.

"So that means you probably have. I always figured you could tell a psycho just by looking. Do you think that's true?"

"I think that's simply something we tell ourselves so we don't have to be jumping at every shadow. But keep in mind how reporters can generally dig up at least one neighbor who always says, 'He seemed like such a nice guy. Never bothered anybody. Minded his own business.' Which turned out to be killing people."

"So you don't think you can tell?" Michael stopped in front of the sink to stare at his fuzzy reflection with the room mirrored behind him. Maybe that's all a person ever saw. Just their own image mirrored back to them. At least until the monster in the dark put his face right against the window and let you know for sure he was out there.

"I didn't say that, exactly. The firm has had clients who scared me to look at them and others who did look like that proverbial guy next door until you knew what they'd done. Not that a defense attorney asks for confessions. It's usually better not to hear that 'I did it' line."

"I keep telling you, Sheridan. You're in the wrong line of work."

"Yours is better?"

"At least I'm trying to put murderers away. Not get them off."

"Everybody is entitled to his or her day in court, and that usually means an attorney there with him. Some of the cases you bleed over. Others you don't cry when you lose."

"What's your obnoxious client done?"

"You know I can't talk cases, Michael. Attorney-client confidentiality. But the firm's into more civilized crime now. Corporate intrigue. The junior, very junior, partners handle the run-of-the-mill criminal cases for our clients. Embezzlement, reckless homicide, that sort of thing. If one of our clients were to be involved in a high-profile murder case, and we do definitely hope that never happens, the senior partners would no doubt farm it out to a firm with more resources in criminal cases." Alex laughed a little. "However, sometimes I think I liked the everyday thieves and murderers better than these bigwigs. You didn't have to promise to keep them out of jail. They were ready to plea-bargain just to knock a few years off their sentences."

"Like I keep telling you, you should come to Hidden Springs and research deeds."

"Now there's some high-pressure work." This time Alex's laugh was more relaxed. Then she was serious again. "Look, Michael, I don't know how I can help you with any of this, but if you think of a way, let me know."

"Just be careful."

"I'll double-check my locks and not make appointments with strangers and look at anyone who mentions anything to do with you or Hidden Springs with wary suspicion."

He wasn't sure that would be enough. "You could hire a bodyguard for a couple of weeks. Write it off as a business expense. To keep away that obnoxious client."

"You looking for a job?" She had a smile in her voice.

"Come to Hidden Springs and I'll work for free."

"I'm thinking you've got enough people to guard down there already." She paused a moment, as though considering her next words. "Did you warn Karen?"

"She's on her way to visit her sister in South Carolina and Betty Jean's at her parents', probably sleeping with her finger on the emergency call button on her phone. I'm headed back to spend the night at Aunt Lindy's."

"You think Malinda could be in danger?" She sounded surprised.

"Who knows? But better safe than sorry. I tried to get her to go visit a friend in Boston, but she refused. Said she could take care of herself."

"Against a serial killer?" Now she sounded incredulous.

"You know Aunt Lindy. She loaded Dad's old pistol. I didn't even know she still had it. When I left a while ago to come get Jasper, she had it on the lamp table beside her."

"Then pity the poor man who attempts to bother her. You don't really think this Jackson will go after her, do you?" Worry took over in Alex's voice.

"No." Michael went back in the living room, but instead of sitting down, he paced back and forth in front of his couch. A couple of floorboards creaked under his weight and Jasper raised his head off his paws to give him a puzzled look.

"All of a sudden, you're scaring me, Michael. You don't sound sure enough."

Michael stood still and breathed out a tired sigh. "I'm not sure of anything, Alex. Just stay safe."

That was all he wanted. For everybody to be safe. Michael put the phone back on the base and stared up at the ceiling while a silent prayer rose up inside him. *Lord, please don't let anybody else die.*

Michael picked up his bag, flicked off the lights, and locked up. He had to pick Jasper's front paws up and place them on the backseat of the car, then shove him inside. The dog didn't like riding in the backseat of the patrol car. All the way to town, he panted so much, the seat was sure to be slimy with dog slobber.

Jasper didn't get any happier when Michael fastened his yard chain to a back porch post. As soon as Michael went inside, the dog set up a howl.

Aunt Lindy came down the hall from her bedroom with Grimalkin trailing after her. No sign of the gun. She looked smaller and more vulnerable in her nightclothes without her glasses propped on her nose. Michael didn't ask if the gun was in her robe pocket because he wasn't sure which scared him the most—that she didn't have it with her or that she did.

"Good gracious, Michael. Can't you make that dog hush? Reece Sheridan will call the police on me."

"I am the police," Michael reminded her.

Aunt Lindy didn't smile. "Then give yourself a citation and bring Dog in the house or whatever it takes to make him stop howling."

"You sure Grimalkin won't have a heart attack?"

"Could be you should worry more about Dog than Grimalkin. I'll see that she stays in my bedroom until you get that animal inside to your room. After that, Dog is on his own." She picked up the cat and headed back toward her bedroom.

"Good night, Aunt Lindy."

"Good night, Michael. I'm not sure any of this is one bit necessary." She didn't slam the bedroom door behind her, but she did close it very firmly.

Michael felt sort of like a teenager again as he brought Jasper through the kitchen door and poked around in the cabinet to find an old pan to use for the dog's water dish. Jasper circled the room, sniffing everything. "Best be good, buddy. She has a gun and says she knows how to use it."

When he turned around from filling the pan at the sink, Jasper had his nose pressed against the closed door that led to the front of house. He was standing stiff with his hackles raised. Michael put his hand on his head. "Easy, boy. The cat's not in there and you couldn't chase her if she was."

Jasper made a sound somewhere between a whine and a growl.

Michael opened the door and the dog made a beeline for the staircase and up it without hesitation. "Huh, guess you want to sniff out my room." Michael followed him up the stairs with his bag and the pan, trying not to slosh the water out on the stairs.

The dog streaked past Michael's bedroom toward a door that led up to the attic. The growl turned into barks that bounced off the walls in the hallway.

"Quiet, Jasper." Michael set the water down and went after the dog to grab his collar. Jasper's bark turned back into a low growl. Michael ran his hand along the dog's back, smoothing down his raised hair. "The cat's not up here, and if you keep barking, Aunt Lindy will kick us both out. We'll have to sleep on the porch."

The dog's growl softened into an anxious whine as he looked from the door up at Michael.

"What's the matter with you? No cats up there. Nothing but mice and old books." Michael took hold of the dog's collar again and turned him back down the hall. Once inside the bedroom with the door shut, Jasper made a thorough sniffing inspection all around the room. That seemed to satisfy him as he plopped down on the rug at the foot of the bed with a whiffling sigh of contentment. Grimalkin had obviously not been in this room.

Michael didn't turn on a light as he undressed. Enough light from the street outside slipped in around the curtains to keep darkness at bay. In bed, Michael stared up at the familiar cracks in the ceiling and listened to the old house settle into a midnight silence.

The sounds ought to be as comforting as an old lullaby, but he couldn't fall asleep. Every time he closed his eyes, the photos of the two dead girls popped them back open. Both girls were dead through no fault of their own but because a monster had decided to stalk him.

And now Alex said the monster was planting evidence on him. But why? No one would ever believe he could kill those girls. No one. Then he remembered how Whitt's eyes narrowed on him when he asked Michael about the earring. Still, he'd never once asked Michael where he was on Friday night. That didn't mean the question wouldn't come up the next time he saw Whitt.

Michael's legs felt so jerky he wanted to get up and pace the room, but he lay still. The old floorboards would creak if he got up, and that might wake Aunt Lindy again. Something he did not want to do. Besides, he needed to sleep. A man couldn't think straight without enough sleep, and he needed to think straight.

He slowly blanked out any thought of the murders by pulling up facts about the War Between the States. Confederate troops attacked Fort Sumter on April 12, 1861. Lee surrendered on April 9, 1865. Michael ran through the battles in between. Bull Run, Antietam, Chancellorsville, Gettysburg. His ancestors had fought in each of those places, and with sleep eluding him in this house where they once lived, it seemed only appropriate to let his mind drift to their stories.

Three Hidden Springs Keanes fought for the Union Army, two for the South. Two of the men, cousins, came back to Hidden Springs to finish out their lives as partners in the dry goods business in spite of fighting on opposite sides in the war. Neither ever married. Then there was Uncle Wilbur, whose body lived through the war but whose spirit died at Gettysburg. He never married either.

The fact was, many of his Keane ancestors hadn't seemed too keen on marrying. Every generation had more than its share of bachelors and spinsters until finally the duty of carrying on the Keane name in Hidden Springs was up to Michael. While he was hardly adverse to the idea of a couple of little Keanes underfoot, first he needed a wife. That's where things got complicated, if not impossible, since he was desperately in love with a woman who would laugh at the idea of settling down in Hidden Springs even if he ever did gather up nerve enough to ask her straight out and risk her saying no. Hearing her no would be too final.

He pushed aside worry about asking her the big question. Right now, he just wanted her to be safe so that maybe someday she would have that chance to say no or maybe have a change of heart about small towns.

With his eyes shut, he started to count Civil War statistics again, but this time the facts weren't mere cold numbers. Instead dead soldiers rose up off the fields of battle to march through his mind while the monster lurked behind them, taunting Michael.

He opened his eyes and stared up at the dark air pressing down on him. At the foot of the bed Jasper breathed in and out, unbothered now. He didn't have murderers haunting his thoughts.

Hand it over to the Lord, Aunt Lindy's voice whispered through his mind. She'd told him that many times after the auto accident when he was a teen. At times then, he had wrestled with the question of why a loving, all-powerful God would allow his parents to die when he needed them so very much. When he put that question to Aunt Lindy, she told him all questions couldn't be answered, but that didn't mean he shouldn't pray for wisdom and help. In both bright sunlit times and dark valley times.

The words of his mother's favorite psalm slipped through Michael's mind now, almost like a caress. *The Lord is my shepherd, I shall not want.* But the words slowed and stopped when he got to *Yea, though I walk through the valley of the shadow of death, I will fear no evil; for Thou are with me.* The psalm didn't promise nothing bad would happen in the walk through life. The Bible said every good and perfect gift came from God, but Scripture was plain that evil was in the world and needed to be overcome. Evil was happening with these murders. An evil that Michael, with the Lord's help, was determined to stop.

Michael gave up trying to shut it all away. Instead he pulled up that day on the bridge to concentrate on every detail. He brought up the image of Jackson teetering on the edge, his shirttail half out of rumpled pants that sagged below his potbelly. His thin hair stuck up in crazy angles and his face was stiff with fear. Greasy dirt showed under his thumbnails, as if he'd had to change a tire or work on his engine on the way to the bridge.

Try as he might, Michael could not see the man on the bridge posing Hope and Kim Barbour so meticulously and then printing photos of them to deliver to Michael. The man surely wouldn't chance going to a self-help photo printer where somebody might look over his shoulder and see the photos. It seemed only reasonable to assume he had his own computer and printer, even if he did look like a man so down on his luck he might not have a roof over his head.

The questions chased around in Michael's head until he finally slipped into a fitful sleep where he dreamed about Jackson. The man was laughing as he climbed over the railing on the bridge. Michael ran toward the jumper, but it was like making his way through deep mud. Slowly. Slowly. Even as he went toward him, he wasn't sure if he was going to save him or push him. When, at last, Michael made it to the railing, the man grabbed him and pulled him out into the air. They fell together. Jackson laughed as the river rushed up toward them.

Michael jerked awake before he hit the water.

24

Michael followed Aunt Lindy to school the next morning where she planned to begin getting her classroom ready for the coming school year. He wanted to take her, but she refused to ride in the patrol car with Jasper panting in the backseat. She disappeared inside the school without once looking back at him. He didn't know if she refused to acknowledge his presence because the reason he was there frightened her or if she merely thought his worries foolish.

Aunt Lindy didn't own up to fearing anything except being in water over her head, but a serial killer on the loose was enough to scare anyone. He hadn't told her Alex's bizarre idea that the killer was trying to lay the blame on Michael. The idea was so crazy Michael couldn't summon up the words to talk about it.

Michael beat Betty Jean to the office. He couldn't remember the last time that had happened. He eyed the phone. Maybe he should call to see if she'd left for work, but he didn't want to get her parents in a panic. Instead he was aware of every minute passing as he found the filters and measured out the coffee. The water was still gurgling through the coffeemaker when he heard her footsteps out in the hallway.

"Don't say a word!" She glared at him as she came in the door and slammed the fresh-off-the-press *Gazette* down on her desk. "This has been, without question, the worst morning of my entire life."

Betty Jean, who prided herself on looking as good as she could, as she liked to say, had fallen short of her target this day. Wisps of curls she usually pulled down over her forehead and sprayed into place until a tornado wouldn't budge them were sticking out at odd angles. On top of that, something wasn't quite right about her makeup, although Michael didn't know exactly what.

He wisely chose not to comment on her appearance. "Your mother insist you eat her bacon and eggs?"

"Country ham and biscuits. My diet is wrecked. My hair is a disaster and my nerves are shot." She poured coffee in the Florida mug she'd bought on her vacation last year. She stared at the seashells on the cup. "I think I'll go to Hawaii."

"I think you should. Sounds like fun."

"Tomorrow." She stared over at him, as though daring him to say anything against that.

"I'm thinking Alaska myself."

"Good. Maybe all of us should pack up and leave. Close down Hidden Springs for a couple of weeks." She took a sip of coffee and finally noticed Jasper peeking out from under Michael's desk. "There's a dog under your desk."

"At least you haven't lost your perceptive powers." Michael touched Jasper's head. The dog looked toward Betty Jean and wagged his tail a bit uncertainly as he inched closer to Michael's leg.

"Jasper, I presume." Betty Jean sounded a little calmer. "Does he have a reason to be here?"

"He's under house arrest for disturbing the peace in Aunt Lindy's neighborhood." The dog had walked around stiff-legged all morning at the house, even though Aunt Lindy shut Grimalkin up in her bedroom.

"I'd suggest him being long gone before Uncle Al comes in."

"Is he coming in?"

"You'd have to ask him that. Grandma Potter is better, but he may decide to go fishing." Betty Jean sipped her coffee, then added, "In Florida. And he hasn't even seen the last bunch of pictures." She picked up the *Gazette* and laid it back down. "I can't stand to look at any more pictures."

"Hank have a story about the pictures?"

"He published the picture of Hope, smiling, happy, alive, and the publicity shot of the reporter." She held up the front page for Michael to see. Then she turned the paper around to stare at it. "Poor little thing. I want to cry every time I look at that sweet young thing's picture. She's not much more than a baby. Did they find out who she was?"

"I don't know. Whitt isn't likely to share any information with me."

"What a jerk!"

"No argument from me there." Michael pointed to the paper. "Hank mention Rebecca Ann getting the pictures?"

"Nope. I guess the public's need to know doesn't include them needing to know his daughter was accosted by a serial killer."

"She wasn't exactly accosted. Just used as a messenger." Michael peeked over Betty's Jean's shoulder as he passed behind her desk to fill his coffee cup. "I don't blame Hank for not mentioning Rebecca Ann. No need putting the child in danger."

"She'd already be dead if this psycho wanted her dead."

"You're probably right."

"I'm always right." Betty Jean's words were clipped, short. The phone rang. She scowled at it a couple of seconds, then pushed away from her desk. "You answer it. I'm going to the grill for some chocolate-covered doughnuts."

The chocolate must have helped, because when she came back a little less than an hour later, she brought Michael a cinnamon twist and Jasper a steak bone. "I took it off Judge Routt's plate. Cindy says he has steak every morning for breakfast. Rare. Blood running down into his eggs. Enough to gag a maggot."

"Thanks for the word picture." Michael dropped his doughnut back down on the napkin, but Jasper's appetite wasn't bothered as he settled down to gnaw the bone. "You didn't forget the yearbook, did you? Need to send Eagleton a picture."

"Got it." She pulled the book out of the tote bag she carried her sneakers in to and from work every day, just in case she found time to walk around the block a couple of times. Michael had never seen the shoes out of her bag.

"I called Orbrey Perkins."

"You called Orbrey Perkins?" She glanced over her shoulder as the scanner hummed. "You must be worse off than I am this morning. Nobody in his right mind calls Orbrey Perkins."

"Not unless you want to know something about somebody in Hidden Springs. The man is a wealth of information." Michael had been on the phone with Orbrey nearly a half hour, but it was time well spent.

"Did he remember this guy's family then?"

"He did. Said they lived on a farm over on Gully Wash Road." Michael picked up his doughnut again. "The fire department burned down the old house out there a few years back as a training exercise after the Bronsons bought the farm."

"I remember that. Hank took pictures and made it look like they almost caught the woods on fire. My cousin was one of the volunteer firemen that day and said the flames never even got close to the trees. That man will write anything to try to sell papers." Betty Jean repositioned the annual and hit the scanner button again.

"He does like to make a story dramatic."

"Except this week, I guess." Betty Jean came back to her desk. She pushed the *Gazette* aside and fired up her computer. "Maybe I can enlarge this picture a little."

"That might help." Michael stood up and watched over her shoulder as she brought up Jackie Johnson's high school picture. Nothing there to make a person think serial killer.

"What else did Orbrey tell you about little Jackie here?" Betty Jean pointed at the picture on her computer screen.

"Nothing about him. Just the place and the family. He knew the farm as the Lillard place, but said that name went back, way before the Johnsons. Orbrey figured somebody in the mother's family owned the place and let them live there. Everybody could tell they were down on their luck with no means of paying rent. He couldn't remember her maiden name, but when he asked his wife, she was almost sure she was an Ellis. Virginia Ellis, she said."

"Hmm," Betty Jean murmured as she moved the cursor to enlarge Jackie Johnson's picture. "I can't think of anybody named Ellis around here these days."

"Mrs. Perkins said the only ones she ever knew moved away some years ago. She had no idea where. Neither did Orbrey."

"Then I can't see how any of this helps. Not if nobody knows where this guy's family is now. The name Johnson isn't exactly Zimrock. Probably only a few zillion of them in the country."

"You're right, but it's all we've got. How about your cousin? You talk to her yet?"

"I can't do but one thing at a time." Betty Jean frowned up at him and then back at her screen. "Enlarging this is going to make the picture fuzzy. Do you think they would still have the original photo at the high school? Don't they keep a photo in the student records?"

"I can ask, but I'd be surprised if they have records back to when this guy was in school. Nothing digital back then." He stared at the image on Betty Jean's screen. It could be the man he pulled back from the edge of the bridge.

"He was in one of the FFA Club pictures, but it wouldn't enlarge better than this one. You think he might have had his picture in the *Gazette*? Maybe doing a project with the club or something? Newspapers keep files of pictures forever, don't they?"

"That's an idea. I'll check with Hank. Was he at the Grill?"

"Nope. Cindy hadn't seen him all morning. Said maybe his wife had finally put him on a real diet, but I told her I didn't think that was it. That Barbara had gone to visit her folks." Betty Jean looked up at Michael before he could say anything. "Don't worry. I didn't tell her why, although I don't see what it could hurt. She'll know before the lunch crowd shows up anyway. Nothing stays secret long in Hidden Springs." She looked back at the picture. "You want me to print it out or just send it along to Whitt?"

"Print it first." Michael moved over to the printer and waited for the picture to slide out. He picked it up and stared at the man who had turned his life into a nightmare. "Maybe I should drive to Eagleton to give Whitt the picture. He might tell me what's going on then."

"He can get it on the computer. You're not going anywhere," Betty Jean said matter-of-factly. "I don't care if Alex calls and says she'll marry you if you can get there before dark or else forget it. You're still sticking in Hidden Springs today."

Michael twisted his mouth to hide his smile. "I don't think I'll get a call like that from Alex, but I did talk to her last night."

"I guess you both stuck to cases." Betty Jean rolled her eyes at him.

"What else?" He thought about telling Betty Jean about the earring, but decided there was no need her getting worried about him too.

"If I have to tell you, it's hopeless anyway." Betty Jean leaned closer to the computer screen to study the picture. "I don't know how Miss Keane can be so sure this is Jackson. Maybe if the picture were a little clearer. Why don't you go check with Hank to see if he might have something better? Maybe even one of the guy's father so we could see how this Jackie might look when he got older. He could have gotten his picture in the paper holding a turnip that looked like a cow or something. That kind of thing always makes the paper."

"Jackson might look like his mother."

"Could be. But you should go check on Hank anyway."

Michael looked over at her, but she kept her eyes riveted on her fingers on her keyboard as if she'd forgotten how to type. "Since when did you ever worry about Hank Leland?"

"Well, you saw him yesterday." She peeked up at Michael and then back at her keyboard. "The poor man was in a shape. What if he had a coronary in his sleep or something?"

"Quite frankly, I figured you'd think that was good news."

"Come on, Michael." Betty Jean slapped her hand flat against her chest. "You make me sound heartless."

"I thought you were when it came to Hank."

She waved him toward the door. "Just go check on him already and let me get this picture sent to our Eagleton friends. Then I'll start looking up every Jackson or Ellis in the state. I tried to look last night, but I forgot my folks don't have wireless." She clicked a few keys without looking up. "And don't expect me to babysit your dog. I like cats. Not dogs."

"Right." Michael hooked the leash on Jasper's collar and glanced back over at Betty Jean. "By the way, while you're searching on there, see if you can find out if that doctor, Philip Colson, has ever written any books."

"He's not going to call again, is he?" Betty Jean peered over her computer monitor at Michael.

"I don't know why he would. I've told him Whitt's in charge of the investigation, but he did leave a message on my answering machine last night."

"What did he want?"

"Best I could make out he was drumming up business by offering me a cut rate in case I needed his services."

"Civic-minded of him." Betty Jean made a face. "But to be honest, he sounds like he might need a little counseling himself."

"I guess if I had to listen to very many stories like Jackson's, that might push me over the edge." He wasn't sure he wasn't tottering on the edge already.

"Do you think Jackson told him anything that could help us find him?" Betty Jean waved toward her computer.

"If he did, Colson hasn't shared that information with me or Whitt either, as far as I know. Whitt thinks the doctor is digging for information because he's writing a book."

"Yeah, that's what you said last night. Okay. I'll check his name on the internet to see if he's published."

"Don't make it a priority. It's not important. I'm just curious." He was almost out the door when Betty Jean called after him. "Don't you dare tell Hank I told you to check on him. I wouldn't want him to think he could start hanging around here trying to get the scoop on what's going on."

At the newspaper office, Hank pointed at Jasper. "He can't come in here unless he's a seeing-eye dog."

Michael led Jasper on into Hank's office. "Police dog will have to do." He moved a pile of papers off a chair and sat down in front of the editor's desk. Jasper glanced around and settled at Michael's feet as if he knew he'd never be able to sniff everything in the room.

Hank didn't argue. He didn't look capable of arguing.

"You okay, Hank?"

"No, I'm not okay." Hank glared at Michael with bloodshot eyes. "How could I be okay? A man who murders girls touched my daughter. My wife has packed up and taken that daughter and left me. I'm afraid to look at the mail on my desk, and this is the shoddiest piece of newspaper work I've ever done." He picked up the *Gazette* and shook it at Michael.

Jasper sat up and peered across the desk at Hank, a low growl sounding in his throat.

"And now I've got dogs growling at me in my own office." Hank's voice went up a level as he glared at Jasper. "I hate dogs."

"Why?" Michael put his hand on Jasper's head.

"Why what?" Hank gave Michael a puzzled look. He'd obviously slept in the office or not slept at all. His desk was littered with empty Styrofoam coffee cups and soft drink cans, but as far as Michael could tell, no new food wrappers gave evidence of him eating anything in the last twenty-four hours.

"Why do you hate dogs?"

For a second, Michael thought Hank was going to come across the desk after him, but then he leaned back in his chair. It creaked under his weight. "You sound like that psychiatrist, psychologist—whatever he is."

"Dr. Colson?"

"The very one." Hank picked up his letter opener and tapped it on his desk. "'And how did that make you feel, Mr. Leland? To get those pictures. Did you like looking at dead girls? How would you have felt if one of them had been your daughter? You did say you had a daughter, didn't you, Mr. Leland?'"

"You shouldn't have told him about the pictures. Not with the investigation ongoing."

"I don't know what I told him." Hank dropped his head into his hands. "I don't know anything this morning."

"You need something to eat. Come on. I'll buy you breakfast at the Grill."

"I can't let the town see me like this. They might start

feeling sorry for me and then they'd never believe anything
I wrote ever again."

"You're not making sense, Hank, but if you won't go to
the Grill, let me drive you home."

"With that dog?" Hank cast a leery look at Jasper sitting
at attention, watching him. "I don't think so. Besides, I'm
tired. I'm distraught. I may even be pathetic. But I'm not
drunk. I can drive myself home."

"Then do it. Go home. Barbara and Rebecca Ann are safe
in Atlanta by now, aren't they?" Hank nodded and Michael
went on. "Then turn off your phone and get some sleep."

"But I might need to take some pictures. Something might
happen."

"Aren't you the one always saying nothing ever happens
in Hidden Springs?"

"Oh, for the good old days."

The phone out in the front office rang a couple of times
before Annie Watson answered it. The sound of her voice
drifting back to them was low and somehow reassuring.
Something the same as last week. Annie had been the same
for years, taking ads over the phone, promising people space
in the paper for newsworthy stories or events.

Hank poked his finger down on the *Gazette*. "Did you
read this? I wimped out, Michael. Didn't put half of what I
could have put in the story. I lost my nerve."

"No, you were being sensible. No need having anything
about Rebecca Ann in the paper. Not in this kind of story."

"But don't you see? Everybody in Hidden Springs will
know about it sooner or later anyway. They'll hear what
really happened, and they'll see that I've lost my nerve."

"They'll understand you're a dad watching out for his daughter. That you're a dad who loves that daughter."

"That's just it." Misery deepened every line of Hank's face. "I can't close my eyes, Michael. Every time I close my eyes, I see that first poor little girl. Hope. Only it's not her face. It's Rebecca Ann's."

25

Annie Watson stuck her head inside the editor's office door. "Sorry to interrupt, Hank, but Michael has a call."

Annie looked toward Michael but was thrown off balance by the sight of Jasper, as if she hadn't just watched the dog parade through the front office moments ago. Michael doubted that she had ever allowed a dog inside the newspaper office. Ever. It took her a minute to remember her message. "Buck Garrett. He claims it's imperative he speak with you immediately."

With a last frown at Jasper, she ducked back out the door. Hank looked almost shell-shocked as he spoke in a near whisper. "You think it's another one?"

Michael picked up the phone on Hank's desk without answering him. Too late he thought he should have followed Annie back out to the front to take the call. Hank might not be on the top of his game, but he was still a newspaperman.

"Michael here." Michael turned so Hank couldn't see his face.

"You forget to turn your cell phone on again, kid?" Buck growled.

"No, forgot to plug it in last night. It's charging back at the office. You could have radioed."

"And have every Tom, Dick, and Harry listening in. Don't know why they don't outlaw those scanner radios."

"You've got me now. So what's up?"

Buck wasn't one to waste words on the phone. "Some fisherman called in. Spotted a blue car. Might be an older model Olds or Plymouth, abandoned down by the lake."

"Why abandoned? Could be somebody fishing off the bank."

"Claimed it was there last night and in the same exact spot this a.m. With water up over the car's front wheels like somebody tried to drive it into the lake."

"He go over for a better look?"

"Said he thought about it, but was worried it might be rocky around there. He wasn't curious enough to chance tearing up his boat. Probably one of those megabuck jobs. Price could pay my Billie Jo's tuition all four years."

"Local guy?"

"Nobody's got money for that kind of boat around here. The guy is down from Ohio. Rented a tourist cabin on Patterson's Creek for a few days."

"He spot anybody in or around the car?"

"Said not. Said he idled his boat for a few minutes but nothing ever moved in the car."

"Could be asleep."

"Or dead." Buck didn't mince words. "I'm headed out that way. Might take some finding from the bozo's directions."

"What did he say about the place besides rocky?"

"He didn't know for sure it was rocky. Just worried it might be. City slicker. First time on the lake."

"He had to tell you something."

"Yeah. Around a little point. Not far from where a finger of the lake separates off into a big back pool. Come to think of it, that sounds like the one that flows back in toward your place. Seems I remember an old road past your place down to the lake."

"Nobody has used it for years. You'd drag off a car's oil pan driving down there."

"Maybe this guy didn't care. Especially if he had plans to drive into the lake." Buck paused a minute. "The description of the car matches. You want to call Eagleton?"

"Let's check it out first. "

"All right by me. Meet you at the turnoff to your place in fifteen minutes." Buck hung up.

On the other side of the desk, Hank sat straight in his chair, his editor's antenna full up. "What's he found?"

Michael tugged on Jasper's leash to get the dog on his feet. "Just an abandoned car."

"What's so important about that?"

"Probably nothing. But we have to check it out." Michael looked over at Hank. "Go home and get some sleep. Anything happens you'll have plenty of time to find out all the details before next week's *Gazette* comes out."

"Nobody can be a real newspaperman and only put out a weekly paper." Hank reached for his camera. "How about I tag along?"

"Free country, but it's probably nothing but an old junker nobody's noticed out there in all the bushes. Could have been there all summer."

"I hope so, Michael." He draped the camera around his neck. "There's nobody any readier than me to go back to taking pictures of Lester waving kids across the street in front of the elementary school or of the lopsided volcano little Suzy made for her science project. Nobody."

Michael picked up Hank's phone again to call Betty Jean. He really needed to remember to charge his cell, but no time to go back to the office now to grab it. He told Betty Jean where he was going and that she could contact him on the radio if she needed anything. Before he hung up, he asked, "You track anything down on our guy?"

"Not looking good. I was right about there being a zillion Johnsons in this world. I'm working on the mother's name now. Sarah's checking out the driver's license records over at the circuit clerk's office. We didn't need a court order for that, did we?" She rushed ahead of his answer. "Don't answer that. It's already done now. What about the car? Where was it licensed?"

"Buck ran a check on that without turning up anything."

"Yes, but you know those state people. They probably did a routine 'who cares if we find it or not' check and so didn't look in the back records."

"I'm sure Whitt was more thorough."

"And wouldn't tell us if he found beans," Betty Jean said.

"The license number is there in my notes."

"Notes for the report you haven't entered in the computer yet, that I daresay nobody but you can decipher." Betty Jean's sigh came over the line. "I'll call T.R. He'll have the number on his tow bill."

He started to hang up but decided to answer the question she wouldn't ask. "Things are okay up the street. Weird but okay."

"Good. Weird is normal." She hung up without saying goodbye.

Michael didn't use his lights or siren on the way to the lake. He didn't want to acknowledge the feeling of dread rising inside him. He even drove a little under the speed limit. In spite of the heat, he left the air off and put down the windows. He let Jasper ride in the front to stick his head out in the wind.

Hank poked along behind him in his beat-up old van. He'd be stuck when he got to the lake because no way could that car navigate the old wagon trace down past Michael's house. Bushes had grown up to almost swallow the deep, narrow ruts. Michael didn't see how any car could get down that road. Buck had to be wrong about the location, even if the description did fit.

Buck, in his four-wheel-drive truck, was waiting at the turnoff down to Michael's place. Michael eased up beside him and Buck rolled down his window. He motioned back toward Hank, who rolled to a stop behind Michael. "What's he doing here?"

"He thinks there might be a photo opportunity."

"He's not riding down there in my truck."

"Fine with me," Michael said. "I'll leave my car and Jasper at the house."

"How come you're letting the dog ride shotgun with you anyway?"

"It's a long story. I'll tell you later."

Michael pulled back out on the road and headed down his lane in front of Buck. Hank followed a respectful distance behind them. Hank didn't mind jerking everybody else's chain, but he didn't mess with Buck. Then again, hardly anybody messed with Buck without paying a price, except maybe his own daughter, Billie Jo. Buck had a long memory, and Hank said he couldn't put out a newspaper without a driver's license.

When Michael stopped in front of his house, he had to tug Jasper out of the car by his collar. Once on the ground, Jasper stalked around the yard stiff-legged, sniffing everything with his fur ruffed up on his neck. Michael made a quick survey of the place, but nothing looked disturbed. The dog must be catching Michael's unease.

"Stay, Jasper." Michael held his palm out toward the dog and climbed up into Buck's truck.

"What's with your dog? He acts like he doesn't know he's home."

"Things have been kind of strange lately." Michael leaned out the window and yelled at Hank. "You better wait here. The road's rough from here on to the lake. You'll never make it in your van."

"You could let me ride in the back." Hank started to open his door, but Buck gunned the truck and bounced over the first ruts into the bushes.

"There goes my paint job," he muttered.

"Maybe we should have looked for tracks before we drove back here. Might not even be the right place."

"Yeah, that might be smart, but let's get out of sight of cameraman or he'll be climbing up in the back of my truck and then, like as not, sue me when I pitch him out. Why didn't you lock him in a closet or something to keep him from following you?"

"Why'd you call me at his office?"

"That's where you were. Without your phone." Buck checked his rearview mirror. Satisfied he'd put enough bushes and trees between them and Hank, he braked. He left the motor running and opened the door to climb out. "Let's see what we can find."

The rainy weather that had muddied the river a couple of weeks ago had given way to hot, dry days. The ground was July hard, with cracks in the dirt between the weeds.

Still, even though there were no visible tracks in the ruts of the road, it was plain something had pushed through the bushes not long ago. Wilted leaves clung to the broken branches, and up the way a little from Buck's truck, Michael spied a rusty muffler and tailpipe.

Michael picked it up. "Whoever drove back here didn't drive out."

"How do you know? Losing a muffler doesn't keep a car from running."

"It's not the muffler. It's the bushes. They're all shoved one way."

"You're a regular Boy Scout." Buck headed back to his truck. "So guess we'd better go see what shoved them."

Michael followed Buck, but he didn't want to. He wanted to walk off into the trees and away from it all.

Something crashed through the brush behind them and both Michael and Buck had their hands on their guns when Jasper came out into the open. Buck moved his hand away from his gun and flexed his fingers a few times.

"Might be you should teach that dog of yours to bark before he jumps out of the bushes. He could catch a bullet." Buck got in his truck. "Come on, Mike. We best get a move on it. I expect old cameraman is probably hoofing along after us too."

Michael pitched the muffler and tailpipe in the back of the truck and wished he was back at the office, listening to

Lester talk about being an umpire at the T-ball games. A simple small-town life. That was all he wanted. A place where people went to church on Sundays and didn't have to worry about evil creeping out from who knew where to cast a dark shadow over their town. He climbed back into the truck.

A prayer rose within him, unbidden. *No more, Lord. Please.*

The car was just like the one Jackie Johnson had left at the bridge. Michael was trying to make out the license plate numbers when Buck swore under his breath.

"That headrest has hair."

26

Michael didn't want to get out of the truck. He didn't want to see whose face went with the long blonde hair draped over the seat.

Buck gripped the steering wheel. "As hot as it's been, this could be bad."

Michael didn't say anything. What was there to say?

Buck blew out a long breath. "Guess we better call in the troops. You got your radio?"

Michael pulled it out of his belt. "No signal. How about your cell phone?"

Buck fished the phone out of his pocket. "Nothing. Too far from civilization out here, I guess. You get a signal back at your house?"

"Not a good one. Usually have to be almost out to the main road before you can be sure a call will go through. That's why I forget to charge my phone up. I use my landline."

Buck turned off the key. They sat there as if they were deciding nothing more important than where they might throw in their lines for the best chance to catch some fish. A boat sped past out in the middle of the lake, slapping the water up against the rocky bank and the car's front tires. A blue jay squawked out a warning that the place had been invaded, and a couple of flies buzzed through the truck's open window to circle their heads. Jasper appeared on the road behind them and whined at the truck before he moved past them to check out the car.

Buck pulled up on his door handle. "Guess we can't let a dog show more nerve than us, Mike. Let's go take a look-see."

Michael climbed out of the truck and followed Buck toward the car. Dread pressed down on him until he could hardly breathe. Nobody had called in anybody missing. Nobody could be missing in Hidden Springs two days without somebody noticing. Even so, he had no doubt he was going to know the blonde in the car.

The windows were all closed, but that didn't keep the smell from leaking out to them. Michael put his hand in front of his nose and tried to take shallow breaths.

Beside him, Buck choked out a cough and turned away from the car. "Oh, man!"

Michael clamped his throat closed and made himself look. The face was barely recognizable. The gunshot wound was to the side of her head closest to the window. Jackson must have caught her by surprise. But what was she doing with him to begin with?

Without the hair, Michael might not have known her. She was dressed in a red knit sleeveless top and a short white skirt. Her hands were folded over her chest just like in the pictures of Hope and Kim Barbour. When Michael held his breath and leaned closer, he could see the nylon fishing line holding her hands in place.

"Wait, Mike." Buck stepped back another couple of feet.

"Don't open that." He whipped out his handkerchief to cover his nose. "Better let the troops get here before we disturb the crime scene."

"Right." Michael looked away from the woman's body in the car out at the clear, blue lake. He'd never seen the water look so inviting. "I wish I could just jump in the lake."

"Yeah. Probably couldn't smell this underwater. Any idea who she is?"

"Julie Lynne Hoskins." Michael shut his eyes and remembered how the woman had flaunted her beautiful body to shock her Hidden Springs fans after the play in Eagleton. So sleek. So beautiful. So alive.

Michael turned away from the car. He was glad when Jasper leaped up to plant his paws on his chest. Usually he kneed the dog when he jumped up on him, but not this time. He ruffled the dog's ears, then buried his face in his fur to breathe in his dog smell.

"She from Hidden Springs?" Buck was back at his truck, his hand on the door handle. "I don't recognize the name."

Michael raised his head away from Jasper. He couldn't hide from it forever. "She grew up here. Went to school with me. She's an actress now. Was an actress. Starred in that play over in Eagleton last week."

"The play you were driving the old church ladies to when you saw the jumper?"

"The very one."

"How would Jackson know that?"

"Hank probably put something about the play in the *Gazette* article. I don't know. I never read it." He pushed Jasper off his chest. "But one of the women was Julie Lynne's aunt. That's why they decided to go." Michael looked over his shoulder toward the car. "I feel like we ought to cover her up."

"Nobody out here to see her who hasn't already seen it all." Buck didn't look back at the car. "Look, we're going to have to drive out of here to get a signal to call this in."

"You go. I'll stay here to secure the scene." Michael fished his house key out of his pocket and handed it to Buck. "You can go in my house and call on my landline if you can't pick up a signal on your cell phone. Or you can use the radio in my cruiser. Better tell Betty Jean to call Justin."

"His hearse won't get through that road," Buck said.

"Right. Guess you'll have to wait and let him ride down here with you in your truck."

"My truck?" Buck swallowed hard, realizing what that meant. The body was going to have to be carried out some way. "We should have come down in your old rust bucket."

"The keys are in it." Michael shrugged. "I haven't driven it for a few days, but if you can get it started, you can drive it down here if you want."

"What'll I tell old cameraman? He sees Justin, we won't be able to keep him away."

"He won't want to take a picture of this."

"That man would take a picture of anything," Buck grumbled as he got in his truck and slammed the door extra hard. He turned around and was gone up the rough road.

The sound of the truck faded away and left nothing but the buzzing of flies in Michael's ears. He studied the ground as he walked in half circles behind the car. Jasper seemed to know it wasn't the time to chase squirrels or dig for moles and followed close behind him.

Michael doubted he'd find anything, but he needed to be

moving. Doing something. He couldn't bear the thought of Julie Lynne in that car. Because of him.

He'd made his fourth sweep of the area without finding anything more interesting than a garter snake slipping out of sight in the weeds when he heard someone coming. Walking. He wasn't surprised when Hank came around the curve into sight. Michael stopped and waited.

Rivulets of sweat were running down Hank's face and his shirt was plastered to his back. "It's hotter than blue blazes out here." He stopped in front of Michael and pulled his shirttail up to wipe his face. It took him a minute to find a spot dry enough. "And a lot farther back here than Buck said."

"He tell you to walk in?"

"Yeah." Hank dabbed at his face again, but he couldn't keep ahead of the sweat. "Said you'd found Jackson's car and that it wasn't far. A stroll in the park, he said. Buck has a great sense of humor." Hank looked toward the car. "What is that awful smell?"

"Julie Lynne Hoskins."

All the color drained out of the editor's face and his eyes rolled back in his head. He made a strange noise as he wobbled up and back on his feet like one of those round-bottomed kids' toys.

"Easy, Hank." Michael grabbed the man's arms, but no way could he keep him on his feet. He lowered him to a sitting position on the ground. He wished for the smelling salts in his emergency kit back in his cruiser, but he'd have to make do without them. "Put your head down between your knees and breathe in and out. You better not be having a heart attack."

Hank did as he was told. After a few minutes of slow breaths, he raised his head. Color had flooded back to his face. "I'm all right, Michael. It's just . . ." Hank peeped toward the car and went pale again. "It's just that I can't keep from thinking that could be Rebecca Ann."

"But it's not." Michael made his voice firm. "Rebecca Ann is safe, away from it all. So get hold of yourself."

"You're right, Michael. Sorry." Hank fingered the camera strap around his neck. "I guess I should take some pictures."

"Not until we get the body covered."

Hank didn't argue. He stayed where he was on the ground and looked around. "Do you think Jackson walked out of here?"

"I don't know. I'm guessing he did."

"All the way out to the road?" Hank frowned. "Then what? He thumb a ride with some local yokel? And why would he pick this place? You think he knew you lived down here?"

"Yeah, I think he did." Michael didn't bother answering Hank's other questions, but he had to believe if Jackson walked out of here back to the highway, somebody would have seen him. Could be he had tied a boat up somewhere before bringing the car down to the lake. The man seemed fast and organized.

"Do you think he's got somebody helping him?" Hank went on with his questions. "It just seems like all this gets weirder and weirder. I know that Eagleton detective didn't think Rebecca Ann knew what she was talking about when she said the man who gave her the pictures didn't look like the picture of Jackson in the paper, but the girl is a lot like me. She notices things and remembers faces."

"Whitt will be here. You can tell him what you think, but psycho killers are generally loners."

Hank didn't act as if he heard him. Instead he kept talking as though trying to figure it all out. "And now he had to get out of here and it's a long walk back to civilization. Somebody would have seen him."

"Maybe he had a canoe or kayak tied on top of the car."

"The Jackson we saw on the bridge?" Hank turned disbelieving eyes on Michael. "You think that guy would even fit in a kayak?"

"Who knows? The man is full of surprises." Michael looked back at the lake as if it might reveal some unseen clue. "He didn't look like somebody who could kill three women and take those posed pictures either."

"That's the truth. And then figure out how to get those pictures into the hands of a newspaperman." Hank wiped the sweat off his forehead. "It's like we're talking about two different people or maybe a half-dozen different people. You think this Jackson has a multiple personality? That Dr. Colson said something about that when he called me."

"That might explain it." Michael dropped down beside Hank. Jasper shoved up against him. He'd taken a dip in the lake, and Michael welcomed his wet dog smell. He looked over at Hank. "Do you really hate dogs?"

"Sometimes I wonder about you, Mike." Hank frowned at him. "What difference does it make whether I like dogs or not?"

"None. None at all. Just curious."

"But better than talking about dead women, I guess." Hank blew out a long breath. "So if you want to talk dogs, we can talk about dogs."

"I like dogs." Michael ran his hand down Jasper's back.

"You must have never got bit." Hank didn't wait for Michael to say anything. "Well, I have. Used to get bit all the time when I delivered papers for my granddaddy back when I was a kid. Anyway, this one little dog lay in wait for me every time and then did his best to grab the back of my leg. I wanted to quit taking the paper to that house, but Granddad said it was just a little dog and all I had to do was kick it a few times and it wouldn't bother me anymore."

"Did it work?"

"I almost threw my leg out of joint kicking at that dog, but he was a quick little rascal. I never landed the first kick." Hank was silent for a minute before he went on. "Then one day I got there and somebody had run over the dog. Flattened him right out in front of the gate to his yard. You'd have thought I'd be glad, but it was a funny thing. Instead, I got all teary-eyed and wished the scoundrel was biting my ankle. People are weird, aren't they?"

"Can't argue with that."

Hank was quiet as he plucked some grass blades. "You asked your question. Now I get to ask mine."

"Fair enough."

The editor shifted on the ground like a stick had started poking his rear. He kept his gaze on the ground. "You go to church, Mike. You even sort of date a preacher woman. Tell me." Hank looked over at Michael and then quickly back at the grass in his hand. "You think God does this kind of thing to punish us? You know, because we skip church to go to a ballgame or whatever. Or get too busy to pray and give the Big Guy enough credit for the good things in our lives."

"No."

Hank looked at him again. "Is that all you've got to say? No. I need more than that."

"I'm no theologian, Hank. You'd do better asking Karen."

"Karen's not here. You are." Hank pointed toward the car. "And she is. Very dead maybe because I put her name in the paper."

"Or because I pulled a jumper back from the brink."

"So has God got something against us? You and me."

Michael wanted to just say no again. Leave it at that. Some things couldn't be explained, but Hank was staring at him, expecting more. More than Michael knew to give. "I don't think so, Hank. Bad things happen. Sometimes because they just happen. And sometimes like this." Michael motioned toward the car. "Because of somebody evil. Some kind of monster."

"Who'd have ever thought we'd have to worry about that kind of monster here in Hidden Springs?"

"Not me."

"But God could stop it, couldn't he?"

"Maybe he's depending on us to do that. To stop it. Good over evil."

"You think we're good enough?" Hank picked up a rock and scraped out a little hole in the ground beside them.

"With the Lord's help, maybe. At least I hope so. I sincerely hope so."

"Yeah. Me too." Hank gave the rock a pitch. "Me too."

They sat there then without saying anything as bees buzzed past them and a mockingbird ran through his songs in a tree behind them. The sun climbed higher in the sky and waves of heat rose up off the car. Michael thought he should go check for marks that might indicate a canoe had been tied

on top of the car, but he didn't get up. He stayed there between Hank and Jasper and took shallow breaths that kept
the smell from being as bad.

After a long time, Hank spoke. "Where do you think he
sent the pictures?"

27

The sun was straight up when Buck brought Justin in. He took a quick look through the window at the body and agreed with Buck and Michael they should wait for the Eagleton homicide people to get there. Once would be enough to open that door.

"It's not like there's any question as to cause of death," Justin said. "Gunshot to the head. Death instantaneous."

"How long ago?" Michael asked.

"Hard to say," Justin hedged.

Michael didn't know why he asked. The fact was, Justin would have no idea. The only reason he was coroner was because he was the local funeral director. The people of Hidden Springs thought it logical to vote him in as coroner since he'd be the one collecting the bodies for the funeral home anyway. Plus, they figured he was the only man in town who didn't mind looking at dead people, but Michael knew better. He'd been beside Justin at enough accident scenes to know the only time the man didn't mind being coroner was when he could say a person died of natural causes in his or her sleep.

People who died of unnatural causes made Justin nervous, and poor Julie Lynne's very unnatural death made him very nervous. While they waited for Whitt to show up, the tall, thin man wore a path in the grass and weeds in front of the tree where Hank and Michael slouched in the shade. Buck had gone back out to the highway to usher in the Eagleton troops. It was his truck, and he wasn't about to stay anywhere close to that car if he could come up with a reason not to.

Michael slapped at a mosquito and wondered if drinking lake water really made a person as sick as the health people warned. He asked Hank what he thought.

Hank kept his eyes shut and didn't act as if he heard him. Michael studied Hank's chest. His breathing didn't appear labored, but something was wrong with the man. Asking questions about God and not once pulling out his little notebook and pen to jot down any details for next week's *Gazette*. He hadn't even taken a picture of the car.

Justin stopped pacing in front of them to look at Hank. "Is he all right?"

"Right as rain." Hank spoke without opening his eyes. "And they say it'll make you puke your guts out."

"What is he talking about?" Justin frowned.

"Lake water," Michael said. "It makes you wonder how Civil War soldiers made it. They drank anything wet wherever they could find it. Ponds. Rivers. Puddles."

"They didn't all make it. They died like flies. History books say more from disease than cannon fire." Justin glanced at Michael and then back at Hank. "He doesn't look right as rain, but who could be right as anything with what's been happening around here lately?"

Justin started in on how Hidden Springs had changed as he took off pacing in circles again. He never used to have to worry about putting people in body bags. He just laid them out on a stretcher with a cover over them and carried them to the funeral home. People died the way they were supposed to, from heart attacks or pneumonia. Nobody went around shooting anybody else unless it was a hunting accident or something. Accidents happened. That was for sure. He'd seen his share of bad things, of course, but those tragedies weren't something a person needed to dwell on. At any rate, there wasn't all this crime.

Didn't Michael think he should do something about it? After all, he was the sheriff's right-hand man, wasn't he? Everybody knew, Justin grumbled, that Alvin didn't have any experience with this sort of thing. He had started out as sheriff not long after Justin took over as coroner. And anyway, how could this car get past Michael's house without Michael noticing it? Weren't law officers trained to notice things?

The questions circled with Justin, and it seemed natural when the buzzards appeared overhead to drift in wide, looping circles above their head and then float in a lazy eight on the wind to fly over Michael's place. That made Michael remember the dead animal or fish he needed to locate and get out of his yard.

Justin went on walking and talking. Hank sat with his eyes closed. Michael had never seen him quiet for so long. But then, wasn't he sitting there like a lump, doing nothing too? Maybe he should try to come up with answers to some of the questions, whether Justin's or his own, and start acting like a policeman instead of cowering in his patch of shade as if he'd never seen a dead person. Even in Hidden Springs, dead people weren't all that uncommon, in spite of what Justin was saying.

Hadn't Michael been there when they found Ernest Callahan in his shack of a house after the mailman finally reported the old man hadn't collected his mail for days? Justin had been there too, but that must be one of those things the coroner didn't like to dwell on. Death visited Hidden Springs the same as any other place, and Michael looked in its face all the time. He took pictures of traffic fatalities for the insurance companies, usually victims he knew. Murder had even come to call on Hidden Springs last year.

But Michael had never felt as if the person was dead because of him. Julie Lynne was dead because Michael took those ladies to her play. Plain and simple. Or maybe not so simple.

He had never been a person to dance away from the truth. He didn't now, and there was no reason for him to shy away from his duties as a law officer. He should have at least brought his camera with him to take pictures of the scene for the report he'd have to file.

He poked the man beside him. "Hank, can I use your camera?"

Without opening his eyes, Hank pulled the camera loop from around his neck and handed the camera to Michael. "Have at it. I can't focus on that car right now."

"I'll get the county to buy you a new memory card."

"In our lifetime?"

"Not sure about that, but maybe you can leave it to your heirs." At least the editor was showing some signs of his old self. "Why don't you walk on back to your car and go home? You need to get some sleep."

"What do you think I've been doing all afternoon? You don't think I've been keeping my eyes closed because I'm too chicken to look, do you?"

"No, not at all."

Hank eased open one eye to look at Michael. "It's my job to be here, Michael, the same as it is yours."

"Neither one of us doing much of a job then, are we?" Michael pushed up off the ground.

"Shut up and go take pictures." When Michael started away, he added, "Hold the camera still or they'll all be fuzzy."

Michael tried not to see Julie Lynne as he focused the shots. It wasn't all that hard, since the body in the car bore little resemblance to the woman he'd seen last week.

He was focusing in on the lake water licking the front tires of the car when Buck's truck burst out of the bushes into the little clearing. Buck braked to a sudden stop, bouncing Whitt and Chekowski forward on the seat beside him. Michael stayed where he was and looked back at the lake.

The water was a lighter blue now than earlier, as if the bright afternoon sun had faded its color. A bird flew down to kiss the surface of the lake a couple of times before it rose back up into the sky. Michael raised the camera up and focused on the water touching against the white blue of the sky on the horizon. He clicked the shutter a few times, then slipped the memory card out and into his shirt pocket. Hank would be out of luck if he didn't carry another memory card with him.

He pulled in a breath and squared his shoulders. Time to go hear what Whitt had to say.

"I think we are officially in the boondocks, Chekowski." Whitt put his hands on his hips and looked around.

"It's definitely country, sir." Chekowski took a peek toward the car as the color drained from her face.

"Well, let's look at what you've got, Deputy." Whitt acknowledged Michael's presence for the first time. The detective moved toward the car and peered in the window for a long minute. "Not a pretty sight."

Michael watched him without saying anything. Instead he kept his eye on Chekowski, who had gone even paler. She looked ready to faint.

Whitt straightened up. "You or any of these other country bumpkins touch the car, Keane?"

"No. We thought you might want to bring in techs."

"Yeah. They're on the way, but I guess we're in your jurisdiction now. Leastways your state cop buddy says so." He glanced around. "A place like this seems too far out for any jurisdiction."

"No way to know where she might have been killed, but little doubt the same guy is responsible. Makes it still your case."

Whitt settled his gaze on Michael and a corner of his lip went up in something that approached a smile. "Good that you're seeing things straight."

Michael met his stare. He refused to let the man intimidate him. The sight of Julie Lynne was intimidating enough.

With a bark of a laugh, Whitt turned back to the car. "No telling when the techs will get here or even if they will. They're not used to the boonies. So we might as well get it over with. They can go over the car after we tow it out and sweep the area for a murder weapon if it isn't conveniently in the car. 'Course if I'd been Jackson, I'd have pitched it in the lake." Whitt frowned and looked around. "The million-dollar question is how he dumped the car and then got out of here. It's got to be twenty miles or more back to the interstate."

Michael didn't offer an answer. Let the man come up with his own theories.

Opening the door was even worse than they'd imagined. First off, all the doors were locked. Michael smashed a hole in the back window with Buck's tire jack handle in order to reach in to unlock the door next to Julie Lynne's body. He was thankful the lock was easy to reach on the door ledge and that his stomach was empty.

Justin's face went a funny shade of gray and beads of sweat popped out on his forehead as he positioned the body bag on the ground. He pulled on rubber gloves and held out a second pair. "I'll need help," he said to none of them in particular.

Michael took the gloves. It was the least he could do for Julie Lynne. Besides, nobody else stepped forward. Buck was on his knees by the lake, dousing his head in the water. Hank was on his feet hugging the tree they'd been sitting under. Chekowski had her notebook over her nose, her eyes wide and fixed.

"Don't forget to breathe, Chekowski," Whitt ordered without a look back at her. "This isn't one of the better ones, but it may not be the worst you ever see if you stay in homicide."

Whitt stepped nearer the car to watch as Justin and Michael carefully maneuvered the body out of the seat and onto the body bag.

"Different weapon." Whitt leaned over the body for a

closer look. "Not as neat a wound. My guess is she was a victim before the reporter woman. Body might have been stashed in the trunk when the perp delivered those pictures to the girl yesterday. Then he must have brought the car out here to plant it in your backyard, Keane."

Whitt paused, maybe to see if Michael had anything to say. He didn't.

"Quite a trick—getting her positioned like that with decomposition and all. Not something I'd want to do." Whitt straightened up but didn't back away from the body. "Officer Garrett said she was an actress. Name Julie Lynne Hoskins, and that you knew her. That she was from around these parts."

Michael didn't bother answering as he helped Justin pull the bag up until it entombed Julie Lynne. He stripped off the gloves and dropped them into the plastic bag Justin held out to him. Then he went over to the lake, knelt down, and plunged his hands into the water. When he dug his fingers down into the cool lake bottom, mud swirled up to cloud the clear water and nearly hide his hands.

Whitt followed him over to the lake's edge. "You can't wash that kind of thing off."

Michael pulled his fingers out of the mud and swished them around before he lifted his hands out of the water and gave them a shake. He stood up and kept his eyes on the lake. "I hadn't seen her since we were juniors in high school until the play last week in Eagleton."

"Yeah, that's what Garrett told me. That you and your church ladies were headed to the city to see her strut her stuff when you so fortuitously kept our psycho from ending it all."

Michael turned to look directly at Whitt. "What else do you want to know?"

"Everything." Whitt's eyes narrowed on Michael. "Only everything."

"Like what?" He tried to sound like he cared, but he didn't. He just wanted to be away from this place. Away from Whitt.

"Like how come this guy has decided to draw his bead on you? Like are you sure you never met him before? Like how has he managed to kill three women pow, pow, pow?" Whitt made a gun with his thumb and finger and pretended to shoot it off. "That fast. Three women he picked out because you knew them."

"I didn't know Hope."

"Victim one," Whitt corrected. "You say you didn't know her, and yet her earring ends up in your washing machine. Not only has this killer offed three women in little more than a week, he's stirred you right in the middle of the mix. He has to be a pro."

"A pro?" Michael frowned.

"Right. Jackson's my name. Killing's my game." Whitt raised his voice in a little singsong chant.

"That doesn't sound right. Pros don't kill unless money is involved."

"You might think that, but could be this guy was having a slow year." Whitt shrugged. "The whole thing defies any kind of logic, if you can ever apply logic to murder. Maybe the biggest question of all is, how come we've never seen anything about this guy before if he's such a killing machine?"

Whitt looked at Chekowski when she stepped up beside them, no longer looking like she might dump her breakfast any minute. "What do you think is the most important question to answer, Chekowski?"

"How did he get out of here?" She looked around as if that seemed an impossibility to her. She let her gaze fall on Michael. "What do you think is the most important question to answer, Deputy Keane?"

"Where is he now?"

28

When the afternoon shadows began lengthening, Whitt gave the nod to T.R. to drag the car out, even though the crime scene technicians hadn't shown up.

Whitt shoved his phone back in his pocket after trying to call them for the tenth time. "No telling where they are. Probably made a wrong turn and ended up in the next county. Maybe the next state." He went on in a mutter that was almost a growl. "How anybody can live in a place without a phone signal."

Chekowski looked down at her own phone and then rubbed off the screen as if that might make the signal come in. "We did go over the whole area already, sir. Inch by inch."

"Without finding anything but bugs and blasted beggar lice." Whitt picked a few of the sticktights off his pants leg. "And no wonder, after everybody and his brother tramped around in here before we came on the scene. Guess protecting a crime scene is not one of the deputy courses."

Michael let him talk. It didn't matter what the man said. There hadn't been anything to find except the car. He'd walked the lake edge. No sign of any kind of canoe or boat being slid out into the water, but the ground was hard or the killer could have slid the canoe off the top of the car directly into the water. If that's how he got back out to civilization. Where phones worked. Where murders happened.

Whitt and Chekowski rode in the cab with Buck back to their car parked at Michael's house. Hank, who quit hugging his tree long enough to fish a new memory card out of his pocket and take pictures of T.R. attaching the tow lines to the car, climbed in T.R.'s truck to ride out with him. Michael and Justin climbed into the back of Buck's truck with poor Julie Lynne. Before he closed the truck's tailgate, Michael motioned for Jasper to jump up with them, but the dog whined and backed away.

The dog loped along happily behind the truck and Michael wished he could jump out of the truck bed and walk along with him. Instead, he dodged low-hanging branches that whipped out at the truck and tried not to think about the body in the bag at his feet. He and Justin didn't talk. Perhaps in respect for the dead or perhaps because there was nothing to say.

Michael glanced back at the lake before the bushes swallowed them up. Blue water lightly kissed the bank where the car had sat. A heavy rain would completely rid the place of any sign of what had been there. For some reason, that made Michael feel better.

At his house, Michael helped Justin load the body bag into the hearse. He was glad to see the coroner's taillights disappear as he headed up the lane toward the highway. Buck followed him out, anxious to find a car wash.

Whitt leaned against his car and looked around. "Pretty isolated out here, Deputy."

"It's quiet. Peaceful. Normally." Michael turned on the garden hose attached to his outside faucet to fill up Jasper's water dish.

The dog lapped at the water without much enthusiasm. He'd had no qualms about slaking his thirst with lake water. Michael leaned over and let the spout of water from the hose fill his mouth. Hank gave Whitt and Chekowski a sideways glance when Michael held the hose out toward them and reached for it first. He took a long drink, then let the water splash over his face.

"What's he doing still here?" Whitt glared at Hank as if seeing him for the first time instead of having already threatened him with arrest for obstruction of justice if he stepped one foot in Whitt's way.

Hank stared back at Whitt. "A good reporter can smell a story a mile away, and that one wasn't hard to smell. In fact, I can still smell it."

Chekowski sniffed one of her arms. "Do odors like that cling to you? You know, like smoke."

"I don't think that's what you're smelling." Michael took the hose back from Hank and offered it to Whitt and Chekowski. When Whitt gave his head a little shake, Chekowski moistened her lips and lowered her hand back down to her side. "Somebody must have dumped some fish down by the lake. Or could be my dog dragged something up into the yard. Dogs like the smell."

The thought of the smell again must have been enough to make Chekowski risk Whitt's displeasure. She grabbed the hose and leaned over to let the water run across her nose and mouth.

Whitt frowned and opened his mouth, but Michael

jumped in front of whatever the man was going to say. "Are we through here, Detective, or do you have more questions?"

"I don't have anything but questions, Deputy. My problem is finding somebody with answers."

"Wonder where the pictures are?" Hank spoke up.

Whitt stared daggers at him. "Maybe you should try to smell them out in your mailbox, newshound."

Hank's face flashed red as he took a step toward Whitt. He rubbed his hands dry on his pants and fingered the camera strap around his neck as if ready to use his most lethal weapon. "Now look here, Mr. Hotshot Detective. I'm just trying to do my job for the people of Hidden Springs by reporting the news, and if you'd do your job a little better, maybe none of us would be here and that poor woman would be on a stage somewhere instead of—" Hank ran out of steam and finished weakly—"instead of where she is."

Whitt surprised Michael by laughing. Honest "that's funny" laughter. He didn't think the man had that kind of laughter in him, an opinion obviously shared by Chekowski from the look on her face as she stared up from the water hose at her boss.

"'Ace Newshound Meets Hotshot Detective.'" Whitt gave a snort to choke off his laugh. "Some headline. Might even make me think about skimming the story." His eyes narrowed on Hank. "How often does that rag of yours comes out?"

Hank's shoulders slumped. "Once a week. Not again till next Wednesday."

"Could be by then we'll have Jackson, and I'll give you an exclusive, Ace."

Hank came as close to smiling as he had all day. "I'll hold you to your word on that, Hotshot."

"Till then, do me a favor and disappear." Every hint of a smile was gone from Whitt's face. "I'm sure your deputy here will give you a press briefing in the morning."

"Sure, Hank. I'll call you in the morning if anything else turns up." Michael took the hose from Chekowski and turned off the faucet without offering it to Whitt again.

"No more bodies." The color drained out of Hank's face. "Please, no more bodies." He turned toward his old van, then looked back at Whitt. "Your men will surely find something in the car, won't you? Some lead to get a line on this Jackson before he has a chance to kill again."

"Could be, Ace. Like I said, the deputy here will let you know."

Fat chance that Whitt would ever share any information with Michael to pass along to anybody, but Michael didn't say so.

"But will the leads lead anywhere?" Whitt muttered as he watched Hank's van bounce away toward the highway. The man settled his back more comfortably against his car, as though he were a neighbor who had stopped by to shoot the breeze for a while. "What is it they say about the probability of catching a murderer, Chekowski?"

"That if you don't catch the perpetrator in the first twenty-four or thirty-six hours, the odds go down that you ever will." Chekowski pulled a tissue out of a hidden pocket and swiped the last drops of water off her face.

"One thing about this guy. He keeps giving us a fresh twenty-four to work with," Whitt said.

Twilight crept out of the woods to surround them, but Michael didn't invite them into his house. If Whitt wanted to third-degree him, he'd have to do it at the office and not here. Michael didn't want them poking around his house, passing judgment on how he lived. He wasn't in the mood to listen to Whitt's questions and hear the undercurrent of blame in what the man was asking.

What Michael wanted was a shower. A long, hot shower. And then to talk to Alex. Or even better, see her. Pete Ballard, his partner on the force in the city, used to say that a man needed a woman to get over a bad death scene. He claimed the act of making babies was a man's only defense against the bald truth of violent death. Of course, it wouldn't matter if Alex was standing right beside him. She wouldn't be thinking about making any babies with him.

He remembered what Betty Jean had said about how he couldn't leave town even if Alex called and said she'd marry him if he could get to her apartment before the day was over. Betty Jean was wrong. He'd be on the road in an instant and let the chips fall where they may. Not that he ever expected that to happen. Right now, he just hoped she'd answer her phone when he called.

Back behind his house, the frogs began their nightly serenade to see if they could outsing the crickets already chirping full strength. Somewhere in the woods, a screech owl joined in.

Chekowski jumped and her hand hovered near the holster under her jacket. "What was that?"

"Relax, Chekowski. Just an owl." Whitt raised his head a little to listen. "I thought you said it was quiet out here, Deputy."

"Quiet except for nature's noise. Nothing man-made."

Whitt tilted his head a little. "I hear traffic."

"The interstate," Michael admitted. "A constant, unfortunate background sound."

"How far away from here?"

"About three miles as the crow flies, but it would be rough walking." Michael looked to the east toward the sound of traffic.

"Think our man could have walked it?"

"I don't know. Jackson didn't impress me as somebody who'd attempt walking across town, but then he didn't look like a man who could entice three young women to go anywhere with him either." Michael shrugged. "So who knows?"

"You find out anything about that Jackie Johnson? The one you think might be Jackson?" Whitt turned his eyes back to Michael.

"The woman in our office is trying to track down his family. I don't know if she's had any success since I've been out of contact most of the day. She'll have gone home now." Michael hoped Betty Jean had sense enough to go back to her parents' house in spite of the country ham and biscuits. "I can give her a call if you want."

Whitt looked at his watch. "Morning will do. It doesn't look as if we're going to answer your question tonight anyway."

"My question?"

"Yeah. Where is he? That's what you said we needed to know, isn't it? Right up there with what he's planning next."

"Maybe he'll take the night off," Chekowski offered. She looked dead on her feet and as eager to be home taking a hot shower as Michael was.

"He already took a night off." Whitt glanced at her and then back at Michael. "You'd agree with that, wouldn't you, Deputy? This Julie actress whatever-her-name definitely quit breathing before our pretty Ms. Barbour. Maybe even before victim one."

"Seems a possibility."

"But if that's true, why didn't this woman's picture surface before the others?" Chekowski asked.

"Who knows?" Whitt said. "Could be the guy didn't want us to see the pictures until after we found the body."

"Maybe there aren't any pictures this time," Michael said.

"Don't count on that, Deputy. Our guy likes his pictures. I figure it's just a question of where they'll surface."

After Whitt and Chekowski finally followed the others away up the lane back to Eagleton, Michael unlocked his front door and went inside. Jasper went straight for his food dish.

"Give me a minute, boy." Michael grabbed the phone and dialed Aunt Lindy's number. He listened to it ring as he poured the dog food out for Jasper.

Of course, she was all right, Aunt Lindy told him. And yes, she could reach out and put her hand on the gun and she certainly would do just that at the first suspicious sound. He needn't worry about that. So it was entirely unnecessary for him to babysit her. However, if he wanted to be closer to the office, then he was welcome to come back to town for the night. And wasn't it awful about poor Julie Lynne? She'd looked so happy when they saw her at the play.

Michael didn't know why he was surprised that she already knew about Julie Lynne. That kind of news was sure to flash through Hidden Springs at the speed of light. Aunt Lindy had heard it at the grocery store, she said. She didn't really know much. Just that somebody had discovered the poor girl's body down at the lake, and it looked like this

Jackson was responsible. At least the man everybody was calling Jackson. She reminded Michael that the man's name was really Jackie Johnson and Michael had surely followed up on that, hadn't he?

Oh yes, and she had some messages for him. Betty Jean wanted him to call first chance he got. She'd tried to reach him all day, but he must have been out of range. No, Betty Jean hadn't sounded in a panic and hadn't said the first word about any suspicious envelopes. Karen had called not ten minutes ago to say it was a good thing she was at her sister's house since Janet was feeling some twinges. The baby might be planning an imminent arrival.

And by the way, Alexandria had called looking for him, but she wouldn't leave a message. Said she'd call back if she couldn't reach him at the log house. She didn't sound quite like herself, so it might be a good idea for Michael to give her a call before it got too late.

Michael looked at the flashing message light on the phone, told Aunt Lindy he'd see her in about an hour, and hung up.

He hit the play message button and Betty Jean asked him to call as soon as he could, but Aunt Lindy was right. She didn't sound panicked. She must have found out something about Jackson, but she hadn't gotten pictures.

Michael frowned at the sound of Dr. Colson's voice on the next message. "Just wondering if you'd considered my offer of counseling yet." The man just would not give up. Michael cut him off, moving on to the next message. A hang-up, maybe Aunt Lindy.

Then the sheriff's voice boomed out from the machine. "Sorry I haven't been around to help during all this, Mike, but I know I can depend on you to keep things under control up there. If you need me and can't get me on my cell, Betty Jean has the number down here."

Michael frowned and wondered where "down here" was. Maybe the sheriff had gone to Florida. Michael and Betty Jean had been too slow getting out of the gate and now they were stuck. At least he was. Who knew about Betty Jean? If she found pictures on her doorstep at home, she'd be off to Hawaii as fast as she could pack her swimsuit.

If only they could find Jackson and end this mess. How many places were there for a man on the run to stay in Eagleton? Maybe he was hiding out in one of the tourist cabins around the lake. Could be he was even the fisherman who had called in about spotting the car. Michael should have already checked that out.

Alex's voice came on the next message. While she didn't exactly sound panicked, she definitely sounded strained. "All right, Michael. I don't like this. An envelope of pictures showed up at the office today. In the regular mail. My secretary fainted. Hit her head on the side of the desk on the way down. Five stitches and a worker's comp claim, no doubt. I've seen worse. Pictures, I mean, but I didn't like seeing my name and office address on that envelope. Return address just had Mike. Cute, huh?"

She paused as though waiting for him to answer, and Michael leaned closer to the machine to be sure he wasn't missing anything. She pulled in a breath and went on. "What am I supposed to do with them? Turn them over to the police here? No need you calling me. I'm turning off my cell and not going home. I'm certainly not leaving a message on your machine saying where I am. The security of your phone line is suspect. Very suspect. But I will call you. Never fear. I'm

doing enough of the fearing part on this end. It's a few minutes past four. Betty Jean is texting me a picture of this guy
pronto. If he's out there stalking me, I want to see him first."

Michael hit the replay button and listened to her message
again, hating the miles between them. How could he protect
her if she was there and he was here? The hard part of it all
was that if it hadn't been for him, she wouldn't need protecting. At least not from Jackson.

29

Michael had to look up Betty Jean's parents' number in the phone book.

"About time you called," Betty Jean said after her father handed her the phone. "I about wore my fingers out trying to call you this afternoon."

"You talk to Alex?"

"She's not happy either. Said anybody who couldn't get a phone call didn't live where somebody should live. I guess I could've told her you left your phone at the office, but I figured she'd freak at that. Not that it would have mattered. I tried the radio and Buck's phone too. No signal anywhere out there."

"You knew where we were. You could have sent Lester down to the lake with a message."

"I might have considered it, but he had to take his mother to the doctor over in Eagleton. A good son like Lester can't refuse his mama no matter what else might be happening in the county."

"Lester is a good son."

"That's what I just said, isn't it?"

Betty Jean sounded like she'd had a long day. Michael didn't try to tell her his was worse, even though it had to be. The image of Julie Lynne's body flashed in front of his eyes while Betty Jean went on.

"Uncle Al needs to quit worrying about money and hire another deputy. Anyway, I did try to get that Detective Whitt's number, but those people in Eagleton don't believe in cooperation between law enforcement agencies. Wouldn't give me anything but a promise to relay a message for him to call me."

"It wouldn't have mattered. His phone wouldn't work either. Signals don't reach out there. Makes it a good place to be sometimes."

"Except for poor Julie Lynne, I guess." Betty Jean blew out a tired-sounding breath.

"Okay. You've made your point. I'm listening now. Did you tell Alex what to do with the pictures?"

"She sent copies via overnight mail, but her firm was turning the originals over to the local authorities. She guaranteed the package would be here in the morning. Guess she knows how to do things fast, but I'm not opening it. You can open it when you get in."

"You should have told her to send it to Eagleton. It's Whitt's case." Michael stared at his windows with the curtains still tightly closed from the last time he'd been there. He checked the kitchen sink. It wasn't dripping.

"How can you say that?" Betty Jean's voice rose a little. "Julie Lynne was murdered here. At least her body ended up here. That gives you jurisdiction."

"I don't want jurisdiction. I just want the man found. Before he takes more pictures."

"No argument with you on that." Betty Jean was quiet for a few seconds. "I tracked down Jackie Johnson's mother."

"You are a miracle worker. Did you talk to her?" Michael felt a flicker of hope. Maybe they would track the guy down after all.

"Yeah. I called Uncle Al and he said to go ahead and see what I could find out from her."

"So do we have the right man? Is Jackson actually Jackie Johnson?"

"Mrs. Johnson said she hadn't seen Jackie for maybe six months, but back then he did have a blue car. She didn't know the make or model. Said he bought it used, but to her, all cars look alike these days. Back when she was young, you could tell cars apart—"

"Are you going to get to a point?" Michael said.

"Thought you wanted the full report. Anyway, she said Jackie is a salesman who goes all over the country and that she doesn't think he even has his own place, that he just stays in motels since he's on the road so much. She had a number for him, but the last time she tried to call him, the number didn't work."

"Didn't work?"

"Been disconnected. But she says he calls her most every week and when she asked about the phone number, he told her he'd lost his phone and was using a friend's. No, she didn't know who the friend was." Betty Jean answered Michael's question before he could ask it. "Said he'd been married once, but not now. Has a kid somewhere in Michigan, but the mother won't let him see her. If Mrs. Johnson is to be believed, the ex-wife is the source of all poor Jackie's problems."

"What problems?" Michael looked at the clock. He needed to get to Aunt Lindy's house. But he also knew Betty Jean couldn't be rushed. She had to give the information the way she received it.

"Not being able to settle down. Financial woes. She knew he was having money problems because he borrowed money from her a couple of months ago. Claimed he was in a tight spot, but that he had some big clients on the line and he'd pay her back with extra in no time at all. You know, all the sucker lines."

"She hear from him the last week or so?" That was the question in need of an answer.

"Nope. Said she was worried about him. That he always called on either Saturday or Sunday. She didn't go to church Sunday night because she didn't want to miss his call. Her friends told her she was silly, but she said if her Jackie called, she was going to be there. Besides, so what if she missed a sermon? She could probably teach that new preacher they had now a thing or two about the Bible anyway."

"Is this leading anywhere?" Michael tried to tamp down his impatience.

"Afraid not. She talked a long time, but she didn't know many particulars. Not the name of the company where he worked. Not what he sold or where the home office was located. She did describe little Jackie. Sounds like our man."

"You didn't tell her why you were looking for him, did you?"

"I had to tell her something." Betty Jean hesitated a minute. "So I said we were looking for him as a possible witness to a crime. That's not exactly a lie and you can't very well call up a man's mother and blurt out that he's going around killing people. She got upset enough with what I did tell her. Said her little Jackie would never do anything against the law. That if anybody said anything different, they were lying and trying to frame him again."

"Again?"

"Yeah. She wouldn't explain that. Cut me off when I tried to ask, but I'm thinking little Jackie must have put in some time behind bars in somebody's jail somewhere. I'll run a records check on him tomorrow. It would help if you had fingerprints."

"There should be plenty in his car. Whitt's men are no doubt going over it now."

"Then why aren't you there watching? Jurisdiction, remember?"

"I'll let you explain jurisdiction to Whitt next time you talk to him. Besides, Buck is probably there guarding our interests." Michael looked at the clock again.

"You're letting the state police one-up us?"

"We're not in competition with the state police. We have a great working relationship."

"Yeah, yeah. Save it for the newspapers."

"Alex didn't tell you where she was going?"

"Said she wasn't sure yet." Betty Jean sounded worried. "I think she was scared."

"Sensible of her, I'd say." Michael's heart skipped a beat, thinking about how Alex had reason to be scared.

"Yeah." The line between them hummed with silence. Then Betty Jean said, "Who'd have ever thought he would go after Julie Lynne?"

"Not me. But I suppose he got her name out of the *Gazette*. Did Hank put in his article that we were on the way to her play when I played the hero and kept Jackson from jumping?"

"I can't believe you never read that story, but actually Hank did make a big deal out of Julie Lynne, the former Hidden Springs nobody, now an accomplished actress." Betty Jean blew out another breath and went on sounding as weary as Michael felt. "You want me to go over that paper and see who else is mentioned that this nut might decide to do in? It'll still be around here somewhere. Mom never throws anything away."

"Couldn't hurt."

Betty Jean was silent for a second. "He quoted your aunt."

"I know. Aunt Lindy told me, but I just talked to her and she's okay. You stay okay too, Betty Jean. Don't fall for any lines about having to come meet me or anybody else to help or anything."

"I never fall for lines." Betty Jean attempted a little laugh.

"I mean it. This guy is smart. He might not look it, but he is. He found Alex."

"I know." Betty Jean's voice suddenly sounded small and far away. "She's scared. I'm scared. We're all scared. Find him, Michael. Soon."

After he hung up, Michael headed for the shower. He didn't want to show up at Aunt Lindy's with this rank smell clinging to him. He was unbuttoning his uniform shirt when he remembered the dead fish or whatever outside. He might as well take care of it while he was in his ruined clothes. It shouldn't take long.

He made Jasper stay inside, to the dog's distress, but the last thing he needed was the dog finding the rotten thing and rolling in it. That would mean a bath for Jasper too before he could get to Aunt Lindy's. Michael played his flashlight over the yard without spotting anything out of the ordinary. He took a few sniffs to determine which way to search. The air seemed fouler coming up from the lake, so he headed toward the dock. It was probably just as he thought. A deserted string of fish.

Whatever it was, he was ready to find it and clear the air. He wanted to smell sweet grass and wild roses and cedar trees again. Not this smell of death that was on him, around him, soaking through him.

The odor was strong as he walked up on the dock. He flashed the light around. Nothing there. He pointed the light down and stared out at the lake. The water ripples sparkled undisturbed in the bright moonlight. Nothing floated there. He probed the cracks between the planks of the dock with the flashlight beam. Still nothing.

He didn't have time for this. Who knew what this Jackson, Johnson, whatever his name was, might be planning or even doing while Michael searched for dead fish? The thought of Aunt Lindy alone in her big old house flashed through Michael's mind.

He was ready to head back to the house when he spotted a flash of orange between the planks. Michael climbed down and got on his knees to look underneath the dock. An old towel was caught in the mud against the back poles of the dock. Michael let his breath out in relief. He wasn't exactly sure what he'd been afraid of finding, but he had been afraid.

Michael sat back and stared out at the lake again. The odor was still in the air, stronger than ever. He played the light on the ground around the dock and finally spotted the pile of fish somebody must have decided were too small for cleaning and left out of the water in the August heat. He'd have to find out what kids had been down here fishing and tell them not to leave a mess like that again. But at least he found it and, with a plank from under the deck, shoved it all into the lake where the bottom-feeding fish would take care of it in short order.

He slowly rolled the flashlight beam along the lake bank to be sure he'd found all the dead fish. When he turned away from the lake, the light landed on his rowboat chained to a tree. The boat was upside down and the sight of the tall weeds around it made Michael guilty. He was obviously letting his rowing muscles wither away.

Some kid, probably the one who threw away the fish, had been developing his muscles though. The boat had been moved recently. The weeds were mashed down around it. Could be the kid had left more fish or spoiled bait under the boat. He might as well make sure before he headed to Aunt Lindy's. A less stubborn woman would have gone to Boston. A less stubborn woman wouldn't be Aunt Lindy.

He didn't see the shoe until he stumbled over it. The black loafer was run over on the inside heel and a couple of sizes smaller than Michael wore. The toe was scuffed and covered with grass stain, but the supple leather showed no sign of being in the lake. That seemed to rule out the shoe floating up into the yard during the last big rain weeks ago.

For a long moment, he kept his flashlight pointed at the shoe, but then he slowly played the light over to the rowboat a few feet away. A matching shoe peeped out from under the boat.

Michael had never thought he lacked backbone. Whatever needed to be done, he did it without shrinking away from

the task. But it was all he could do to make himself lean over
and grasp the edge of the rowboat to lift it up.

He flipped the boat over on the grass and stared into the
fixed eyes of the man he'd pulled back from the edge of the
bridge. He had claimed to want to find Jackie Johnson. Now
he had.

30

Michael stared at the body of the man he'd last seen being loaded in the Hidden Springs ambulance. The night fell like a shroud around him. The stars quit shining. The frogs stopped croaking, and the lake water no longer caressed the bank.

It had to be some kind of nightmare. *Please, Lord, let that be true.* All of it nothing more than a nightmare from the start and he would wake up in a little bit. Then before he was halfway through eating his breakfast cereal, the whole thing would slide off into that dream never-never land to be forgotten forever. Julie Lynne would be flaunting her perfect body on some new stage. And who knew? The others might never have even existed except in the dream.

After he'd come out of the coma when he was fifteen, he often had to test to see if he was in the present or dreaming. He had to weigh and balance his memories to decide if something had really happened or might be some leftover from the black sleep sneaking into his thoughts. But he wasn't dreaming now, as much as he wanted to be.

He forced himself to lean down for a closer look. Blood

was dried and caked on the man's shirt, but none on the ground. Jackie Johnson had died long before reaching this hiding place. Johnson wasn't a small man, and whoever put his body under the boat must have had a struggle to hide it there. Why put it under the boat anyway? Why not just weight the body down and drop it in the lake? But then, why any of it?

Michael straightened up and stared out at the lake. The moon must have started shining again, because light glinted off something close to the water's edge. Michael knew what it was even before he walked down to look, but he had to look, the same as he'd had to lift up the boat and see the body. Half covered in mud at the edge of the water was one of his Civil War sabers. No blood stained its blade, but Michael didn't need to go back and bare the mortal wound in the man's midsection to know he was looking at the murder weapon.

Dear Father in heaven. He didn't know if he said the words aloud or only let them slide through his head. No more prayer words followed behind. Maybe they were enough.

Michael left the saber in the mud. He kicked off his shoes and stripped down to his shorts. As he waded out into the lake, he focused his mind completely on the cool, velvety water closing around his legs. When he was chest deep, he started swimming and pushed through the water until he was well away from the bank. Below him the water stretched down deep and cool.

He flipped over on his back and floated, staring straight up at the stars. With the water gently lapping against him, he pulled in slow breaths and did his best to block out everything except the lake and the stars.

But the question wouldn't be shut out. It screamed at him from every side. If not Jackie Johnson, then who? The who echoed through his head until it seemed to be bouncing off everything around him. Who? Who?

He let his feet sink and treaded water while he stared back toward his house. The body was there, a deep shadow under the tree.

And what did you do after you found the body? Michael could hear Whitt's voice inside his head.

Went swimming, of course. What else could a man do when a monster who no longer had a face was laughing in the trees around him? But the lake couldn't insulate him from the monster laughter. It bubbled out through the water to mock him.

Michael sank below the lake's surface and swam as fast as he could toward the dock. He must have lost his mind. How could he try to escape in the lake while a monster was stalking the people he loved most? A monster they wouldn't expect or recognize.

Without a glance in the direction of the body, Michael grabbed up his clothes and ran across the yard. Johnson wasn't going anywhere. What Michael had to figure out was what the monster who'd put him there planned next.

He dumped his uniform on the porch and took the fastest shower on record after he called 911 to have the dispatcher call in the troops. Justin, Buck, Eagleton. It was going to be a long night.

He dialed Aunt Lindy's number, then held the phone between his ear and shoulder while he jerked on jeans. His heart didn't start beating right until he heard her hello.

"Where are you, Michael? I thought you were coming here for the night."

"Something's happened. Call Reece and ask him to come over to stay with you until I get there."

"I'll do no such thing." It was easy to hear Aunt Lindy's frown in her voice.

"Then you go over there. That would be better anyway. Call him up and tell him to come walk you over to his house."

"What is the matter with you, Michael? You know I'm not going to call Reece Sheridan in the middle of the night to come protect me. The poor man's hardly in any physical condition to protect himself, much less anybody else. Besides, that Jackie Johnson isn't going to bother me."

"You're right there." Michael pressed the phone harder against his ear. He needed to make Aunt Lindy realize the danger. "Jackie Johnson isn't going to bother anybody. He's dead."

"Dead?" Aunt Lindy sounded surprised.

"That's what I said. I found him under my rowboat." He tried to keep his voice calm, but how could a man stay calm with a dead man in his backyard? A man killed with a saber from his own house. Michael looked toward the cabinet that stored his antique weapons. The doors were closed and locked the same as always.

"Rowboat? You're not making sense, Michael. What's this about a rowboat?" Aunt Lindy was using her stop-the-nonsense teacher's voice.

Michael pulled in a breath. "Jackie Johnson's body was under my rowboat."

"Your rowboat?" Her voice rose a little with disbelief.

"Yes. Dead. Under my rowboat in my yard."

She recaptured her matter-of-fact tone. "I take it he didn't crawl under there and happen to expire on his own." When Michael didn't say anything, she went on. "So who put him there?"

"I have no idea, Aunt Lindy. Until a little while ago, I didn't know there was another who."

"All right. We don't know who. Do we know why? Why go to the trouble of hiding him under your rowboat?"

"And use Uncle Wilbur's Civil War saber to see that he didn't crawl out from under it."

"Uncle Wilbur's saber? Oh my." Aunt Lindy's voice was strained. "I don't like the sound of any of this. Do you have any possible suspects in mind?"

"I don't, but Detective Whitt will."

"Whitt. He's the man on the news after that poor reporter was killed." Aunt Lindy let the silence hum on the line a moment. "I think I will call Reece after all."

"Good. And don't open the door for anyone else no matter what they tell you. Promise?"

"Michael, I do believe you are trying to frighten me."

"Is it working?"

"Yes."

"Good," Michael said again. "Have you heard from Alex since we talked last?"

"No."

"If she calls, tell her what I told you and make sure she knows to be afraid too. And very careful. Tell her . . ." Michael let his words die off. Then he went on. "Tell her I'm sorry I got her into this."

After Michael clicked off the phone, he went to the gun cabinet. The locked doors showed no sign of being forced open. He didn't know when he'd last looked down into the cabinet where he could see the saber on the bottom shelf. Two days. Three. Maybe a week. But now he stared at the empty space where the saber always lay and thought of the stories he'd been told about his uncle Wilbur.

They said Wilbur claimed he never fired a shot that he didn't worry one of his Rebel brothers might be on the other side in his line of fire. So when they both fought at Gettysburg and his brother, Pascal, was killed, Wilbur went half mad with grief. Well-meaning people told him it couldn't have been his bullet that ended Pascal's life, but Wilbur took no solace in their empty words. He told them his bullets could have killed somebody's brother.

Michael hadn't killed anybody, but somebody was going to a lot of trouble to make it look as if he had. Why? And who? Most of all, who?

At the first sign of flashing lights in the distance, he stepped out on his front porch to wait. Jasper barely bothered to bark when Buck pulled up into the yard.

Justin was right behind him, and after another twenty minutes, Whitt rolled in, this time with his techs in tow. Lights and camera time.

Michael pointed out the body and the probable murder weapon and stood back as the spotlights went on and the cameras started flashing. One woman nobody bothered to introduce wrapped yellow police line tape around his trees back and forth like a giant web.

Buck went down to take a look at the corpse and then stepped over the police tape to come stand beside Michael. He waved his hand at the yellow tape. "Not much need of this out here, but I guess the stuff's cheap."

"I guess," Michael said.

Buck was silent a minute. "You don't think he offed himself, do you?"

"And then crawled under my rowboat?" Michael looked at Buck, who kept his eyes on the people surrounding the body. "Not likely."

"Yeah. Then what do you think did happen?"

"I think there's a monster out in the bushes we didn't even know was there and I think he's laughing."

"Laughing?" Buck turned to stare at him.

"Laughing." Michael looked from him to the woods. "This is a game to whoever's doing it. He's playing gotcha and I'm it. At least, I hope I'm it."

"What do you mean?"

Michael turned back to Buck. "I want it to be me he goes after next."

Justin sidled up beside them. "I'm not running for reelection next year. I don't care if people think it's my duty or not."

"Nobody else will run," Buck said.

"Then the judge or the governor or whoever will just have to appoint somebody. Anybody but me." Justin headed toward his hearse to get the gurney. "I'll need somebody to help me again."

"Why don't you hire an assistant?" Buck called after him.

Justin didn't look around. "Never needed an assistant before today."

Buck blew out a breath. "Guess it's my turn, huh?"

"It's not mine." Michael kept his feet planted where they were.

Buck punched his shoulder lightly. "Don't worry, kid. We'll catch this joker. Nobody can go around killing people the way this perp has been without leaving some trails. We'll just follow those trails straight to him."

Michael didn't bother saying anything. He knew where the trails were leading. The monster had made sure of that.

Whitt dropped any semblance of professional courtesy when he came over to question Michael. "You ready to tell me what's going on here, Keane?"

"I told you. I came out to locate the source of the bad odor in my yard. I found some fish some kid had left down by the dock, and then when I headed back to the house, I saw Jackson under my boat. Or Johnson."

"And the probable murder weapon we found down by the lake? The saber. You said that was yours."

"One of my ancestors carried it in the Civil War."

"Your uncle Wilton, I think you said."

"Wilbur," Michael corrected as if it mattered.

"Right. Got that, Chekowski?" Whitt looked at his partner, who was scribbling notes as Whitt talked. He didn't expect her to answer him and she didn't.

The lights they strung up pushed back the night but left deep shadows around the edges of the yard. Michael refrained from telling the detective it might be a little late to get a statement from Wilbur. A hundred-years-plus too late. Instead he kept his mouth shut and waited for whatever the man would say next.

"You hadn't noticed it missing? It's not exactly a pocket knife. Seems you'd notice it missing."

"I hadn't actually looked inside the cabinet for a few days. I did check to be sure the doors were locked on Monday when I came in and my dog seemed unusually nervous. The night before I found the earring."

"So you don't think it was lifted that night?"

"I can't be sure. I didn't look inside the cabinet to see if everything was there. Assumed nothing would be missing since the doors were closed and locked."

"And they were."

"They were."

"You did say you started locking your doors after that."

"The door was locked," Michael said. "Not that night but after that."

"So do you have a broken window? A splintered doorjamb?"

"Not that I've seen."

Whitt stared at him, shielding his eyes from the glare of the light with his hand. "I think you'd notice that."

"I haven't examined all my windows." Michael didn't flinch under the man's stare. "The lock's a simple one. Probably wouldn't hold out much challenge to anybody with some lock picks. The same with the lock on the cabinet."

Whitt pressed his lips together and gazed over Michael's shoulder toward the woods beyond the house. Michael wondered if he saw nothing but dark shadows or if he could see the monster lurking there laughing at them. Then again, Whitt probably had no awareness of the trees there at all. He was looking inward at the facts he'd piled up in his head. Finally he blew out his breath and looked back at Michael. "What do you think is going on here?"

"I wish I knew, Detective Whitt."

Michael met his eyes. Whitt looked away first, glancing over his shoulder to where the lights were brightest around the body. "Sure does ruin the view. Right, Chekowski?"

"Yes, sir." She sounded surprised that Whitt had even noticed there was a view to see.

The man turned back toward Michael but stared at the ground as if he might discover some new truth there. "You know what it looks like, don't you, Keane?"

"No." Michael kept his voice flat. He knew very well where the conversation was heading. "What does it look like?"

Whitt pulled his gaze up off the ground to settle his eyes on Michael. "Two bodies in your backyard or the same as. Evidence for the first killing in your pocket. You admit to owning a probable murder weapon. Two, maybe even three, of the victims knew you and had reason to trust you."

Behind Whitt, Chekowski stopped scribbling in her notebook and stared at her boss.

With his back to the lights, Michael's face was shadowed. He turned a bit so Whitt could see his face in full light. He didn't blink. "I'm not a murderer, Whitt, and even more telling, I'm not an idiot."

"Most murderers aren't. Idiots, I mean." Whitt stared back at him as unblinking as Michael.

"But if I was the murderer, I'd have to be an idiot to hand over the earring to you and to put Johnson's body under my boat and then pretend I'd simply found him there."

Whitt pursed his lips again. "What would you have done?"

"Buried him in the woods or weighted him down and sunk him in a deep cove of the lake. I'd have pushed that Oldsmobile into the lake with my old truck and you'd be down to two bodies to worry about."

"Maybe you were going to. You just didn't get it done quick enough."

"So I call in you and your crew to make sure I don't have time?" Michael waved his hand at the people swarming over his yard.

Whitt looked toward where Justin was finally loading the body on his gurney. "Stranger things have happened. And somebody, might even have been you, threw out the idea that this killer—" Whitt paused and fixed his gaze back on Michael—"this perp might be one of those . . ."

Chekowski spoke up when he hesitated. "Multiple personalities, sir."

"Yeah, whatever. The shrinks are always hunting excuses." He leaned a little closer to Michael.

Michael didn't give an inch or say a word.

"I know you don't have any kind of smudge on your record. Squeaky clean as far as the computers know."

"You checked?" Michael stared him down.

Whitt backed up and shrugged a little. "I wanted to see why you left the Columbus police force to come back to this tiny dot on the map. Didn't seem the normal thing for a man to do."

"Normal for me. My roots are here." Michael finally looked away from Whitt to stare out toward the lake. It was hard to see the water past the glare of the lights, but he knew it was there. "Do you have more questions? Or are we finished here?"

"You know we're not." Whitt sounded almost sorry. "You know I have to at least hold you for questioning on this. Hard to ignore the evidence."

"You'll be making a terrible mistake." Michael had known it was coming, but it was still a punch in the gut.

"Sir, are you . . ." Chekowski let her sentence sputter out at a look from Whitt.

"Read him his rights, Chekowski."

"That won't be necessary." Michael resisted the impulse to punch Whitt in the nose. "I know my rights."

31

When Buck came over to them after helping Justin load the body, Whitt told him to take Michael in.

"What the . . . ?" Buck's mouth dropped open as he looked from Whitt to Michael. "He's kidding, right?"

Michael let Whitt answer.

"I never kid, Officer Garrett. Do I, Chekowski?"

"No sir," Chekowski said.

"This man is under arrest." Whitt fixed his gaze on Buck. "I strongly suggest you use your handcuffs. The suspect may be dangerous."

Buck looked straight at Whitt. "I left my cuffs in my other car."

"Get this straight, Officer." Whitt moved a step closer to Buck. "I know it may be difficult for you to imagine your friend a murderer, but the evidence is impossible to ignore."

"Murderer! Mike here? You've lost your marbles, Whitt." Buck shook his head. "The man we're after is no plain, average, run-of-the-mill murderer. He's a full-blown psycho."

"The more reason to treat any and all suspects with the

utmost caution. I assume you do want to wake up in the morning to go out and catch your quota of speeders."

Buck bristled at the detective's tone and gave him an earful.

Michael leaned against Buck's car and listened. He considered more than once just walking around the car, getting in, and driving off. Buck had pitched the keys on the dash. Michael would put on the siren and lights and wake up everybody in Keane County and Hidden Springs on the way to Aunt Lindy's. He kept thinking about her alone in that house. Even if she had gone to get Reece, what help would he be? Aunt Lindy was right. These days, the old lawyer could barely land a good-sized crappie. He would be no match for a monster.

Whitt surprised Michael by suddenly giving in to Buck. "All right, Garrett. Tell you what. You can hold him over at the Hidden Springs jail tonight and bring him to Eagleton tomorrow morning. That will give Keane time to arrange to have an attorney present when he's interrogated. Unless he wants to give his statement this evening. Chekowski could make arrangements if that's the case."

Michael didn't bother answering him. Instead he gave Jasper's ears a rub and pointed the dog toward the porch. The dog whined but did as he was told.

"Will he be all right? The dog, I mean," Chekowski said, but she was looking at Michael.

"He'll be fine." Michael tried to believe that he himself would be as fine.

"I can't believe I'm doing this," Buck muttered as he went around the car to get in under the wheel. "Come on, Michael. Let's get this over with."

Michael climbed in the front seat beside Buck without

glancing back at Whitt. As they started up the lane, Michael said, "Think they'll search my house before they leave?"

"You worried about them finding something you don't want found? We can go back if you want. You can say you decided to put the dog in the house or something." Buck sounded uncomfortable.

"Relax, Buck. I don't have any contraband hidden in my closets. But whoever is doing this may have planted something for them to find."

"No more bodies, I hope." Buck's hands tightened on the wheel as he glanced over at Michael.

"Probably not. I was thinking more of a murder weapon or two." Michael should have looked around his house instead of just waiting for sirens. In fact, now when he thought about it, he wondered why he'd waited at all. He should have gone straight to Aunt Lindy's. They could have tracked him down there to arrest him. "After you take me in, will you go by and check on Aunt Lindy?"

"You don't think the guy would go after her?" Buck sounded shocked.

"I don't know. Alex got the pictures. Julie Lynne's pictures. At her office in Washington." Michael rubbed his forehead. "I should have told Whitt that. He'll say I was concealing evidence or something."

"Whitt's a jerk, but he's not stupid. He'll come to his senses by morning and let you go."

"But what about till then?"

"You mean what will the real murderer do?" Buck was quiet as he pulled out on the highway. "If the guy is trying to pin this on you, he won't do anything as long as you're in jail."

"I hope you're right, Buck."

"Then again, he may not know you're in jail."

"I think he'll know."

"How?" Buck flicked on his flashing lights but left the siren off.

"I don't know that." There was too much Michael didn't know.

"Who do you think it is, Mike?"

"As Detective Whitt has already deduced, there's nobody out there who could possibly be a suspect except me." Michael stared out at the blue lights reflecting off everything they passed.

"We know it's not you. So there has to be somebody else out there."

"But who?"

The question chased along with them as Buck sped toward Hidden Springs. Who?

They roused Burton Fuller out of bed to open the jail. After he jerked on a pair of floppy brown pants and stuck his feet into untied shoes without bothering with socks or a shirt in the July heat, he led the way to the booking area of the jail.

He yawned, scratched through the wiry gray hairs on his chest, and looked at Buck and Michael. "Okay. I'm awake. Where's my customer?"

"I guess that's me," Michael said.

Burton frowned. "I mean the guy you want me to lock up."

Michael pointed at Buck. "He's the arresting officer."

"Come on, boys. An old man like me needs his sleep. Now go get whoever it is you want me to lock up so we can get this over with." Burton's frown got fiercer.

Buck put his arm around the jailor's shoulders. "It's a long story, Burton, and one that doesn't make enough sense to tell. So just do all of us a favor and let Mike here sleep in one of your rooms tonight. I'll come back in the morning and get everything straightened out."

Michael took the change and his pocketknife out of his pockets. His gun and badge were back at the house. Whitt's techs had probably stuck them in plastic evidence bags by now, along with his antique gun collection. He should have unlocked the gun cabinet for them. Not that it mattered. He had more to worry about than a splintered cabinet door.

"I need to make a telephone call," he told Burton.

Burton rocked back and forth on his feet, still looking like he thought he was in the middle of some kind of practical joke. He ran his hand through the few strands of hair left on top of his head. "You call anybody you want to, Michael. You know where the phone is."

Michael looked at the clock. A few minutes past midnight. He hesitated, then dialed the number. Aunt Lindy answered on the first ring to tell him of course she hadn't gone to bed not knowing where he was or what was happening. And yes, she was safe inside with every door locked, the windows bolted, and straight chairs wedged tightly under the doorknobs for insurance. Yes, she had called Reece, but he must have already turned in for the night because his infernal machine picked up on the second ring. She'd even left a message. Not that it would do any good if he was asleep, but Reece was an early riser. She'd call him at first light. No, she hadn't heard from Alexandria. And where exactly was he?

"At the jail," Michael said. "Things are a little strange right now. I'll explain in the morning. Just remember if anybody tries to get in the house, shoot first and worry about who they are later."

"Don't you think that might be a bit drastic, Michael?" Her voice wobbled between concerned and skeptical.

"Not tonight, Aunt Lindy. And aim to kill."

The skeptical won out. "I'm perfectly safe, Michael. From the sound of your voice, you best worry about yourself."

After Aunt Lindy hung up, Michael held the phone a moment and wondered if he should call anyone else. But he didn't know where Alex was and what could he tell Betty Jean that she didn't already know. Maybe Buck was right. As long as Michael was behind bars, the monster wouldn't kill again.

Michael put down the phone and walked back down the hallway to the first cell. He stepped inside and pulled the door shut behind him. The lock clanged shut and monster laughter echoed inside his head. It could be he had just made the biggest mistake of his life.

Buck looked through the bars. "Hang in there, Mike. We'll get it worked out in the morning. And don't worry about Miss Keane. I'll make a sweep by there on my way out of town to check out the neighborhood."

After Buck left, Burton frowned and raked his fingers through his hair again. He jerked up his pants. "I guess I'll just sleep out there on the cot in the front room. So holler if you need anything." He started away, then looked back at Michael. "I ain't got my calendar mixed up and this is really April Fool's Day?"

"Don't worry, Burton. You're in the clear. Doing your job the way you were elected to do."

"That's what I've always tried to do." Burton shoved his

hands in his pockets. "But I always thought you did too. It just ain't right seeing you behind them bars."

"It's like Buck says. We'll figure it out in the morning, but that bigshot detective from Eagleton wants me locked up tonight."

Burton still hesitated. "This ain't the way things is supposed to be."

"I know, but you can't tell those big-city cops anything. There's no explaining things to them."

With a last sad shake of his head, the jailor shuffled on back to the front office. The cot squeaked as the man settled in it. A few minutes later, he was snoring.

Michael glanced at the prisoner's cot. No way he could sleep. He paced the few steps back and forth across the cell, did some deep-knee bends, but nothing kept him from wanting to bang his head into the bars. He shouldn't have locked himself in here. Burton wouldn't have done it if he hadn't let him. Michael had done nothing but make mistakes since he pulled Johnson back from the railing of the bridge.

But it wasn't Johnson doing this. It had never been Johnson. That man had just been the poor down-on-his-luck derelict that he'd looked like. But if not him, who? No suspects came to mind. Nothing made sense. Not since the first envelope of pictures landed on Betty Jean's desk.

He had to stop trying to figure things out in a rational way. Instead he needed to think like the monster. What would the murderer do next? Could be he might just move on, laughing at the wreck he'd made of Michael's life. Michael let that thought rise up inside him like an unspoken prayer. But somehow, Michael didn't think that was going to happen.

He had the awful feeling the monster was on the prowl in Hidden Springs.

But if the killer was going to pin the blame on Michael, he couldn't do anything while Michael was locked up in jail. Michael tried to cling to that thought, but it was like grasping at a silky ribbon whipping in the wind. And somewhere the monster laughed.

He was about to shout to wake up Burton and convince him to unlock the cell when somebody started pounding on the outside door.

The cot squeaked as Burton got up and headed for the door, muttering dark words Michael couldn't quite make out.

"Wait, Burton," Michael called. What if it was the monster tracking Michael down to finish things off? The voice through the door sounded familiar, but then the monster could be someone he knew.

"Hold your horses, Michael. I got to see who's at the door." Burton shuffled away.

Michael had never felt as helpless in his life. Locked up. With no options but pleading for God's mercy. Aunt Lindy would have told him that should have been his first option. Michael shut his eyes and sent up a silent prayer.

Burton pulled open the door. "Leland? What are you doing here? Can't the news wait till morning?"

Hank sounded excited. "Thank goodness, you heard me. I was passing the courthouse and I think I saw smoke coming out of the clerk's office. I couldn't get inside to check it out. The front door's locked, but you have keys, don't you?"

"You really saw smoke?"

"I'm not sure, Burton. That's why I didn't call the fire department. I didn't want to wake everybody up to bring out the truck for a false alarm. But I think you should check to see for sure, don't you?"

Burton started to say something, but Hank pushed his words out ahead of the jailor's. "We can't be wasting time. What if it is a fire? All those old deed books. Up in smoke."

"I guess you're right." Burton's voice faded as he headed down the steps toward the back of the courthouse.

Then Hank was in front of Michael staring at him through the bars. "He said you were in here, but I really didn't believe it until now. And me without my camera."

32

"Is the courthouse on fire?" Michael asked.

"Nah. But I had to get in somehow, and you know Burton would slam the door in my face this time of night. A fire was the first thing I could think of. He said you're in for murder. That can't be true, can it?"

"Right now I'm in temporary custody until I can be interrogated, but Whitt seems to think I might be the killer. Who is this 'he'? Buck?"

"Buck Garrett call me?" Hank slapped his hand against his chest. "This cell has affected your thinking."

Michael stepped closer to the bars. He wanted to reach through and grab Hank, make him tell him what he needed to know. "Then who called you?"

"That's just it. I don't know. The voice was weird. Like something computer generated. But the good news is, he said you wouldn't have to worry. That by daylight, everybody would know you didn't do it, and you'd be off the hook."

Michael grabbed hold of the bars and felt sick. "Get me out of here, Hank. Now!"

Hank looked a little scared as he stared at Michael. "What's wrong with you? I thought I was bringing you good news."

"Think, Hank." Michael forced himself to stay calm. "He's going to kill somebody."

The color drained out of Hank's face. "Who?"

"How do I know?" Michael couldn't keep his voice from rising. "Just get the key and unlock this door."

Hank grabbed the key off the hook where Burton kept it just inside the door in the front office. He stuck it in the lock, his hands shaking so badly he could barely turn it. "Can they put me in jail for this?"

"Helping a prisoner escape. Of course they can. But this should keep you out of trouble." Michael pushed open the door, then grabbed Hank and shoved him into the cell where he fell against the cot.

"Wait, Michael. You might need help." Hank scrambled up to rush the door, but Michael had it shut and locked.

"I did, and I thank you."

Michael ignored Hank's ongoing protests. He found Burton's gun under his cot and waited until the jailer climbed back up the steps, grumbling under his breath. Michael stayed out of sight until the man was through the door. Then he stepped in behind him. "I'm really sorry about this, but things have changed. I can't let you keep me in jail after all."

Burton frowned. "How'd you get out? The door was locked, wasn't it?"

"It was locked." Michael kept the gun down at his side, pointed at the floor. "Now you need to head on back and get in the cell."

"I'm not going to let you lock me up." Burton frowned

with a shake of his head. "It don't look good, a jailer getting locked up in his own jail."

"It'll look better than you letting me walk out of here without stopping me. Trust me on this one, Burton."

"Why can't you just wait till morning?" Burton wasn't budging.

"I can't. Aunt Lindy might be in danger."

"Then why don't we call for help?"

"Because they might not believe me and make you lock me back up." Michael nodded toward the cells. "I can't take that chance. Not tonight."

Burton's gaze went to the gun Michael still had pointed at the floor. "I ain't afraid of that gun, Michael. You wouldn't shoot me."

Michael raised the gun up and looked at it. "You're right. I won't shoot you, but if I have to, I'll hit you. So just go on and get in the cell. You can sleep the rest of the night back there. I'll come let you out first thing in the morning. Nobody will ever know except you and me and Hank."

"If Leland knows, everybody in Hidden Springs will know. Sending me on a wild-goose chase like that. Where is he anyhow?"

"Where I was, and if nothing happens before the night is over, he won't write it in the paper. I'll see to it. And if something does happen, he'll make you a hero in the piece."

Burton looked at Michael for a long moment, then gave in and walked back to the second cell. He glared at Hank as he went in and pulled the door shut. "I can't remember the last time both of these had somebody in them."

Hank paid no attention to Burton. Instead he grabbed the cell door and tried to push it open. "Listen to me, Mi-

310

chael. If you're right, you're going to need help. Let me go with you."

Michael didn't answer him as he headed toward the door. Hank called after him. "If you won't take me, call Buck. He'll believe you. This whole thing could be a trap."

With his hand on the door, Michael hesitated. Hank was right. The monster was probably still thinking three steps ahead of him. He went back to Burton's desk and called Sally Jo, the night dispatcher. In a flat voice that revealed none of the emotion roiling through him, he asked her to call Buck and tell him to check out Aunt Lindy's house. Buck would know something was up, but maybe if the monster was monitoring the police scanner, he would think Michael was still behind bars.

Hank stopped shaking the cell door. "Be careful, Michael. This guy, he's some kind of a . . ."

"Monster," Michael finished for Hank as he went out the door.

Just as Michael hoped, Hank's keys were in the ignition of his old van. He slipped behind the wheel and was relieved when the motor rumbled awake. Hank was badly in need of a new muffler, so Michael let the car sputter to a stop at the end of Keane Street. Michael wanted to go in silently to check for anything out of the ordinary before he went to the door.

The neighborhood was quiet. No lights on except for a soft nightlight here and there. Nothing gave the smallest hint of anything wrong as Michael slipped through the familiar backyards. Even so, Michael stayed hidden in the deep shadows away from the streetlights.

When he made his way through the yard next to Aunt Lindy's house, Miss June's dog was yapping for all he was worth somewhere in the house. But the little dog was always yapping at something. Nobody ever took much notice of his barking. Not even Miss June. Still, Michael stopped at the end of her hedge and studied the area around Aunt Lindy's house. He'd heard the dog before he stepped into Miss June's yard.

The warm, silky night air carried the scent of roses from Aunt Lindy's and Miss June's gardens. Light from the streetlights spread a glow out on the sidewalk and road. No car moved, and no unknown vehicles were anywhere in sight. A car moved past out on Broadway, but it didn't slow to make the turn onto Keane Street.

Everything looked the same as always. Peaceful. Ordinary. The only noise was the dog yapping behind him, and even that was so commonplace, it wouldn't sound any kind of warning to anybody in the neighborhood. Yet, alarm bells were clamoring inside Michael's head.

He crept up the driveway and across the yard to the porch that stretched across the front of the old house. The porch was stone, so no creaking boards betrayed his presence. He fished out the door key that Aunt Lindy hid under a loose piece of chinking between the stones.

Miss June's dog stopped barking. In the suddenly ominous silence, Michael's breathing sounded too loud. He held his breath as he peered through the side panels beside the solid wood door, but he couldn't see through the etched glass window. He turned the key in the lock. Aunt Lindy should be shooting at him by now or at least demanding to know who he was. Then again, if she was in her bedroom in the back of the house, she probably wouldn't hear him.

He quietly turned the knob and pushed gently on the door. It didn't budge. The chair Aunt Lindy had propped under the knob held. Michael ran around to the back door where the glass storm door was locked. All the windows looked secure. Unless the man went down the chimney, Aunt Lindy had to be safe inside.

He stopped worrying about making noise and banged on the back door. Nothing. He knocked again, even harder, but no lights came on. She must be sound asleep. He went back to the front door and rang the doorbell. Even through the door the chimes sounded loud. She had to hear that. His heart started beating faster as he listened for her footsteps inside. Nothing.

"Aunt Lindy, it's me, Michael. Open the door."

His voice broke the silence of the night, and Miss June's dog started yapping again. No sound came from within the house. No light flicked on. The lack of an answer pounded against his ears.

He pulled the gun out of his belt and turned the doorknob. The chair had been moved. The door swung open easily.

Aunt Lindy was tied to a chair directly in front of him, visible in the light spilling in from the streetlight behind Michael. A wide piece of clear tape covered her mouth. Anger warred with panic in her eyes.

"So nice of you to finally join us." A hand came out of the shadows behind Aunt Lindy to press the end of a gun barrel to her head. "If you would be so kind as to drop your gun and slide it this way."

Aunt Lindy contorted her face, trying to stop Michael. He knew what she was trying to tell him. Shoot him. Let her die. Stop him from killing again, because if Michael gave up his gun, they were both going to die.

Michael dropped the gun to the floor and kicked it toward

the man's shape in the shadows. He'd have to find another way.

Tears edged out of Aunt Lindy's eyes and trickled down her wrinkled cheeks.

The man reached down and picked up the gun, but Michael still couldn't see his face.

"Please shut the door behind you. We wouldn't want anyone to happen by and be privy to our private affairs, now, would we?"

"Who are you?" The man's voice sounded familiar and strange at the same time.

"Don't you know? I'm the hero destroyer." The man laughed and stepped out of the shadows into the light.

33

"Dr. Colson?" Michael stared at the man who emerged from the shadows.

The man laughed. "You do well to sound surprised. But no, not Dr. Colson. The doctor was a timid little man. He could never have accomplished any of the things I've achieved under the guise of his good name. Regretfully enough, it was Philip Colson's time to pass on a number of years ago."

Michael couldn't spare any worry for whatever had happened to the real Dr. Colson. "What do you want with us?" he demanded.

"Only everything." The man ran a slender finger encased in a latex glove down the gun barrel and then across Aunt Lindy's temple. She jerked away from his touch. "Your aunt was not an easy subject. If my appearance hadn't been so unexpected, I do believe she might have shot me." The man's smile chilled Michael's blood. "It's so much nicer when there's a bit of challenge."

Michael stared at the man's face while he frantically tried to come up with a plan to get the gun pointed away from Aunt Lindy's head. He took a tiny step back and bumped against the straight chair that moments ago must have been jammed under the doorknob.

"Sit down, if you like." The man motioned toward the chair with his free hand. "I'm sure you have more questions you would like answered. How did I get in? Why am I doing this? How many people have I ushered out of life? The questions vary somewhat, but I do like giving my people the chance to ask. It somehow helps for them to realize they aren't alone in this great game of death."

Michael felt the back of the chair behind him, but no way was he going to sit down. He had to stay on his feet to have any chance of taking out the man. The man's lips turned up at the corners as he waited for Michael to say something. To play his games. Michael didn't want to give him that satisfaction, but he needed time.

"So how did you get in? My aunt assured me all the doors were locked." Michael kept his eyes on the man. It was better not to look at Aunt Lindy. He needed to stay as cold-blooded as the murderer to have a chance against him.

"Doors all locked. Windows intact. Breaking windows is entirely too messy, and if one is not extremely careful, one can get cut. It has never seemed wise to leave any of my own blood at a murder scene. That pesky DNA, you know." Again the chilling smile. "The fact is, I was already in. Attics in old houses like this are so cozy, don't you think? One doesn't even have to be particularly quiet, because those who live in old houses pay scant attention to the odd squeak and creak above their heads."

"How long have you been here?" Michael felt sick, thinking the man might have been right over his head the night before and he hadn't even known.

"Only a few days. In and out, of course. Dr. Colson is attending an educational seminar at the Hilton in Eagleton. He's the keynote speaker there later today. I think his topic is going to be how unexpected events in life can be a threat to one's health. He is considering presenting a case study about how even saving someone's life, perhaps a stranger's, can be extremely stressful to our regular routine. Dr. Colson is a much sought-after speaker." The man looked too smug. "He has such great insight about life-and-death matters."

Michael's hands wanted to curl into fists, but he forced them to stay relaxed. Buck would be on the way. He just had to keep the man talking. "What is your real name then?"

"My birth name was Carl Corley. Not that names matter. I've often found the need to shed a name much the way a snake sheds its skin when it begins to feel uncomfortable. As a matter of fact, the kind couple who adopted me when I was ten changed my name to David."

The man hesitated a moment with a bit of a perplexed look, then went on. "At least, I think it was David. Definitely something biblical. I suggested Judas, but the dear woman who wanted to be my mother explained that wouldn't be appropriate. Later I agreed. Judas felt much too much remorse. At any rate, they had hopes that shedding my first name would help me forget my tragic past."

"What tragic past?" Michael tried to sound interested.

"A couple of months before the nice Brysons took me in, my father executed my mother. I was his witness. As best I recall, he was upset because the milk had gone sour in the refrigerator. And then, since there was no milk for our cereal, he decided to eliminate our need for food. He shot me as well, but his aim was a bit off. The bullet only creased the side of my head."

The man swept his finger across the side of his forehead. He was obviously enjoying recounting his story. "I had the presence of mind to lie quite still on the kitchen floor. While it wasn't a life-threatening wound, it was messy. My blood spilled out on my mother's just-mopped floor. Along with hers. Blood congeals very quickly. Did you know that?" The man peered over at Michael. "But of course, you did. Policemen see congealed blood all the time. But somehow, it's different when it's your own."

"You didn't die."

"Many have wished they could rewrite that portion of my story, but alas, I did not die. I was very convincing however. My father thought it so. He even sounded somewhat contrite. From his muttering, I think he planned to kill himself too but lacked the courage to put the gun to his head. So the sorrowful man went to the source of all his courage or comfort. The bottle. Have you ever had to find courage in a bottle?"

When Michael didn't answer, he answered for him. "I'd guess not. You're a man with an ample supply of courage, aren't you? Even now your mind is racing to figure out how to make a courageous rescue." The man made a sound that could have been a laugh. "I regret to tell you how futile that is. I always win. As I did that long ago day when my father thought to kill his own seed. Don't you want to know what happened next?"

"The police came and rescued you?"

Michael could use some reinforcements to come to their rescue now. He studied the man's hand holding the gun, but it showed no sign of weakness. Aunt Lindy sat very still with her eyes closed. Michael hoped she was praying. Out of the corner of his eyes he saw Aunt Lindy's cat lurking in the dark hallway leading away from the foyer. Grimalkin was crouched low, creeping closer as though stalking a mouse. If only Buck was there instead.

"Hardly." The man seemed amused. "I waited until his head fell over on the table. Then I crept over and eased the gun from under his hand. Regrettably, the movement roused him and he grabbed me. Fortunately, I already had the gun and pressed it into his stomach and pulled the trigger. He fell on top of me and suffered badly for several moments, which I thought only proper given what he'd done to my dear mother. Under him, soaked in his blood, I felt the life go out of him. I've tried to re-create that feeling many times since, but perhaps the first is always the best. Do you agree, Michael? Was your first killing best?"

"I've never had to kill anyone." Michael listened intently for the sound of Buck's car gliding toward the house. Surely Sally Jo had paged him by now. He would be on the way, but would he be soon enough?

"Had to?" The man touched his lower lip with his tongue. "You mean got to, don't you?"

When Michael stared at him without saying anything, the man laughed again. "Oh, that's right. You're in the 'keep them alive' corner. Save a life a day and all your troubles will go away. Didn't work out quite like that this time, did it, Michael?"

"Not quite." Michael tried to visualize what might be beside the door behind him. He needed a weapon. Buck might not show up in time.

"Is my story boring you, Michael? You appear somewhat distracted."

"It's been a long day."

"Yes, I suppose it has. And I can't expect all my people to be as enraptured with my story as that cute little reporter. Kim something, wasn't it?" Corley shifted on his feet a bit to lean against the wall with the gun still pressed against Aunt Lindy's head. "She took copious notes. I think the poor child really believed I was turning myself in to her and giving her an exclusive that would make her famous. Such an enthusiastic thing. Her life energy practically exploded out of her. The young are always the most fun."

"You're a monster." Michael couldn't stop the words.

"A monster?" The man smiled, not upset in the least. "I like that. But if you are tired of my story, we can get on with it. I do need to prepare for my speech later today."

"Dr. Colson's speech." Michael had to keep the man talking. "By the way, what happened to the real Dr. Colson?"

"A laboratory fire in which I, his faithful lab assistant, sadly died. My body, alas, was burned beyond recognition. The two of us looked a great deal alike. People were always asking if we were brothers, and since the scholarly Dr. Colson was so wrapped up in his research on the human brain that he never had time for the social aspects of life, it was quite easy to step into his shoes. The surviving Dr. Colson was so distraught by the fire and the loss of his valued assistant and all his research notes that he went into seclusion for a year. By the time he was up to taking patients again, I doubt you could have found anyone who remembered exactly what the good doctor looked like."

"How long ago was that?" How much time had gone by since he left the jail?

"A bit over ten years, and the last few years, things have been quite dull, you know. It's just too easy with all these willing candidates for my own brand of research coming into the hospital each day. Remember? The poor man whose appendectomy went bad? I never had to go hunting. Even sweet little Hope, your first victim, showed up on my doorstep, begging to be part of the greater plan. Took some of the fun away. That is, until you came to call."

"How's that?" Michael estimated it would take three steps to reach Corley, more than ample time for the man to pull the trigger of the gun he had against Aunt Lindy's temple.

"The perfect crime. Although since no one has ever suspected me, I suppose all of them have been perfect. But this one brought the fun back. And now you've come to save your aunt just as I knew you would. It makes the ideal ending. You shoot her and then yourself. Keanes are no more on Keane Street in Keane County."

"Nobody will ever believe I would shoot Aunt Lindy." Michael looked down at Aunt Lindy. Her eyes were open now. Not exactly scared. More regretful.

"It will be a shock to the citizens of Hidden Springs, but the evidence will convince them. They'll be saying you can never tell about people. By tomorrow afternoon, they'll all be remembering odd things you did that should have alerted them to your psychotic state. And can't you just imagine our detective Whitt's smug face as he stamps 'closed' on his file?"

"And will it be over? Closed?"

"You mean will I stop? What do you think?" Again the

monstrous smile. "Your episode will be closed. At least almost."

"Almost?"

The monster's face took on a look of fake pity. "There's the lovely Alexandria in Washington, DC."

The words hit Michael like a blow and he staggered back, bumping against the chair behind him and scooting it to the side. He grabbed its back to steady himself.

Corley was still talking. "You needn't worry. No one will ever connect her death with you, because you will have already met your untimely end. I haven't decided completely how the last scene will play out. Perhaps a stalker. Beautiful women often must deal with unwanted admirers, especially high-profile women like our Alexandria. I was fortunate to track her down on the internet. She is quite striking."

Michael took a step toward Corley, then stopped. He tamped down on his rage so he could think. He had to find a way.

"There's nothing you can do, Michael." The man shook his head slightly. "Nobody has ever been able to stop me. Nobody."

Michael shot a look at Aunt Lindy. Anger had pushed out the panic in her eyes too. He had to try something. He slid the chair in front of him and gripped the back again as though he still needed support.

"But enough of this," Corley said. "You seem to have heard all you can bear at any rate. Let's get things all tidied up before anybody comes to call."

As if on cue, footsteps sounded on the porch. "Malinda, it's me, Alex." She knocked on the door. "Can I come in?"

The monster's eyes lit up like a child seeing an unexpected

gift under the Christmas tree. "She must have heard me calling," he whispered.

"Run," Michael shouted but he knew she wouldn't.

"What's going on, Michael?" Alex called back. The doorknob was turning.

Aunt Lindy shot a look at the door, then at Michael before her head drooped forward as though in a faint. With a yowl, Grimalkin shot out of the shadows and attacked Corley's leg. The man kicked to dislodge the cat, but Grimalkin must have dug in her claws. The cat yowled again and hung on. Corley let out a yelp and reached down toward the cat. When he did, his other hand holding the gun shifted a bit to the side so that when Aunt Lindy jerked her head up, it butted the gun away from her.

With the chair as a shield, Michael charged Corley. The gun went off, the bullet shattering the side window next to the door. The cat jerked away from Corley and retreated into the hall as Aunt Lindy rocked to the side and crashed to the floor. Michael hurled the chair at the man.

When the chair banged into Corley's chest, he stumbled backward against the wall. He brought the gun up. With a smile, he pointed the gun at Aunt Lindy, helpless on the floor, as Michael sprang toward him.

The gun popped again. Michael didn't know whether he'd hit the man's arm in time to ruin his aim or not. He didn't look. He kept his eyes on the monster's face as he tackled him and knocked him to the floor. Corley scrambled away, but Michael grabbed him. Corley was stronger than Michael expected. The two of them rolled first one way on the floor and then another, the gun between them. Slowly, Corley edged the gun barrel toward Michael's chest.

Sirens sounded in the distance. Buck was coming in no holds barred, but he was still minutes away. Too far. Michael had to be the one to stop Corley. Now.

Michael slackened his hold on the man and fell away from him. Corley's face lit up, thinking he'd won, but Michael slammed his knee into the man's solar plexus. Corley gasped for breath. Michael didn't give him time to recover. With a burst of energy fueled by desperation, Michael threw his weight on Corley to hold him down while he banged the man's hand against the floor until he finally dropped the gun. Michael grabbed the gun and shoved it up under the monster's chin.

The overhead light came on. That had to mean Alex was okay and hadn't been hit by Corley's shot that shattered the glass beside the door.

"If you don't pull the trigger, you'll wish you had." Corley smiled up at Michael even while still panting for breath.

Michael pushed the tip of the gun even harder against the man's skin until his head tipped back.

But it didn't keep Corley from talking. "Go ahead. Pull the trigger. You want to. You're not that different from me."

"Michael." Alex spoke behind him. "Think about what you're doing."

"That's right, Michael. Think," Corley said. "The powers that be will decide I'm mentally unstable. They'll put me away, but in a couple of years I'll convince them I'm totally recovered. I won't even need medication. So there'll be nothing to fog my memory. I can't see you changing your name, even if it did become as uncomfortable as an outgrown skin."

Aunt Lindy was making desperate noises, but Michael dared not look around at her. So he had no idea if she was advising him to shoot or not shoot. He wasn't even sure if Corley wanted him to shoot or not. The man had a detached expression, as if nothing that was happening mattered at all to him.

"You'll wish you had," Corley said. "Isn't that what our friend Jackson said? You'll wish you had let him jump. And wasn't he right?"

"I'm through playing your games." Michael kept the gun under the man's chin as he eased his body off him. He could still shoot if Corley made a wrong move.

"Death is the only way to end the game, Michael."

Buck burst through the door behind them, his gun drawn.

"I hope you didn't leave your handcuffs at home this time, Buck," Michael said without taking his eyes off the monster in front of him.

34

While Buck handcuffed Corley and read him his rights, Michael and Alex righted Aunt Lindy's chair and cut the nylon ropes binding her wrists to the chair posts. Michael reached for the tape over her mouth, but she held up her hand to stop him. With a determined look, she grabbed a corner of the tape and yanked it off. Tears sprang to her eyes and then she was smiling. Grimalkin came back out of the hallway to wind around her legs.

". . . Anything you say can and will be used against you." Buck's voice went on in the background.

"I don't have anything to hide," Corley said. "I stopped by to see if Miss Keane would speak to me about her nephew rescuing a man who turned out to be a murderer when I heard sounds of a scuffle inside. By the time I was able to force open the door, he had her bound and was holding a gun to her head." The man pointed at Michael. "He appears to be mentally unstable."

"I don't know who you are or what you think you're doing, but I suggest you stop talking right now before I forget I've got witnesses." Buck grabbed the man's arm to propel him toward the door.

"Get him out of my house." Aunt Lindy's voice was raspy but firm.

Corley turned to smile directly at Aunt Lindy. "Floorboards creaking will take on a whole new significance now, won't they, Malinda?"

"Move." Buck shoved him through the door.

Michael picked up the gun he'd taken from Burton and followed them out, a wary eye on the man. He didn't know what he expected Corley to do. He surely couldn't shrink his wrists to jerk free of the handcuffs. But whatever happened, Michael wanted to be ready. Buck needed to be ready too.

"Lock him in your car and call for backup, Buck."

Buck frowned over his shoulder at Michael. "I can take him in."

"He sounds as if he doesn't think you're capable of securing a prisoner, Officer Garrett," the killer said.

Michael ignored Corley. "Call for backup or I will. This is not some drunk who just needs to sober up. He kills people for fun and he'd enjoy adding you to his career total. Just think about it. He knows your name. Consider him extremely dangerous."

"Why, Deputy Keane, I can't imagine why you would say such things. My job is to help people. Not hurt them in any way. He must have me confused with himself, Officer Garrett."

"You're the one confused, buster." Buck looked from Corley to Michael. "Who are you going to call, Mike? Lester?"

"Ah, the nice deputy who told me his biggest pleasure in life is to ensure the children get safely across the street when school starts. Did you know he knows all the names and exactly where those sweet children live?" Corley laughed. "It's such a pleasure to talk to someone so helpful when you're new to a place."

Michael turned his eyes back to Corley. The man was a monster. "Put him in the car, Buck."

"You bet." Buck ushered the man down the steps toward his patrol car.

"If he makes the first wrong move, shoot him," Michael said.

Corley stopped to look back at Michael. "I do believe you have a transference problem that really should be analyzed by your favorite therapist, Michael. You lacked the nerve to shoot me yourself a few moments ago, but now you're urging your friend to do it for you."

Michael stared straight at Corley for the first time since he'd relaxed his finger on the trigger of the gun between them. "Be a model prisoner and you won't have anything to worry about from Officer Garrett."

"Oh, I have no worries. None at all," the murderer said. "You're the one who needs to worry. The game isn't over. I'll be back."

He was laughing when Buck folded him into the backseat of his cruiser.

Buck stared through the cruiser window at the man and then unhooked his radio from his belt. "Could be you're right, Mike. I'll call in the troops. Eagleton and all. No need Whitt getting to sleep if we can't. Think I'll just wait right here until they come. Him in there." Buck nodded toward the car. "Me out here. Safer for both of us that way."

When Buck started talking into his radio, Michael went

328

back inside. Corley couldn't get out of the car and there were people he needed to have in front of his eyes again.

Alex was massaging Aunt Lindy's wrists while Grimalkin sat back as though waiting her turn.

"You're the most beautiful sight I've ever seen," Michael said.

"Is he talking to me or you, Malinda?" Alex smiled at Aunt Lindy.

"I think you know the answer to that." Aunt Lindy picked up Grimalkin and laid her cheek against the cat's head. "Good cat," she murmured.

Alex turned to face Michael. "Then, same old line every time I see you." She attempted a smile that looked shaky.

"The truth never changes." Michael kept his eyes on her face, drinking in the sight of her. "But why are you here?"

"To save your bacon as usual." Alex's smile looked easier now.

"And a good thing. I'm just not sure how you knew it needed saving."

"That has a longer, somewhat stranger answer."

"Well, let's hear it." Aunt Lindy spoke up. "The whole night has been strange. A little more strange will fit right in."

Alex flicked a look over at Aunt Lindy and then back at Michael. "It was Hank Leland. He called Uncle Reece's house. He tried here but the line was busy. Uncle Reece had just fallen back to sleep after I disturbed him by showing up in the middle of the night. I didn't have the heart to wake him again. Besides, I looked out and everything appeared peaceful as can be. Not a thing out of the ordinary except the phone wasn't working."

Alex glanced at Aunt Lindy again. "So I thought I'd just

pop over to check on you, Malinda, and see if Michael was here."

Michael frowned at her. "Not the best thing for you to do in the middle of the night with a psycho killer on the loose."

"I guess not, but Mr. Leland neglected to warn me about said psycho killer perhaps lurking in the shadows. However, he did say something about his van being missing." She raised her eyebrows at Michael. "You know anything about that?"

"He shouldn't leave the keys in the ignition," Michael said. "But Hank and Burton were locked up. How did they get out?"

"Mr. Leland did say that he and Burton had somehow gotten locked in the jail, but it seems Burton keeps a spare key in his pocket for just such unexpected eventualities. Anyway, Mr. Leland claimed he had been doing his best to convince Burton to desert his post at the jail to drive him over here to check on you and Malinda, but Burton refused to budge. Something about how Mr. Leland had already sent him on one wild-goose chase and he wasn't about to let him send him on another one."

Michael gave her a wry grin. "Sounds as if Hank had a lot to say. Were you cross-examining him?"

"I may have asked a few questions." Alex swept a stray strand of hair away from her face. "Obviously not the right ones or I would have called for help and waited for reinforcements."

"Lucky for Aunt Lindy and me that you didn't," Michael said.

Behind her, Aunt Lindy set Grimalkin on the floor and got to her feet. She grabbed hold of the chair to keep her balance. When Michael stepped toward her, she waved him away. "I'm fine. Let Alexandria finish her story."

Alex shifted to the side a bit so she could see Aunt Lindy. "All right then. So obviously, I didn't wait. Mr. Leland had indicated that if I didn't see or hear anything out of the ordinary, that there was probably nothing to worry about. He did ask if I could take some photos with my phone if anything unusual was happening. He graciously offered to pay my going rate for my time."

"You're kidding now, aren't you?" When Alex simply smiled, Michael added, "He evidently has no idea what the going rate is for a high-profile attorney. Hank doesn't have that kind of money."

"I've been known to do a little pro bono work from time to time."

"I'd dare Hank Leland or anybody else to take a picture of me right now." Aunt Lindy gave Alex a hard look. "Even you, Alexandria, so if you have a phone in your pocket, you'd best keep it there."

A smile spiraled up inside Michael. It was good to be alive. Good to hear Aunt Lindy laying down the law. "Don't worry, Aunt Lindy. Hank isn't here and nobody's taking pictures."

"Well, Mr. Leland did say that if he couldn't budge Burton, he might attempt to hitch a ride or even walk over here." A grin played around Alex's mouth. "Said it wasn't all that far, but if I understood him correctly, he had left his camera at home and he didn't know what had happened to his phone. Quite unprofessional of him."

"This place is a zoo," Michael said.

"I've been telling you that for years." Alex let the grin win out and her smile lit up her face.

Michael wanted to grab her, feel her next to him. Let their

breath mingle. Instead he stayed where he was. "I just broke
out of jail and stole a car. Will you represent me?"

"Normally, I don't take hopeless cases," she said.

Aunt Lindy stepped up beside Michael to give his arm a
shake. "That's not what you want to ask her."

"Stay out of this, Aunt Lindy," Michael said.

But as usual, Aunt Lindy paid no attention. Her voice
changed, got almost dreamy. "I've always thought October
is the prettiest month for the back garden. The maples are in
full color and we can cover the roses against any early frosts
and still have them too. A nice outdoor wedding. That would
give us three months."

"Malinda!" Alex turned surprised eyes on Aunt Lindy.

Michael looked at Aunt Lindy and thought he should tell
her to slow down too, but the idea didn't sound at all bad
to him.

"Oh bother," Aunt Lindy said. "The two of you still don't
get it, do you? When I was tied to that chair with that gun—
my own gun, by the way—pressed against my head, I thought
I might never see the next generation of Keanes. Then, when
Michael came through the door, I feared there would never
be another generation of Keanes for anybody to see." Aunt
Lindy put her arms around both of them and pulled them
to her in a three-way hug. "As if all that wasn't sorrowful
enough, here comes Alexandria breezing in. I wasn't sure
if she was an answer to prayer or if her appearance would
make an even more tragic ending. I couldn't let him kill you
both. I couldn't."

"So with a little help from Grimalkin, you used your head."
Michael looked down at Aunt Lindy.

"Indeed." Aunt Lindy rubbed the side of her head she'd

bumped against the gun. "You're fortunate I have a feisty cat and a hard head. But there are times to be hard-headed and times not to be." She poked Michael's chest with her finger. "So since by some amazing miracle we're all still breathing, ask the right question."

Michael turned to look straight into Alex's beautiful eyes. "I'm afraid to ask."

"And if you did ask, I'd be afraid to answer," Alex whispered.

"Cowards, the both of you. You barely squeak through the night on the side of life, and you still won't take a chance." Aunt Lindy pushed them both away from her in disgust. "I'm an old lady who's been tied to a chair for much too long. I need to visit the necessary room." She and Grimalkin disappeared down the hallway.

Michael didn't turn Alex loose. "I may be afraid to ask, but I'm not afraid to do this." He pulled her close and covered her mouth softly with his. Lights flashed and sirens sounded.

Alex pulled her head back. "That wasn't just the kiss, was it?"

"I'd like to say yes, but I think Hank must have found a camera and Buck must have called in the clowns and now the circus is starting."

"Oh well, sometimes a circus can be fun." Alex didn't try to pull away from him. She fit perfectly in his arms.

"And sometimes they can be crazy."

"Let's not worry about the circus." She kept her eyes fastened on his. "Or about questions or answers right now. Let's just be thankful both our hearts are still beating."

She caressed his cheek with her fingers and his heart started drumming in his ears. He tightened his arms around her. "Beating in concert."

"Always," she whispered. "No matter where we are."

"But what about Aunt Lindy and October?"

"Shh." She put her fingers over his lips. "I told you no questions right now. Just embrace the moment."

"Embracing sounds good."

"Very good." Alex wrapped her hands around the back of his neck and pulled him close to put her lips on his again.

The lights flashed brighter than ever and sirens rang in his ears. This time it definitely had to be the kiss.

KEEP READING FOR A SNEAK PEEK
OF THE NEXT BOOK IN
THE HIDDEN SPRINGS MYSTERIES

1

When Maggie Greene heard a noise in the big old house below her, she sucked in her breath to listen. It wouldn't do for her to get caught up in the tower room at Miss Fonda's house. She wasn't supposed to be there.

It didn't matter that Miss Fonda had told her it was okay. The old lady's face had lit up when she remembered hiding out in the tower room at age fifteen like Maggie. But Maggie's mother wouldn't think Maggie had any business inside the house unless they were cleaning it for Miss Fonda. So she kept her visits to the tower room a secret.

After Miss Fonda had to go to the Gentle Care Home, Maggie's mother did say Maggie could come feed Miss Fonda's calico cat, Miss Marble, who lived out in the garden shed. But the cat excuse wouldn't help if she got caught inside the house. She'd be in trouble.

The thing was not to get caught. So she stayed very still and listened for what she'd heard. Or thought she'd heard. No sounds now. Old houses could creak and groan for no reason.

Maggie crept over to the window and felt better when she saw the circular drive down below was empty. She rubbed a spot clean on the glass with a corner of her sweater. No telling how long it had been since these windows had been washed. The years of grime didn't let in much of the October sunshine.

She shivered and pulled her sweater tighter around her. But it wasn't actually a feeling-cold shiver. More the kind of shiver that sneaked up on you and made old-timey people like Miss Fonda say somebody must have walked over their grave.

As Maggie started to turn away from the window, a car did pull into the driveway. She took a step back, but she could still see the red and white sign shaped like a house on the car's door. She knew who drove that car. Geraldine Harper.

Everybody in Hidden Springs knew the Realtor. They said she could talk a bulldog into selling his doghouse. Maggie had heard her sales pitch back when her parents had hoped to move out of the trailer park and buy a house. That was before Maggie's father lost his job. Since then, there wasn't any talk about new houses, just worries about paying the lot rent at the trailer park.

That didn't keep Mrs. Harper from calling now and again about this or that perfect house. Calls that nearly always led to arguments between Maggie's parents. A couple of weeks ago she stopped by the trailer where Maggie's father told her in no uncertain terms to stop bothering them about houses. The woman gave him back as good as she got and then kicked their little dog when he sidled up to her, his tail wagging friendly as anything.

She'd probably kick Miss Marble too if she spotted the cat, but maybe the cat would stay hidden. Like Maggie. If Mrs. Harper caught Maggie in Miss Fonda's house, things were going to be bad. Really bad. Surely Mrs. Harper wouldn't climb up to the tower, even if she did look over the rest of the house. She had on a skirt and shoes with a little heel. A woman had to dress for success, she'd told Maggie's class last year on career day. But she definitely wasn't dressed for climbing the rickety ladder up to the tower room.

All Maggie had to do was stay quiet. Very quiet. And hope the woman left soon. She needed to be home before her mother came in from her job at the Fast Serve. The "doing homework at the library" excuse didn't work past closing time.

The woman pulled her briefcase and purse out of the car and headed toward the front steps. She must have a key. Maggie couldn't believe Miss Fonda wanted to sell her house. She loved this house. She was always begging to go home whenever Maggie went to visit her.

Maggie couldn't see Mrs. Harper after she stepped up on the porch. She couldn't hear her either. The tower room was a long way from the front door. But what about the back door? That was how Maggie had come in. If Mrs. Harper found it unlocked, she might blame Maggie's mother. Say she was careless. They might fire her mother.

Maggie's heart was already beating too hard when she heard somebody coming up the steps to the third floor. Too soon for Mrs. Harper. She would just be coming in the front hall where the grand staircase rose up to the second floor. But somebody was in the hall just below. A board creaked. The one in front of the room that led up to the tower. Maggie always stepped over it, but whoever was there now didn't.

Mrs. Harper must have heard the board creak too. Her voice came up the stairway. "Who's there?"

Nobody answered. Certainly not Maggie. And not who-ever had just stepped on the squeaky floorboard. Maggie wasn't sure she could have answered if she'd wanted to. Her throat was too tight.

The door opened in the room below Maggie and something crashed to the floor. Probably the lamp on that table beside the door. It sounded like a bomb going off in the silent house.

"Who's there?" Mrs. Harper's feet pounded on the steps.

Maggie desperately hoped whoever it was wouldn't decide to hide in the tower room. Her heart banged against her ribs, and she put a hand over her mouth to keep her breathing from sounding so loud.

Relief rushed through her when the door creaked open and the floorboard squeaked again. Where before the steps had sounded furtive, now they were hurried. Mrs. Harper's heels clattered on the wooden stairs up to the third floor. Those steps were narrow and steep, nothing like the sweeping broad staircase from the first to the second floor.

Maggie dared to move over to the tower's trapdoor and ease it up a few inches. She didn't know why. She couldn't see anything, but maybe she could hear what was happening.

"What are you doing here?" Mrs. Harper's voice was strident.

The other person must not have found a place to hide. Whoever it was mumbled something, but Maggie couldn't make out any words.

"Stealing is more like it." Mrs. Harper sounded angry. "I'll not let you get away with it."

Maggie did hear the other person then. Panicked sounding. Maybe a woman's voice. Maybe not. "I can explain."

"You can explain it to the sheriff."

"Wait!"

Mrs. Harper didn't wait. Her heels clicked purposely on

the floorboards as she moved away. The other person rushed after her.

A shriek. Thumps. The whole upstairs seemed to shake as the bumps kept on. Then it was quiet. Too quiet.

Maggie lowered the trapdoor and scooted away from it. She waited. Down below, a door opened and shut. Not on the third floor. On the first floor. Somebody leaving the house. Maggie counted to one hundred slowly. Once. Twice. Still no noise. Maggie peeked out the window. Mrs. Harper's car sat in the same place in the driveway.

What if the woman was hurt? She might have fallen. Something had made all that noise. Maggie couldn't just stay hidden and not help her. It didn't matter whether she liked Mrs. Harper or not.

She took a deep breath and squeezed her hands into fists to keep her fingers from trembling. Her breathing was too loud again.

You're fifteen, Maggie. Stop acting like a scared three-year-old.

The trapdoor creaked when she lifted it. Maggie froze for a few seconds, but nobody shouted. She put her foot on the first rung of the ladder, but then climbed back into the tower room to hide her notebook. She'd never worried about that before, but nobody had ever come into the house while she was there until today.

She spotted a crack between the wallboards and stuck the notebook in it. When she turned it loose, it sank out of sight. Well hidden. With a big breath for courage, she climbed down into the room where she stood still. All she could hear was her own breathing.

With her foot, she scooted aside the broken lamp and

went out into the hallway. She made sure to step over the squeaky board.

The silence pounded against her ears. She'd never been afraid in the house, even though people said it was haunted. People had died there. Miss Fonda told her that, but that didn't mean they were hanging around now. Maggie didn't believe in ghosts. She really didn't, but right that moment, she was having trouble being absolutely sure.

"Mrs. Harper, are you all right?" Her voice, not much more than a whisper, sounded loud in Maggie's ears. She shouldn't have said anything. If Mrs. Harper had followed the other person outside, Maggie might slip away without anybody knowing she was there.

A little hope took wing inside her as she reached the top of the stairs. Hope that sank as fast as it rose.

Mrs. Harper was on her back at the bottom of the steps. She wasn't moving. At all. Maggie grabbed the railing and half stumbled, half slid down to stoop by the woman.

"Mrs. Harper?" Again her voice was barely audible, but that didn't matter. The woman stared up at Maggie with fixed eyes.

Maggie had never seen a dead person out of a casket. She wanted to scream but that wouldn't help. Nothing was going to help.

She should tell somebody, but how? She didn't have a cell phone. Not with her family struggling to buy groceries. Maybe the other person did. The one who had chased after Mrs. Harper to keep her from calling the sheriff.

But that person must have walked past Mrs. Harper and on out the door without doing anything. Maybe worried like Maggie about getting in trouble. Afraid like Maggie.

Maggie stood up. It wasn't like she could do anything for Mrs. Harper. The woman was dead. A shudder shook through Maggie, and she rubbed her hands up and down her arms. She could leave and nobody would be the wiser.

A chill followed her down the stairs. Her feet got heavier with every step. Whether she got in trouble or not, she couldn't leave without telling somebody. When Maggie spotted the white cell phone in an outside pocket of Mrs. Harper's handbag beside the front entrance, it seemed the perfect answer. She didn't even have to unzip anything. She gingerly picked it up and punched in 911. The beeps sounded deafening in the silent house.

"What's your emergency?"

The woman's voice made Maggie jump. She must have hit the speaker button. She didn't want to say anything. She thought they just came when you dialed 911.

The woman on the other end of the line repeated her question. "Respond if you can."

Maggie held the phone close to her mouth. "She can't. She's dead."

"Who's speaking? What's your location?" The woman sounded matter-of-fact, as though she heard about people being dead every day.

Maggie didn't answer. Instead she clicked the phone off so she couldn't hear the questions. She started to put it down, but then she remembered some of those police shows on television. She pulled her sweater sleeve down to hold the phone while she wiped it off on her shirt. Her fingerprints were all over the house, but nobody would be suspicious of that since she helped her mother clean there. The 911 voice didn't have to know who Maggie was. That wouldn't help Mrs. Harper.

Maggie propped the phone against Mrs. Harper's purse. The police would have caller ID. They could find Mrs. Harper easy enough, since her car was right out front. But Maggie didn't want them to find her too.

She slipped through the house and outside. Her hands were shaking so much that she had to try three times to get the key in the hole to lock the back door.

When she turned away from the house and looked around, she didn't see anybody. Not even Miss Marble. She ran across the yard and ducked through the opening in the shrubs.

She didn't think about whether anybody saw her.

Acknowledgments

Ever since I can remember I've wanted to write stories. Over the years, dozens, perhaps hundreds of characters have marched through my head, pulling me along to tell their stories. But a story needs more than a writer. It needs readers to let those characters spring to life in their own minds. So I thank each of you who went on this suspense-filled mystery ride with Michael. You make my storytelling complete.

I am forever grateful to the Lord who gifted me with an imagination to come up with stories and then gave me the ability to write them down. That's a thank-you for each and every day.

Thank you also to my editor, Lonnie Hull DuPont, who stands ready to make my stories better with her insightful comments. Barb Barnes's careful line-by-line editing has made me a better writer. Erin Bartels has a way of pulling out the best words for the back cover to entice a reader, while Cheryl Van Andel and the art department wrap my stories in a great cover each and every time. I'm thankful for the whole team at Revell and Baker who help make my stories into books and then get those books in front of readers. You're the best.

I'm also fortunate to have a wonderful agent, Wendy Lawton, whose middle name must be Encourager. An agent ever ready to go the extra mile for her clients while also praying for them is a blessing. Thank you, Wendy.

And of course, I have to thank my husband, Darrell, and all my family for their support and understanding over the years. I dedicated this book to my two sisters, because here in our hometown they have to continually put up with being asked, "Are you the one who writes the books?"

A. H. Gabhart is a pseudonym for Ann H. Gabhart, the bestselling author of more than twenty-five novels for adults and young adults. *Angel Sister*, Ann's first Rosey Corner book, was a nominee for inspirational novel of 2011 by *RT Book Reviews* magazine. Her Shaker novel, *The Outsider*, was a Christian Book Awards finalist in the fiction category. She lives on a farm not far from where she was born in rural Kentucky. She and her husband are blessed with three children, three in-law children, and nine grandchildren. Ann loves reading books, watching her grandkids grow up, and walking with her dog, Oscar.

Ann likes to connect with readers on her Facebook page, www.facebook.com/anngabhart, where you can peek over her shoulder for her "Sunday mornings coming down," or walk along to see what she might spot on her walks, or laugh with her on Friday smiles day. Find out more about Ann's books and check out her blog posts at www.annhgabhart.com.

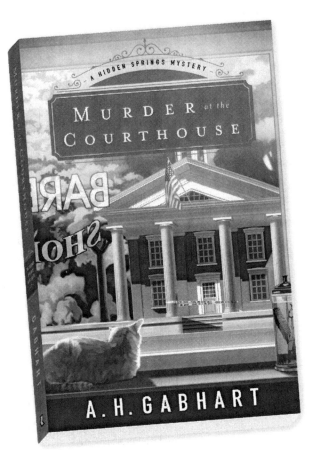

If You Liked *Murder at the Courthouse*, You May Also Like **The Cate Kinkaid Files**

Nothing Will Be the Same after the Summer of 1964...

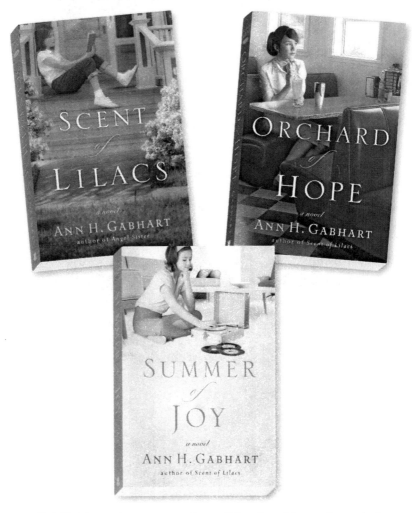

Hollyhill, Kentucky, seems to be well insulated from the turbulent world beyond its quiet streets. Life-changing events rarely happen here, and when they do, they are few and far between. But for Jocie Brooke and her family, they happen all at once.

"A RICH AND REWARDING READ YOU WON'T WANT TO MISS!"

—JUDITH MILLER,

AWARD-WINNING AUTHOR OF THE REFINED BY LOVE SERIES

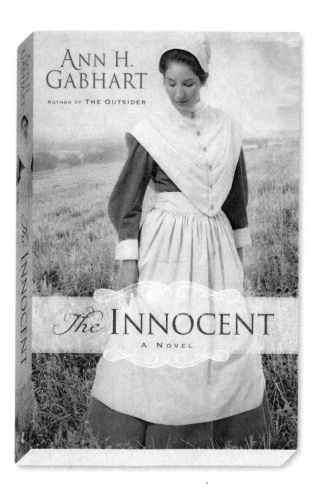

Meet A. H. Gabhart at
www.AnnHGabhart.com
Be the First to Learn about New Releases,
Read Her Blog, and Sign Up for Her Newsletter

Connect with Ann at
f Ann H Gabhart
t AnnHGabhart